The Amazing
Super Wolf

Roxanne Smolen

Published by: moonRox, Inc.
Cover Design: Y. Nikolova at Ammonia Book Covers

This is a work of fiction and is produced from the author's imagination. People, places, and things mentioned in this novel are used in a fictional manner.

ISBN 978-0-9915673-9-3

Thank you for supporting author rights.

For more information about Roxanne Smolen
go to www.roxannesmolen.com

Contents

ONE

October 26, 2008, Loxahatchee, Florida

I pressed my back against the tree trunk, my gun close to my chest. The night air cooled my sweaty skin. I smelled pine and palm trees, rabbit and raccoon. And her. Creeping through the forest. Quiet footsteps disturbed the brush. *Just a bit closer, little girl. Closer and I'll have you.* I took a slow breath and focused all my senses.

And something weird happened. I did more than hear her moving behind me. I *saw* her. Not with my eyes. With something else. Her silhouette slipped through the trees, and I sensed it like radar, like heat sensors. Her body language told me which way she would step before she did.

What was going on?

I shook my head to clear it, spun from behind the tree, and fired. The paintball splatted against her chest. But not with paint. These were filled with Brittany's improved Wolfsbane Brew, designed to incapacitate a werewolf whether in wolf form or not.

Ayanna's back arched with the impact, and for a moment, I thought she might turn to the Dark Side. For us, the Dark Side meant our wolf beast guise—a seven-foot wolfman with claws and fangs. But her eyes met mine, and she fired.

Her shot struck my arm. It burned like fire. The potion coursed through my body, trying to paralyze me, trying to disrupt my connection to Mother Moon.

I said, "Ow!"

"Ow yourself," Ayanna called. "Those things sting."

"You did great, though. You didn't lose control once."

Her dark face split into a grin. Pride and pleasure swelled through the *link,* the psychic bond that connected the pack.

My pack. Despite my protests, I was the leader of my little band of werewolves. An honor I didn't want or deserve. But I was the one with superpowers. And apparently, my skills were still growing.

Had I actually seen Ayanna's spectral image through the trees? What was that all about?

I rubbed my arm, frowning. "That's enough for tonight. School tomorrow."

She tramped toward me through the brush. "I have an examination in algebra. But it's all rubbish. I'm miles beyond them in my studies."

I nodded in mock sympathy. I knew she secretly liked school, liked being the best in class, enjoyed the other kids' awe of her exotic British accent.

"Great," I told her. "I expect good grades."

"Yes, big brother," she sang.

I caught the sarcasm. I wasn't her brother.

With my arm draped around her shoulders, we traipsed back to her house. We were in the woods behind her property. More specifically, near the boggy pond where we always met. We lived in Loxahatchee, Florida, a small town in the northernmost region of the Everglades. Like in any small town, everybody knew everybody. But few people realized we were werewolves, and I intended to keep it that way.

The trees petered out at the edge of a wide yard. Ayanna and her parents, Dick and Chloe

Richardson, lived on an old horse farm with expansive pastures and tumbled-down fences. The yard looked even more open now. Their ranch-style house had been demolished in a tropical storm. All that was left was the cement foundation. Her father used the flat slab as a parking lot. His battered Winnebago was there along with his Lexus. My uncle often parked his truck there as well. Ayanna and her family lived in the renovated horse stable.

We reached the back door with its thick fisheye window. It was always unlocked for us.

I handed Ayanna my paintball gun. "See you tomorrow."

She beamed at me. The *look* my girlfriend, Brittany, always warned me about. But Ayanna understood that I loved her like a sister. We were both okay with that.

I hopped on my bike and pedaled away. A year ago, if you had told me I'd be tooling around town on a candy-apple-red bicycle, I would've laughed. My friends at my old school in Massachusetts would've laughed, too. They probably all had cars by now. I tried not to think about it too much. They were a bunch of rich snobs anyway.

The ride home was pleasant enough. There

was no traffic at that time of night. No one to see me. Leaving me free to use my super wolf speed. I could move faster than any human. The wind was cool in my hair. The stars were bright overhead. I sped down the flat asphalt as if it were a raceway. As if I could escape my misgivings. But they crept into my thoughts anyway.

My powers were growing again. Cripes! Why did everything happen to me? I'd just have to hide them, that's all. I've had to hide things before.

I slowed when I reached my sub-division. I lived with my Uncle Bob and his girlfriend, Rita. They rented a small, blue house at the end of a cul-de-sac. The yard backed into the surrounding forest. The perfect place for a family of werewolves. I dropped my bike on its appointed spot in the front lawn and tiptoed up the wooden steps. I needn't have bothered being so quiet–Uncle Bob met me at the door.

My uncle was a few inches shorter than me. His steel-gray hair curled where it hit his collar. He'd been watching *The Tonight Show* without sound, probably so he wouldn't disturb Rita. "Getting in kind of late, aren't you?"

"I was with Ayanna."

"Have a seat. I want to talk to you about responsibilities."

Ugh. Just hearing that word made me want to hyperventilate. I sat on the couch. He sat on the old recliner across from me.

"I'm your legal guardian," he said. "It's my responsibility to see that you are fed, clothed, and have a roof over your head. In return, it's your responsibility to get good grades in school. That's your responsibility to your father, to me, but more importantly, to yourself. Instead, you go out at night and—"

"I was with *Ayanna*. I was teaching her—"

"So, you feel that Ayanna is your responsibility?"

"No!" I chopped my hand down. "I am not responsible for her."

"Then who is?"

I paused. "Her parents?"

"Exactly." He pointed at me with both hands. "Ayanna's parents are responsible for Ayanna. And what are you responsible for?"

"Good grades," I said dully.

"That's right."

"But what about being a pack leader?"

"Being a pack leader doesn't make you a teacher. It makes you a boss. You guide. You protect. And if you want that girl trained, you damned well tell her parents to do it."

"Because I'm the boss."

"There you go." He stood. "Good talk."

I watched him walk down the hallway and disappear into his room. I didn't want to be anyone's boss. I wanted to be a normal sixteen-year-old kid. I wanted to hang out with my girlfriend and chill. What would that even be like? No responsibilities. No worries.

I went to my room and plopped down on my bed. I couldn't sleep, so I called Brittany.

She yawned as she answered the phone. "There you are. I was beginning to think something happened to you."

"Sorry. I lost track of time."

"I bet Bob wasn't pleased."

"He doesn't want me to take Ayanna out anymore. He says her parents should train her. But how can they when neither of them is an alpha?"

She yawned again. "That is a dilemma."

"He says I should be the boss."

"And you don't agree?"

"I can't tell everyone what to do. It's not my thing. Besides, as far as I can see, being a pack leader isn't about bossing people around, it's about trying to please everyone."

"You can't please everyone."

"Tell me about it." I sighed. "I feel like I'm being pulled in five directions."

"Well, you're the boss. What do you want to do?"

"Run away. Just you and me. I want to go somewhere… else."

"I always wanted to travel."

She understood. She always did. No judging. No criticism. "I love you, Brittany."

"I love you, too. And I would go anywhere for you. But in the meantime, I'm going back to sleep. See you in my dreams."

I set down the phone, smiling. As I drifted off to slumberland, I imagined us somewhere that was the opposite of South Florida. Cold instead of hot. Mountainous instead of flat. Just the two of us. What would that even be like?

TWO

Bright and early Monday morning, I drove to school in my uncle's truck. A normal procedure this semester. Lately, Uncle Bob had been having me drive everywhere on my learner's permit. I was nervous at first, but now I didn't mind so much.

In the seat beside me, Uncle Bob slurped his coffee. "I wish you would reconsider naming me first lieutenant of the pack," he said.

I glanced at him. "Why?"

He gave an exasperated snort. "So, I can advise you."

"You can advise me even if you're not my lieutenant," I said. "I welcome it. In fact, I plan to have a wolf democracy."

He sputtered and nearly spilled his coffee. "That just isn't done."

"Then we'll be the first. What's the worst that could happen?"

"Someone might attack?"

"I can protect us," I said. "Besides, no one knows we're here."

"Lavinia's pack in Georgia knows where we are."

I thought about Lavinia and her son Tommy Lee. A werewolf's abilities came from the mother's side of the family. Tommy Lee had inherited his mother's werewolf traits, but he wasn't very good at it. A real newbie. "Yeah," I said, "but they're our friends."

He grunted in agreement.

I pulled to the drop-off point in front of the school and put the gearshift in *park*. "Touchdown. The crowd goes wild."

"Good job," Uncle Bob said. "I think you're ready. If you want me to, I'll make the appointment for you to get your driver's license after school today."

My stomach went all tingly inside, and I chided myself for it. I was the leader of the pack, for Pete's sake. I wasn't supposed to get nervous about stuff.

"All right," I said, not looking at him. "In that case, I'll leave my bike in the truck bed."

We both hopped down, and he circled around to the driver's side.

"I'll pick you up at three o'clock," he said.

"All right," I said again, a little dazed. *I was going to get my driver's license*.

I walked across the schoolyard. Seminole Bluffs High School was a one-story building with a football field in back. Home of the Hawks. The front was an expanse of white concrete with occasional holes cut out for scraggly trees. Kids milled about. A bus had just let out.

To the side, Eff scowled at me. Efrem Higgins was an ex-football star. He'd been my enemy, then my friend, now my enemy again. A few weeks ago, he'd found out I was a werewolf. Some people might be horrified at that revelation. Eff was pissed. I guess he thought I'd tricked him by keeping it a secret.

I avoided his glare by entering the school. The halls were packed, and the noise level went up two decibels. I slipped through the crowd. It was way easier than it should have been. As if I could anticipate which way people would go— and I wondered if I was influencing them, using my powers to unconsciously move them out of my way. I didn't want to control people like that— although it was convenient.

As always, Ayanna waited for me outside her first class. Two girls stood with her, but they hurried inside the room when they saw me. I was glad Ayanna was making friends. She'd been homeschooled all her life, and her social skills were even worse than mine.

"Hi," I said.

"Good morning. How did you sleep?"

"Like a rock."

She cocked her head and frowned. "Pardon?"

"Never mind." I grinned. "Did your parents give you trouble about getting in late last night?"

"They were both asleep. You?"

"Nothing I can't handle."

"Good. We can go out tonight, then."

"Not tonight. Let's take a break."

"Oh." Her smile fell.

And there it was again—the feeling that I needed to please everyone. And I was failing.

I nudged her arm. "Hey, next time you see me, I might have my driver's license."

"That's a milestone."

"Won't mean much. I still won't have a car."

The warning bell rang.

"I have to get to class," I said. "Good luck in algebra."

I felt her gaze on my back as I walked away.

At last, the best part of the school day arrived—lunch. I was on Lunch B, so by the time 12:30 rolled around, I was starved. But that's not why I looked forward to it. I bypassed the conga line at the hot food, grabbed a couple of apples from the new salad bar area, and hurried to my usual table in the back of the room.

Brittany was already there. She looked beautiful. She was growing her hair out, and it fell in a dark swag. She wore less makeup lately. Her eyes weren't so black, her lips not so purple. But they still tasted as sweet. I kissed her softly as I sat beside her.

"Hi," I said.

"Hi." She smiled, and her nose crinkled just right. "I forgot to ask last night. How was your paintball session with Ayanna?"

"Great. The new potion works really well." I placed one of my apples on her tray.

She reciprocated by giving me one of her yogurts. "I can tweak it further if you want me to."

"You can?"

"Sure. The more Lynette teaches me about herbs and potions, the more everything seems

13

to fall together."

Brittany's Aunt Lynette had degrees in herbology and holistic medicine. She was also a Wiccan Priestess. She and Brittany didn't always get along, which made it tough when you lived together. But lately, they seemed friendly enough.

I said, "I wish I were as comfortable being a pack master as you are being a potential witch queen."

"Did something happen?"

I drew a deep breath. "It's just that lately—"

"Hi, Brittany." A girl stopped at our table.

"Oh, hi, Monica," Brittany said.

"I heard you started blogging over the summer."

"Yeah. It's all about herbs and their properties. How to mix them. You know."

Monica narrowed her eyes. "Herbs as in cooking?"

"No," Brittany drawled. "More like in potions."

"Ah." She brightened. "That sounds interesting. Maybe I'll look it up."

"Great. Thanks."

I smiled indulgently as Monica walked away then hunched my shoulders and leaned closer. "As I was saying, my werewolf powers seem to be getting stronger. Every day it's something new. And I just don't–"

"Brittany, did I hear this right?" Another girl strode to our table. Her companion lagged behind. "You want to be a pharmacist?"

"Apothecary." Brittany nodded. "I'm studying herbalism."

Her face scrunched. "Herbs as in cooking?"

"No, Emily. Medical herbs. Natural remedies. That sort of thing."

"Oh." The second girl popped up. "That makes much more sense. I didn't think you could cook."

I said, "Actually, she's a terrific cook."

"Well, check out Mister Over Protective," Emily said.

The girls giggled and wandered off.

I said, "Anyway, lately it's like I can read people's minds. Like I know what they're going to do before they do it. And I started thinking. What if I'm not reading their minds but projecting mine. What if I'm influencing–"

"So, Brittany, you're like a blogger now?"

Three more girls appeared.

Brittany said, "Hi, Susan. Yeah, I'm blogging about herbs."

Susan cocked her hip and held out a finger.

"So, it's like a cooking show?"

"No, it's not a cooking show," I barked. "What kind of question is that?"

"I was just asking. Sheesh." Susan and her cohorts ambled away.

I raised my hands. "What is wrong with people?"

"Forget about them," Brittany said. "So, you're afraid you're taking thralls."

My anger deflated. She got me. She always got me. I nodded. "Inadvertently."

"This is serious. You need to find out all you can about it."

"How? It's not like someone will have *a blog*." I regretted my choice of words as soon as I said them.

She looked hurt. "Someone might."

I sighed and opened my yogurt. We ate in silence for a few moments.

"Okay," she said. "You're afraid you're mentally influencing people. What else?"

"I know when someone's lying. I smell it in their sweat."

"Like a chemical reaction."

"I guess."

"That sound's helpful. What else?"

"The *link* to my pack is stronger. If I put my

16

mind to it, I think I could communicate with them in real time."

"That sounds helpful, too. Do all alpha wolves have these powers?"

"Maybe. I don't know. But here's the thing. Power corrupts. And I don't want to wake up one morning to find out I'm the bad guy."

She placed her hand over mine. "I understand. I do. I felt the same way when I found out I was a super powerful witch. But we can't hide from who we are. All we can do is learn to use our abilities responsibly. Practice makes perfect, right?"

I nodded. I would *never* practice making a thrall.

She pulled her hand away. "Don't look now, but Eff is staring at us again."

"I hope he's not going to make trouble."

"He called last night urging me to break up with you," she said. "He didn't use the word werewolf. He just said you weren't who you seemed."

"My uncle would freak if he found out Eff knew about him." A familiar weight landed in my stomach. I pushed it away. "Speaking of my uncle, he's going to take me to get my driver's license after school today."

"That's great. You must be excited."

I scowled. "What's the point if I don't have a car?"

"Baby steps." She got to her feet. "Call me tonight and tell me how it went. Smitten you."

"Smitten you."

THREE

After school, Uncle Bob, Rita, and I drove out to the DMV in Royal Palm Beach for my official road test. I rode in the truck bed, as usual.

Rita had flaming red hair and the widest smile I'd ever seen. She had always been my cheerleader, and this afternoon was no different. "You'll be fine," she called to me out the back window. "Just remember to check your mirrors. And keep your hands at ten and two."

"That's not right anymore," Uncle Bob said. "They want you at nine and three because of the airbag."

"It was ten and two when I took the test," she said.

"Sure. Ages ago."

"What do you mean by that?" She poked him.

Then came a mock argument about what driving was like in the covered-wagon era. Their good-natured bickering made me feel even more anxious.

We got to the DMV and went to the area for people with appointments. My examiner was a woman of few words. She sat shotgun in my uncle's truck, her only indication that I should begin. I ran over the curb during my three-point-turn, and I wasn't exactly centered in the designated parking space, but she didn't even look up from her clipboard.

We went out on the road. Royal Palm Beach was like a mini city. It had parks and stores and movie theaters. I followed the examiner's instructions, turning right here, turning left there, making sure I came to a complete stop at the stop signs. After a while, she directed me out of town.

The surrounding area was mainly jackfruit groves and horse ranches crisscrossed with country roads. Some were paved, some not. My examiner chose a paved road. Two lanes of black asphalt, flat and straight. Traffic came toward me on the other side. There were no cars in the lane in front of me. They were all lined up behind. I was doing the speed limit, my sweaty hands firmly at nine and three.

Suddenly the examiner sat up straight and shouted, "Squirrel!"

Time stopped. I peered ahead. The squirrel in question sat on my side of the road. Options ran through my mind.

I could slow down and hope the squirrel ran away. But what if it didn't? Would I have points taken off for winning a game of chicken?

What if the squirrel ran into oncoming traffic? Would I have points taken off for chasing a woodland creature into certain doom?

The squirrel watched me approach, wringing its tiny hands. I didn't want to hurt it. So, relying on my newfound, untried superpowers, I attempted to influence its mind.

It didn't have a coherent thought in its head. As I connected with it, I was hit with a barrage of images–tree, grass, nut, tree, sex, sex, SEX.

I tried to project a thought. *Run away, little squirrel. Run into the trees*.

Instead, the little monster ran straight toward my truck, leaped up, did a backflip like a freaking ninja, and landed on the hood. It bounced once then hit the windshield–SPLAT–all four legs extended.

"Eek!" the examiner shrieked.

"Awk!" I answered.

The squirrel pressed its beady eye against the glass and stared at me. I turned on the windshield wipers. It latched onto the wiper blade and swung back and forth.

Feigning calm, I flipped on the turn signal and pulled to the side of the road. The trailing line of cars zoomed past. All twenty-seven of them. A few slowed down long enough to give me dirty looks.

I turned off the wipers. Ninja squirrel slid down the windshield. It chittered at me, tail twitching.

The examiner said, "That's unusual. I wonder what made it do that?"

I glared at it. *You communicate in images? Try this one*. I projected an image of me in my wolf form.

The squirrel's jaw dropped. Its little eyes widened. Then it leaped off the hood and disappeared into the trees.

I ran my hand over my face, trying to keep my emotions out of the *link*. Hopefully, Ayanna hadn't picked up on what had happened. I would never hear the end of it. I turned on my turn signal, checked my blind spots, and inched onto the road.

"Excellent," the examiner said. "We can go back now. Turn right at the next intersection."

We returned to the DMV. And just like that, I had a driver's license. The picture made me look like a dork, but at that moment, I didn't even care.

"Congratulations." My uncle thumped me on the back.

Rita gave me her wide smile. "We should go out to dinner to celebrate."

I paused. My birthday was coming up, and I'd hoped they'd take me out then. We couldn't afford to go out to eat twice in one week.

But Uncle Bob hopped into the back of the truck, my designated spot, and waggled his brows. "Dinner it is. You drive, Cody."

I drove to the Coffee Café, which was my uncle's favorite diner. I held the door open for them as we entered. The place was small. It had a long counter where I sat when I came in alone, a few tables in the middle of the room, and a line of booths under the windows. It smelled like coffee and bacon even though breakfast was hours ago.

Anne, the waitress, smiled and waved. "Well, if it isn't my favorite family. Come on over. I got a place for you right here."

We slid into the proffered booth. A big jack-o-lantern was painted on the window with poster paint. Daylight filtered through and tinted the table orange.

Anne brought over the menus.

"We're celebrating tonight," Uncle Bob told her. "Cody just got his driver's license."

"That's wonderful!" Anne hugged me against her ample bosom and kissed my cheek.

I was feeling kind of proud of myself after all the fuss they were making.

Uncle Bob said to get whatever I wanted, so I ordered the smothered steak, which was a half-pound hamburger patty covered with onions and gravy over a bed of mashed potatoes. Delicious as always. I wolfed it down then sat back, patting my stomach. I was stuffed.

Then Anne walked toward me through the tables, her face alight, carrying a huge piece of chocolate cake with a birthday candle on it. She moved slowly so she wouldn't put out the flame, all the while singing off-key. "Congratulations to you. Congratulations to you. Congratulations, dear Cody. Congratulations to youuu." On the final, drawn out *you*, she set the cake before me.

There was a smattering of applause from the other diners.

"Thank you," I sputtered, flabbergasted.

I found there's always room for cake.

Afterward, I drove home. Uncle Bob and Rita settled in front of the television. They'd missed the beginning of *Jeopardy*. I went to my room to call Brittany.

"Hi," I said.

Her smile lit up my phone. "How'd it go?"

"I got it."

"I knew you would."

"Maybe we can go on a real date now," I said. "Like dinner and a movie."

"Sounds great. I'll pencil you in."

"When?"

"When what?"

"When can we go on a date?"

She chuckled. "Let me check my social calendar. I can't go right now. I'm busy talking to my boyfriend. And remember that tomorrow is the dark moon, so I'll have rituals with Lynette and Myra."

"Dark moon on Tuesday. Check."

"Oh, and I have my early birthday party on Sunday. Did you invite Ayanna and her parents?"

"Yes, but I'll remind them." I frowned. *My* birthday was on Thursday, but she didn't mention it. Didn't she remember?

The next morning, I drove to school. My uncle rode shotgun as usual. Getting my driver's license didn't change my life. Not that I'd expected it to.

I wrestled my bike out of the back of the truck and walked it to the bike rack. Eff came out of the parking lot and stopped dead, staring at me. Maybe he thought I'd wolf out, and he'd catch me in the act. I considered approaching him and starting a conversation. Prove to him I was the same kid he was friends with before. But, nah. That would make it worse. I dropped my gaze and locked up my bike.

Inside the school, the halls were as noisy as ever. I made my way to Ayanna. She stood with the same two girls. They gave me blinding smiles before disappearing into the classroom. I hoped they didn't think I was her boyfriend.

"Good morning," Ayanna said.

"Hey." I nodded. "I got my driver's license."

"I thought as much. The *link* fairly hummed with pride. And what was that about a squirrel?"

"It was nothing."

"Are you sure? It felt like you were rather

perplexed. I would be happy to go out and give it a stern talking to."

My cheeks warmed. "How was your algebra exam?"

She smiled. "I believe I performed admirably."

"That's good. We'll make an A student of you yet."

"I'm more concerned with my extracurricular activities. You should come over tonight. We can practice with the paintball guns. Work on our concentration."

"Not tonight."

"Why not? It will be dark. And Brittany will be busy."

I was tempted. I really was. But I was the one who talked her parents into sending her to a public school. So, I was responsible for keeping her grades up. Plus, I didn't want to hear about it from Uncle Bob again. "We'll go soon. But you don't need me with you to practice concentration. Are you doing that meditation thing I showed you?"

"Almost constantly." She smiled. She was pretty when she smiled.

"Well, keep it up. It's important to strengthen your connection to Mother Moon." I looked around as the bell rang. "I better go. Don't forget Brittany's birthday party this Sunday. They'll have food."

"I wouldn't miss it."

With a nod and a grin, I hurried to my first class.

Lunchtime came, and I sat with Brittany at our special table. We exchanged yogurt and apples.

As we ate, I said, "Are we still study partners? Because we haven't been studying much so far this semester."

"Well," she drawled, "we don't have classes together this semester. Besides, I won't have as much time for schoolwork this year with the blog and all."

"The blog."

"It needs a lot of attention. I can't study witchcraft and American History at the same time. What's the point of schoolwork anyway? I can't afford to go to college."

"You could go to a community college. We both could. What happened to your dream of becoming a graphic artist?" For that matter, what happened to my dream of becoming a doctor? What would I do now that I'm a werewolf?

"Things change," she murmured. "Interests change. I'm really into making potions. It's like working a puzzle, learning how all the pieces fit together."

"You can study herbology in school. Or even chemistry."

Brittany sighed as if deep in thought. The yogurt container slipped from her grasp, bounced on her tray, and spattered her Michael Meyers t-shirt with pink slime.

"Darn it," she said. "I'd better go clean this up." She kissed my cheek and stood. "Don't forget—rituals this evening. So, call early."

I called Brittany after dinner. It was the best time. She'd be fasting so my call wouldn't disturb her meal. And the sun was still out.

"Hi," I said. "Ready for your big night?"

"We still have to take a bath."

I imagined the three women in the hot tub together. "By any chance, is this one of the naked ceremonies?"

"Why?"

"I could come over. Lend you a hand."

She giggled. "Cody."

"What? We hardly see each other except at school."

"Speaking of which, I've been thinking about what you said about my grades, and I decided the best way to get back at my father is to get straight A's in my senior year."

I nodded. Brittany's father used to punish her for good grades, saying he didn't want a show-off know-it-all for a daughter.

"That's great," I said. "Let's get together to study this Thursday." Maybe once she saw me, it would jog her memory that it was my birthday.

"Thursday? Um, no. I might be busy that day. This is my first Halloween as a Wiccan, and I'm not sure what rites they observe."

"But Thursday is October thirtieth." *My birthday.*

"Exactly."

"All right." I sighed and shook my head. Didn't anyone remember?

FOUR

Brittany smiled as she hung up the phone. See? She could keep a secret. Cody's surprise birthday party was going to be perfect.

She stripped to her underwear and grabbed her white ceremonial robe. It was ankle-length and had a hood. She bounded down the stairs. No one was in the kitchen, so she hurried to the back porch.

The screened-in porch was enclosed by filmy curtains which fluttered like ghosts. The ceremonial hot tub where most of their rituals began was surrounded by lit candles. Lynette and Myra stood to one side, eyes closed.

"Oh!" Brittany cried. "I didn't realize I was late."

"Shh," Lynette said.

Brittany winced and draped her robe on the chair with the others. Head down, shoulders hunched, she tiptoed to the pair of witches and stood on Lynette's right.

Lynette murmured something. The only word Brittany recognized was *esbat*. Lynette was a Wiccan Priestess and head of their coven, although she claimed Brittany was more powerful. Powerful enough to become a witch queen. But Brittany was happy to relinquish control of the coven. She had a lot to learn.

So, she watched in silence as Lynette poured a cup of sea salt into the tub's swirling hot water and added three drops of geranium oil, three drops of pine oil, and six drops of magnolia oil. Brittany and Myra took each of Lynette's hands, and they stepped into the tub together.

The water was as warm and fragrant as her grandmother's hug. Grandma used to say that there was a lesson to be learned in every experience. What Brittany had learned from Grandma's passing was that things changed and not always for the better. Sometimes the changes were gradual and sometimes as abrupt as death.

Brittany sat back, eyes closed, and pretended to meditate. But her thoughts swirled as noisily as the water. She understood the basis behind meditation—to clear the mind of negativity so as to experience peace, happiness, and bliss—but she never quite got the hang of it. Once she had even fallen asleep, and Lynette had swatted her ear.

So, she thought some more about her grandmother, then imagined herself as a grandmother, which led to thoughts about marriage and Cody. A witch and a werewolf. Could they make it work? He was always respectful of her rituals, supportive of her quest for knowledge. Why was he so troubled about his expanding powers? Testing his strengths could only lead to a better understanding of them. He should use this opportunity to learn more about what being an alpha wolf was all about. But her job was to listen, not to judge. She would be supportive of him, too.

After twenty minutes or so, Lynette stood. Brittany followed her out of the tub and put on her robe. Hers was plain. Myra's was also white but with quilted sleeves that she could roll back to expose her hands. Lynette's robe was blood red with symbols embroidered in gold along the hem. Once Brittany had asked what the symbols meant, but Lynette skirted the subject.

Myra picked up the sack of supplies and stood behind Brittany. Lynette strapped on the athame, her jeweled ceremonial dagger, and lifted her head. A bright blue aura glowed around her. She looked every bit the priestess she claimed to be. Brittany was told she also had an aura. A white one. But she never saw it.

Brittany followed Lynette outside. A breeze touched her damp skin. Stars speckled the black sky. She closed her eyes and listened to the chirrup of crickets. The song of Nature. *This* was where she could meditate. She could surrender her thoughts here.

With measured steps, Lynette walked across the lawn toward the ritual site. Brittany and Myra filed behind her. The grass beneath their bare feet was kept short and free of debris. In the far end of the huge backyard, a twenty-foot circle had been laid out. It was made of charred boards from the burned-out playhouse that had once stood there—Lynette's playhouse, indelibly imprinted with the love and security of her childhood. Melted wax from countless candles marked the compass points. Inside the circle was dark, rich soil, soft and raked free of sticks and stones.

Brittany and Myra set chunky white candles

on each of the compass points. The corners of the circle. Lynette approached the altar. It was constructed of fist-sized stones from the cobbled walkway that had once led to her playhouse. On top of the altar stood a black Crone candle representing Hecate, Goddess of the Moon. Around the main candle were representations of the four Elements: salt for Earth, incense for Air, a red candle for Fire, and a small bowl of Water. Lynette lit the red candle and the incense with a long wooden match then drew out the athame and held her arms in a Y shape.

That was Brittany's cue to cast the circle. Spilling salt from a canvas bag, she walked the perimeter of the boards. She chanted, "Round and round the circle's cast, joining present, future, and past. A sacred place. A world apart. Where powers merge and magic starts." She closed the circle with a flourish and set the bag next to the rest of their supplies.

With the athame, Lynette drew the shape of a pentagram in the air above the altar. "Elements of Earth, Air, Fire, and Water, I cleanse and consecrate you in the names of the Lord and Lady."

She sheathed her dagger and picked up the

box of wooden matches. With a swish of her robe, she strode to the North compass point and lit the chunky candle. "Hoofed One, Spirit of Earth, come from the mountains of midnight. You are the field of our pleasure, the source of our might. Hoofed One, Spirit of Earth, keep us strong throughout our rite."

She lit the East candle. "Winged One, Spirit of Air, come on the winds of sunrise. You are the gentle Spring breezes, the glory of flight. Winged One, Spirit of Air, keep us wise throughout our rite."

She went to the South candle. "Fierce One, Spirit of Fire, come with your blazing noon passion. You are the flickering candle, the bonfire bright. Fierce One, Spirit of Fire, keep us brave throughout our rite."

Finally, she lit the West. "Swift One, Spirit of Water, come on the waves of sunset. You are the well of deep comfort, the crashing wave's height. Swift One, Spirit of Water, keep us sure throughout our rite."

Brittany and Myra intoned, "So mote it be."

Lynette returned to the altar and lit the black Crone candle. "Hecate, Goddess of the Moon, your daughters are in need of your wisdom and strength this night. We walk with shadows.

Fears and negativity haunt us. We call upon you this night of the dark moon to banish these shadows."

She picked up a bottle of wine and poured a dollop onto the ground. "To the Lord and Lady." Then she filled a silver goblet and held it high. "I drink to the God and Goddess."

Lynette sipped the wine then passed the goblet to Brittany, who sipped and passed it to Myra.

Together, they recited, "Hecate, Honored Crone of Night, we call on you to put things right. Transform our negative thoughts and pain. Help our lives be whole again."

With a sudden shriek of laughter, Myra took off dancing around the circle.

Brittany followed, arms outstretched, spinning in the cool air. She visualized the best moments of her life—the day Cody kissed her in the doorway of the Video Stop, the night he gave her his promise ring in Howard's backyard garden. She imagined the joy she would feel being married to him, having a little girl of their own. Her laughter and exuberance banished the doubts within her until all she knew was happiness.

Panting and spent, Brittany sat with her

sisters before the altar. Stars shone brightly above. The smell of rich loam was all around. Her feet were black with dirt.

Lynette handed her a plate with three small cakes. She said, "May you never hunger."

Brittany took a cake and passed the plate to Myra. "May you never hunger."

Myra repeated the blessing as she passed the plate back to Lynette.

Brittany took a bite. The taste of cinnamon and nutmeg burst over her tongue. The cake was pumpkin spice in honor of the season.

Lynette handed the goblet of wine to Brittany. "May you never thirst."

Brittany sipped the wine and passed it to Myra. "May you never thirst."

Myra passed it back to Lynette and repeated the blessing. They closed their eyes. Meditating again. They were each supposed to contemplate what they were most thankful for. Brittany smiled and started a silent mantra.

I am grateful for Cody's love.

After a few minutes, Lynette stood. With her fingers, she snuffed out the North candle. "Strong One, go by the powers that brought you. As our bright magic fades, depart before the circle is gone." She did the same for the next candle, moving counter-clockwise until all four candles were extinguished.

Brittany walked the perimeter and chanted, "Circle round, now be unbound as I make my way around. Our work is finished for the night, and now we end our magic rite."

Lynette stepped to the black Crone candle on the altar. "We give thanks to the Goddess for guarding our circle and joining our rite. Hail and farewell."

She snuffed out the black candle. As she did, a gust of wind swirled like a long exhalation of breath.

Brittany took Myra's and Lynette's hands. She felt light. Unburdened. Blessed.

Her sisters shared their smiles with her. Together, they said, "The circle is open but unbroken. So mote it be."

FIVE

I woke with a grin Thursday morning and went out to the kitchen. I hoped for a pancake breakfast, but Rita wasn't up. I poured myself a glass of milk and sat at the table. Any minute now they would come out of their room to wish me a happy birthday. They'd have presents, maybe even a cake for breakfast. But no. It was just a regular day to them.

On the drive to school, Uncle Bob didn't mention my birthday. I should have known. He never remembered it while I was growing up, either. When we got to the school drop off, I hopped out to get my bike, and he drove off almost before I pulled it out of the truck bed.

At lunchtime, Brittany talked animatedly about a project she was doing on the life of Pablo Picasso. I was certain I'd told her when my birthday was, but she didn't bring it up. Well, if she didn't remember, I wasn't going to remind her.

By the time school ended, my good mood had soured. I considered biking to Howard's house. Howard Shebala was Uncle Bob's best friend. He ran a perpetual garage sale in his front yard. Maybe I could buy myself a birthday gift. But that would be too weird. So, I rode home. I ran a red light then yelled at the cars for getting in my way. Sweat ran into my eyes, and I cursed the Floridian weather. It was late October, for crying out loud. When was it going to cool off?

I pulled into the subdivision with the vague hope that I'd see my dad's car in the driveway. But no joy. He'd forgotten me, too. The house was silent and empty. I stomped to the kitchen for a glass of water.

An envelope addressed to me was propped up against a coffee cup on the counter. It was from my mother. For a moment, I considered tossing it. My mother and I hadn't spoken since she tried to pawn me off to a mad scientist to cure *my affliction*. But I sighed and tore it open. Inside was a check for seventeen hundred dollars and a handwritten letter.

Dear Cody,

Seventeen years. How the time has flown. This is the first birthday we've been apart. I plan to spend the evening with a glass of wine and a picture album, looking at your precious little face. I sometimes wonder if I did the right thing sending you to live with your uncle. But I truly don't know what else I could do. Cambridge is no place for someone like you.

I hope you and your father have a nice birthday dinner together. Yes, I know he's in South Florida with you. Not too surprising. He's always loved you. And so, I've lost both my men. All that's left for me is my job. It keeps me busy. Love, Mom

I threw the letter into the trash can next to the refrigerator. I kept the check.

Friday was Halloween. I couldn't keep my mind on my studies. I remembered Halloween as a kid. Mickey Martin and I would dress up like zombies or vampires and go door-to-door begging for candy. Sometimes the adults who answered the door would be dressed up as well.

I wondered if they did that in Loxahatchee. Maybe I should answer the door in my wolf beast guise. Give them a thrill.

After a long day of doing nothing, I slumped out of school—and was surprised to find Uncle Bob waiting for me at the bike rack.

"Hey." He grinned. "Would you mind going to the lumberyard with me? I could use a hand with a large order."

Uncle Bob was the local Fix-It Guy, and he kept a running account at the lumberyard. It was one of my favorite places to go. So, we stowed my bike in the truck bed and drove out. The mill was like a playground to me, and my mood lightened as I wandered through stacks of freshly cut wood. I loved working with chisels and planes. In my spare time, I was carving a totem pole out of the trunk of an old orange tree that had fallen in Brittany's yard.

It took us over an hour to get the load of two-by-fours secured in the back of the truck. At long last, we jumped in the truck and trundled home. Uncle Bob drove slowly as if afraid to lose his load. I didn't begrudge the time—I had nothing better to do. Brittany said she planned to stay home tonight.

So, imagine my bewilderment to find her

lime-green VW pulled onto the grass in front of my house. There were other vehicles there, too. Dick's Lexus. Howard's rust truck.

I said, "What's going on?"

Instead of answering, Uncle Bob parked his truck on the lawn behind Howard's. The only car in the driveway was a cherry-red BMW-Z4. Brand new. Had my dad gotten another car?

I climbed down from the truck. The smoky aroma of dinner on the grill greeted me. Brittany and Ayanna rushed along the side of the house yelling "Surprise" in unison. My mouth dropped open. Brittany was dressed like a witch with a huge black hat. Ayanna was a belly dancer in filmy turquoise pants.

I stammered. "Wh-what?"

Brittany kissed my cheek. "You didn't really think we forgot, did you?"

Behind them, the others walked up. I burst out laughing. Howard, a bona fide Navajo medicine man, was dressed like a cowboy. Rita wore a roaring twenties dress complete with a feather boa. Chloe was in 1970's attire—mini-skirt, white go-go boots. Her hair was fluffed into a nice afro. Dick looked like… himself in his usual African dashiki tunic and kufi cap. My dad wore a suit and tie. He was obviously coming straight from work.

Howard shook my hand. "Happy birthday, young *Mai-Coh*."

Rita hugged me. "Happy birthday, Cody."

"Many returns, old man," Dick said.

"Wow!" I blinked, still stunned. "Thanks, everyone."

Dad said, "Sorry I missed you yesterday, but I couldn't get away."

I motioned to the BMW. "I see you got a new car."

"Actually, it's yours." He held out the keys. "Happy birthday, son."

"Are you kidding me?" I cupped the keys in my hands like they were some fragile artifact.

Uncle Bob laughed. "My job was to make sure you got your driver's license in time."

I looked around at their smiling faces. A car? I had a car?

"It's paid for," Dad said, "and I'll keep up the insurance as long as you keep up your grades."

That was no problem—if I influenced the minds of my teachers. Wait, I couldn't actually do something like that. What was I thinking?

"Come on, Cody." Brittany tugged my arm. "Let's go see."

She towed me, stumbling toward the car. My

car. I had a car.

I climbed behind the driver's seat. It was low to the ground. A big difference from my uncle's truck. Red inside and out. With that new car smell.

"Give me a ride around the block," Brittany said, eyes twinkling. "We'll be right back, everybody."

I put the key in the ignition. The car roared then purred. I twisted to look behind and for the first time noticed there was no back seat. I inched down the driveway, scared to death I would wreck the car my first trip out.

But I didn't. By the time I got back to the driveway, I was grinning.

"My turn." Ayanna slid in as Brittany got out.

So, I took her around the block. The neighbors probably thought I was weird. On the other hand, Loxahatchee was such a small town, they probably all knew about the car before I did.

When we got back, I climbed out and circled the bimmer one last time. There was a little road dust on the back panel, and I wiped it off with the corner of my t-shirt. Uncle Bob chuckled and wrapped his arm around my shoulders. We walked to the side yard.

A table had been set up—an old door balanced on two sawhorses. On top of the table was a pile of brightly wrapped presents. They were stacked to resemble the shape of a car with glow-in-the-dark frisbees as wheels.

I stared. "This is amazing."

Ayanna sang, "Open them. Open them."

The others picked up her chant.

So, I sat and opened my presents.

Dad gave me a silver wolf's head keychain.

Howard's gift was a Dolphin football jersey and cap. I tried them on for size.

He laughed. "Now you look like you belong in Florida."

Rita gave me a selection of horror movie DVDs. "B movies," she said. "The B stands for bad."

I grinned. "Just the way I like them."

To a chorus of laughter and applause, I opened my uncle's gift—a car washing kit complete with a soft mitt to spread the wax.

Ayanna got me a *Werewolf of London* t-shirt. She had artfully cut out the werewolf's eyes so the shirt had two holes.

"It will fray properly in time," she promised.

I pulled it on over the football jersey. It gave me *Popeye* arms. "It's perfect. Thank you."

Dick and Chloe bought me a zebra-print bathrobe and slippers.

"For lounging," Dick explained.

The final gift was from Brittany. It was heavy. I unwrapped it to find a case filled with woodworking tools. There was even a small wood burning kit.

"I love it." I kissed her. "And you."

She hugged me. "Happy birthday."

"All right." Uncle Bob dusted off his hands. "Clean off this table. Food's almost ready."

The table was outside my bedroom, so I nudged the window a little higher and set the gifts inside on the floor. Howard and Uncle Bob manned the grill. The other adults sat on lawn chairs, booing and clapping while Ayanna, Brittany, and I played frisbee. We juggled all four discs between us. Brittany's reaction time was definitely not up to werewolf specs.

After a while, Ayanna caught her disc and walked over to me. "Are you aware someone is spying on us from the forest?"

I'd noticed but hoped my pack hadn't picked up on it.

Brittany hustled over. "What are you two whispering about?"

I said, "Eff is watching us from the trees."

She didn't look. "Let him. We aren't doing anything wrong."

Rita called, "Food is ready."

We sat down to a huge meal of barbecue ribs, chicken, and fresh last-of-the-season Florida corn. Eff remained in the woods. I considered inviting him to eat with us. But Uncle Bob hated Eff. I didn't want to make a scene.

I said to Brittany, "You should have asked Aunt Lynette and Myra to come. There's plenty of food."

"Well, as it turns out, there *is* a Wiccan ritual for Halloween," she said. "So, Eileen is taking my place. And before you ask, yes, it's a naked ceremony."

I looked at her. "You're missing it."

"This is more important. Were you really surprised?"

"Blown away." Of course, it helped that it was the day after my actual birthday. I grabbed another chicken leg then licked my fingers. "How about we go out on a date tomorrow night? A real date. Dinner and a movie. I can pick you up in my car." *My car. My God. I have a car.*

She smiled, crinkling her nose in the way that I loved. "Deal."

"All right, then. I'll pick you up at seven." Life

couldn't get more perfect.

A pile of discarded bones grew in the center of the table. The sky turned purple and gold.

Uncle Bob said, "Save room for cake. We have a Publix special."

"Mmm, cake," Ayanna said.

Everyone laughed.

From the front yard, a group of kids chorused, "Trick or treat."

Rita leaped up. "Our first customers."

"Ooh. I want to see their costumes." Chloe followed her out.

I grinned. It was the best Halloween I ever had.

SIX

D r. Torhild Saarsgard breezed into the meeting room. She was half an hour late and judging by the covert glances she received, some of her staff resented that fact. Discipline was failing. Perhaps it was time for another shakeup—bleed off some of the old blood, bring in some new.

The problem was, she couldn't fire her staff members outright. The work they did at the Lindgren Institute was top secret. So, she devised an ingenious way to rid herself of dissenters. She stripped them of rank and sent them to live in general population where their longevity was proportionate to their previous relationships with the lycanthropes. It had the secondary benefit of keeping the rest of her staff in line.

With a cold smile, she sat at the head of the table and swept her gaze over those in attendance, amusing herself with a list of those she might retire.

"Order," called Karl, her personal assistant. "This meeting will now come to order."

He spoke in Swedish, as did all her personnel. Outside of a few Germans, her staff was made up of Swedes, although the institute was technically in Norway.

She said, "I am still awaiting a report on your latest formula, Dr. Ahlgren."

Ahlgren said, "The formula is not the success we envisioned, I'm afraid. While it does retard the lycan's ability to transform, it also limits their healing capabilities."

To his left, Dr. Friberg gave a tinkle of laughter. "So, what you have is a cure for lycanthropy."

"You fool." Saarsgard leaned forward. "I'm not interested in curing them. I want to harvest their powers for the rest of mankind."

Ahlgren looked miserable. "I need more subjects."

"Take them!" Carlsson threw up his hands. "Population is at an all-time high. Ninety-seven lycans. The amount of food they eat."

"Don't start whining about the budget again," Ms. Entropy snapped. "We have limited funds."

He stabbed the table with his forefinger. "You are given a bounty from every nation where we extradite these monsters."

"Yes. A single payment. And when they eat all that, then what?" Entropy turned her attention to Saarsgard. "Madam Director, I implore you to redouble our conscripting efforts. A sustainable income from families looking to house their little secrets makes financial sense."

"I agree," Saarsgard said. "Mr. Olsson, see to it."

Olsson sputtered. "And what should I do, take out an ad? Unless the psychology department provides viable tips–"

Dr. Hellquist chuckled. All eyes turned to him. He glanced around the table as if to make sure he had everyone's attention. "As it happens, I received an interesting tip just this morning. About a super alpha."

A murmur rounded the table.

Ahlgren said, "Super alphas are myths."

"Perhaps." He chuckled again. "But I have reason to suspect it's true. My source claims this super wolf resides in Florida. His name is Cody." His gaze met Saarsgard's. "Wasn't that the name of the boy you went to conscript some months ago?"

She sniffed. "Cody Forester is no longer a werewolf. A shaman took his powers."

"Yes, yes. As you say."

"You doubt me?"

"Oh, you must be correct. It is difficult to believe that someone so esteemed as yourself could be duped by a teenage boy." He slapped down his hand and leaned forward. "However, my informant is most convincing. If Cody Forester is indeed a super alpha—"

"Get out," Saarsgard growled. "All of you."

"Meeting adjourned," Karl announced.

Everyone leaped up and rushed from the room. Hellquist was last to leave. A faint smirk graced his face.

How dare he question her, humiliate her in front of her staff?

But was he right? Had Cody Forester tricked her? She remembered the shaman dancing, the wind rising. Had it all been a ruse?

She couldn't let it stand.

She motioned Karl to her side. "Consign twenty inmates to Dr. Ahlgren's experiments. Yellow flag twenty more."

"Yes, Madam Director."

"But before you do that, activate the troop transport we have on standby. And prepare my Learjet for a trip to Florida. I'll check on Cody Forester myself."

SEVEN

At seven o'clock on Saturday night, I drove slowly over the bumpy dirt road and parked in Brittany's driveway. She lived in a large, two-story home with an enormous screened-in front porch. It was the only house around. Grandpa Earle once owned acres of land, but over the years he'd had to sell it off in parcels to pay his taxes. The house and its wide green lawn were still surrounded by woodland, just not as much as before.

As I got out of the car, Brittany's half-breed dog, Haff, bounded over to greet me. I ruffled his ears. Haff and I weren't always buddies. Werewolves don't usually get along with other animals. But over time we'd learned to trust and respect one another.

I looked up as Brit stepped out of the porch. She wore the black mini-skirt she often wore to school, but instead of army boots, she wore sandals. It made her legs look long and shapely.

"Hi," I said, giving Haff a final pat. "You hungry?"

She smiled. "Starved. Where do you want to eat?"

I could have played the where-do-you-want-to-go game, but Uncle Bob warned me that girls liked it when their dates planned everything. It was kind of a test to see how well we knew them. So, I chose a restaurant I knew she liked. "Olive Garden."

"Ooh." Her smile broadened, and I knew I'd scored a point.

I opened the passenger door and helped her inside. And just like that, we were on our way.

"This is such a nice car," she said.

"Yeah. Do you want me to start picking you up for school? It'd be no problem."

"Of course, it would." She laughed. "I'm all the way on the other side of town. Besides, Baby would be jealous. Let's just drive ourselves for now."

I shrugged and pulled up to a traffic light. It was dusk. The sky was still a little pink, making the trees look black.

"Daylight savings time," she murmured as if reading my thoughts. "Such a pain."

"Benjamin Franklin was a jerk."

"That's a little harsh. Besides, he didn't have anything to do with it."

"He didn't?"

"Look it up." She turned on the radio. "Do you have Sirus?"

"No, so I brought a few CDs. They're in the glove compartment."

She thumbed through the cases. "*Linkin Park*, *My Chemical Romance*, *Fall Out Boy*. Nice selection." She put on *Panic at the Disco* and leaned back humming.

We headed out to Wellington, and before long, we were at the restaurant. The advantages to eating at Olive Garden were they all looked the same, they all tasted the same, and you didn't need a reservation. I hopped out of the car, circled around, and offered Brit my arm. She smiled, and I felt like I'd scored another point. We went inside.

The hostess said she'd have a table for us in ten minutes, so we sat in the bar area and ordered a Dew.

I said, "Are you excited about your birthday

party tomorrow?"

"My actual birthday isn't until Monday, but yeah, we have a nice party planned. Expect to spend the whole day."

"I'm looking forward to it."

"Funny how close our birthdays are."

"What are you talking about? Mine's in October and yours is in November."

She laughed.

"Now, if they were on the same day, that would be something," I said. "We could tell everyone we were twins."

"Or that we met in the hospital nursery and fell in love when we were infants."

"Meant to be." I smiled.

She put her hand over mine. "Predestination. From birth. The stars aligned, and here we are."

"Do Wiccans believe in astrology?"

"Astronomy, yes. Astrology, no."

"Well, if there is such a thing as destiny, then I was destined to be with you. Of course, fifty years from now when you're all gray and wrinkly–"

"Cody." She smacked my arm.

I leaned close. "I'll be gray and wrinkly, too."

The hostess interrupted and led us to our table. Brittany gazed dreamily out the window. It was dark out. Headlights and taillights streamed along the street.

"The movie starts at eight-thirty," I said, more to get her attention than to inform her. "I thought we'd see *The Haunting of Molly Hartley*."

"You know me so well."

"An educated guess."

The server brought us water. We each ordered salad with no onions and lasagna with meat sauce. The server left, and Brittany gazed out the window again. She seemed miles away.

She murmured, "I was thinking of having lasagna at our wedding."

"Wh-what?"

She raised her brows. "You asked me to marry you?"

"Several times, actually. But you never said yes."

Her eyes met mine. A smile touched her lips. "Yes."

I reached across the table and took her hand. It was the best night of my life.

Sunday was the perfect day for a birthday party. A cold front had moved down the state, dropping the temperature ten degrees. The sky was bright blue. The trees were flowering again, and their falling petals made such a mess it was almost like autumn up north.

I decided to leave my car at home to save gas. Before we left, I gave it a quick once-over with a soft cloth from my kit. It looked great in the driveway, but I really wished we had a garage. Maybe I should buy a custom car cover. I climbed into the back of my uncle's truck. As we drove away, I said a silent farewell.

We got to Brittany's house around eleven o'clock and were the last ones there. Uncle Bob parked behind Eileen's woody station wagon. We picked up our presents and headed around the side of the house. The yard seemed bigger without the old orange tree. It had fallen during a recent storm, ripping its roots out of the ground. The massive crater it left behind was now a horseshoe pit.

"Hi!" Brittany bounded over and kissed me.

Howard called, "Presents go over here." As if we couldn't see the stack of boxes and gift bags beneath the halo of crepe paper streamers.

Haff-the-dog stood at the side of the yard barking frantically.

"What's with him?" Uncle Bob asked.

Brittany shrugged. "He's been barking all morning."

Uncle Bob and Rita walked over to Howard and the gift table.

I lowered my voice. "It's Eff."

Brittany gasped and whispered, "Eff is in my woods? Why does he keep spying on us?"

"I think he's trying to catch me doing something wolfish. Probably recording us right now."

"Video?" She widened her eyes in mock alarm. "Is my hair all right?"

I guffawed and gave her a sideways squeeze.

Ayanna sauntered over. "He's back," she crooned.

I said, "Let's just ignore him for now."

"All right," she said, "but sooner or later, you'll have to address it."

I nodded. Eff was getting out of control.

Eileen and William sat at the picnic table beneath a red-and-yellow striped canopy. They waved, and I steered Brittany and Ayanna toward them.

"Howdy," William said.

I said, "How's married life treating you?"

Eileen and William were newlyweds, and

their wedding was instrumental in getting William's parents back together.

As if on cue, Chelsea stepped out the kitchen door carrying two pitchers. "I have the mimosas."

Howard hopped up to help her. They were Native American—Howard was Navajo, Chelsea was Miccosukee, and William was—well, I tease him that he's a sukee-ho. Howard, a powerful medicine man, could turn into a bear using a bear-hide belt. William, wanting to imitate his father, learned to do the same. Actually, William could do a lot of interesting stuff.

Lynette came outside carrying a platter of sandwiches. "Brunch is ready," she called. "These here are my famous ham-and-egg sammies."

According to Lynette, everything she cooked was *famous*.

Myra followed her out with a bowl of fruit salad. They placed the food on the picnic table, and we fell on it like a swarm of ants. The only one eating the fruit was Eileen—she was a vegetarian.

Lynette picked up the empty platter. "Got more in the oven. Be right back."

Eileen said, "Sorry I missed your birthday,

Cody. Did you have fun?"

"Yeah, I'm sorry you missed it, too. But I appreciate you taking Brit's part in the ceremony. My birthday wouldn't have been the same without her." I grinned at Brittany, and she gave me her special smile in return.

Lynette brought out another platter. I was glad for a second sandwich. They were delicious—fried egg, barbecued ham, yellow cheese inside, white cheese on top. You couldn't have too much cheese.

The adults gathered around the mimosa pitchers. Dick's booming laugh rocked the yard.

Haff continued barking at Eff.

"Oh, that dog." Brittany slapped her leg. "Here, Haff. Come here, boy."

The dog kept barking.

I looked over and said, "Come."

Haff stopped mid-bark and trotted over to us with a doggy grin.

"Well." Brittany chuckled. "That was impressive."

Eileen said, "You summoned him like William summons bears."

I shrugged as if to say it was nothing, but inside my thoughts squirmed. Had I done a mind whammy on the dog?

EIGHT

Dr. Saarsgard seethed. She sat in the back of the silver limousine, arms folded, legs crossed, and replayed the day she'd thought Cody Forester had lost his powers.

She'd tried to conscript him through normal channels. His parents hadn't taken much convincing. They believed she was searching for a cure. But Cody fought. He refused to go. She told him the only way she would leave him alone was if he stopped being a werewolf. So, he enlisted the help of a Native American shaman.

Saarsgard shuddered in spite of herself as she remembered the power that radiated from the Indian boy. He had no idea how powerful a shaman he really was. He chanted and danced around his little fire, and the wind rose. A terrifying wind that tore trees from the ground. Cody fell. He started to shift into his wolf form—in the middle of the day, no less. But the shaman doused him with a steaming potion. The transformation halted. The wind died, and Cody was a boy once more.

And she'd believed the shaman had taken away his ability to turn into a wolf. Their performance had been so convincing. The two of them had probably laughed together when she left empty-handed.

She'd always taken Cody for a rather nerdy teenager. Was he actually a super wolf? A super alpha had powers far beyond what a normal werewolf possessed. She never heard of one who could shift during the day, however. Perhaps she was overreacting. Perhaps Cody Forester was no longer a werewolf. But if he was... Only a super alpha could have deceived her.

And now thanks to Hellquist her entire staff knew of her folly. He could have approached her with the information privately, but he chose to confront her in front of her underlings. They were all laughing at her now. But her humiliation would die with them. They wouldn't last two days in the lycan population. She'd have to remember to tell Karl she was recruiting new heads of staff.

The limo slowed and turned onto a gravel driveway, snapping her out of her reverie. She gazed at a familiar blue clapboard house. A little red car sat in the driveway. They pulled in behind it.

Her driver cut the engine. As if it were their cue, her troops burst from the surrounding woodland and spread over the yard. They wore the Institute's distinctive beige-and-white mottled uniforms. A few had stripes on their shoulders. Three soldiers mounted the front steps, bashed in the door, and tossed in a stun grenade. They disappeared inside.

Saarsgard's bodyguard stepped out from the front seat, flexing his muscles. He always sat with the driver of late. He was a werewolf, and she complained publicly that she couldn't tolerate his stink. Although she privately admitted it was probably all in her mind.

Her driver said, "Will you be exiting, Madam?"

"Not at this time. Please have the captain join me when he has a free moment."

The driver got out, circled the back of the limo so as not to obscure her view, and stood beside the passenger door. Moments later, the door opened, and Captain Gary Nilsson slid in opposite her.

Saarsgard said, "I take it no one is home."

"No ma'am," he said. "The house is clear."

She muttered, "Delays, delays."

"Your orders, Madam Director?"

She gazed through the windshield at the house. "Burn it."

"Ma'am?"

"I don't want him to have any place to come back to. I'll go somewhere visible. Have a cup of coffee perhaps. With any luck, he'll come to me."

He opened the door.

"Oh, and Gary," Saarsgard said, "torch the car, too."

I laughed.

Eileen continued. "So, now he comes over every day to see if I'm pregnant yet."

William shook his head. "That Barney. He never was good with auras."

There came a clang and a shout. I looked over at the horseshoe pit where the adults played. They'd finished the mimosas and were working on the bottle of wine Dick brought.

Brittany took my hand. I smiled and kissed her cheek.

Ayanna snorted. "Good. He's finally leaving."

"Who?" asked Eileen.

"Eff," Brittany said. "That boy from school. He's watching us from the trees."

William nodded. "Ah," he said and sat back.

Eileen looked confused. "I thought you were friends with Eff."

"We were," I said, "but he found out I was a werewolf. He's been following me around ever since."

Ayanna said, "Trying to catch you doing something dodgy?"

"Good luck to him," Brittany said. "We're not hurting anyone."

I said, "I think he's taking pictures of me to show to the sheriff."

"Or maybe he'll post them on the Internet," Eileen said. "Like that blogger. What was her name?"

"I should pay him a visit." William grinned. "I could wear my bear-pelt belt."

Laughter rounded our group.

Brittany said, "He would really freak if you turned into a bear in front of him."

I said, "He's not ready for someone like you. I'm hoping he'll get bored and quit on his own."

"No." Ayanna's dark eyes flashed. "You hoped to avoid confrontation. You should have told him to sod off."

I shook my head. "That would only make it worse."

Finished with their game of horseshoes, the adults moseyed toward us.

Aunt Lynette called, "Brit, would you like to open your gifts?"

Ayanna clapped to the tune of "Open them. Open them."

Brittany's cheeks pinked. "Sure."

So, Brittany sat at the picnic table surrounded by gifts, and we sat on lawn chairs surrounding her and the picnic table.

Uncle Bob and Rita gave her candles—all different sizes and colors.

"Wonderful," Brittany said. "I can really use these."

Aunt Lynette and Myra gave her a Samsung smartphone with a slide-out keyboard.

"All set and raring to go," Aunt Lynette said.

Brittany snapped a few pics then beamed. "I love it. Thank you."

Dick and Chloe's gift was a silky, leopard-print bathrobe with slippers.

"For lounging," Dick explained.

When Brittany opened Ayanna's gift, her eyes lit. It was twenty packets of assorted flower and herb seeds.

"I'll put these to good use," Brittany told her.

Ayanna grinned. Genuine pleasure seeped through the *link*, and I was glad for the friendship that was springing up between them.

Howard and Chelsea gave her a recipe box filled with handwritten index cards.

"Herbal remedies," Howard said. "Passed down through generations. Some Navajo, some Miccosukee."

"And a few Seminole," Chelsea said. "From friends."

"Amazing," Brittany murmured as she thumbed through them. "Thank you."

Eileen and William got her a couple of blank books and a purple t-shirt with *Trust Me—I'm A Witch* printed on the front.

Brittany smirked as she held it up to herself. "I'll wear it to school tomorrow."

Finally, she got to my gift. With my father's help and advice, I'd gotten her a black leather doctor's bag filled with vials and flasks.

Brittany gasped. "It's perfect."

I smiled. "Just like you."

ᕍᕍᕍ

"Perfect," Dr. Saarsgard said as the matronly waitress led her to a window seat. It had a clear view of the comings and goings outdoors. "I'll take some coffee."

"Right away, ma'am."

The Coffee Café was a quaint little diner. *Little* being the operative word. Her limo was too long for the parking lot, so her driver waited for her on the street. Her werewolf bodyguard sat at the counter, looking at once nonchalant and vigilant. Outside the window, a woman was painting red-and-green ornaments on the glass. The transparent paint turned the sunlight as red as fire.

Saarsgard imagined Cody Forester returning home to find his house ablaze. Would he know she was responsible? Perhaps she erred by not getting out of the car. If she'd left her scent in the yard, he would certainly search her out. Providing, of course, that he was still a werewolf and could smell such things. Her first impression might yet prove correct.

The waitress brought her a steaming cup of

coffee. Saarsgard nodded in acknowledgment then poured in three packets of sugar. She stirred and sipped, poured in another packet and sipped again.

A teenage boy approached her booth. He was muscular and tan. Her bodyguard tensed. Saarsgard caught his eye and gave a small nod. She would allow this intrusion.

"I saw your limo," the boy said. He spoke boldly, but his hands twitched, belying his nervousness. "Do you remember me?"

And all at once, she did. "Yes. You're the boy who totaled my car and put me in the hospital the last time I was here."

"You were after *him*."

"To whom are we referring?"

"Cody. You knew he was a monster even then."

She sniffed. She'd been trying to abduct Cody Forester, and this boy's interference cost her a lot of time.

"He's a werewolf," the boy said.

"I prefer the term lycanthrope."

He fell silent. She sipped her coffee and let him stew.

He said, "Do you still want him?"

"Do you know where he is?"

His lip curled. "With the rest of his pack."

She set the cup down hard. "He has a pack?"

He blanched and took a step back. "I think so. I mean, his uncle's one for sure. And they've become chummy with the Richardsons."

"Bob Nowak? Is a werewolf?" Saarsgard clenched her jaw.

They'd tricked her. All of them. How could she be so blind? She thought back to when she'd first met the mother—a young doctor looking for a cure. Long before Cody was born. Of course. It made perfect sense now. She'd been looking for a cure for her brother.

"Where are they?" she growled.

To his credit, he didn't run. "They're at a party. A birthday party. But not everyone there is involved."

"Brittany," she murmured. "They're at Brittany Myers' house."

"Don't hurt her," he cried. "She's innocent. She doesn't know."

"Of course, she knows, you stupid boy. She's always known."

🐺🐺🐺

Brittany smiled, surrounded by friends. The

most important people in her life. Lynette stood with Rita and Chloe, educating them about the virtues of St. John's Wort. Myra and Chelsea discussed Miccosukee versus Wiccan wedding customs. Howard and Bob sat at the picnic table trying to teach Dick how to play rummy. Eileen braided Ayanna's hair. Cody and William stood at the grill flipping burgers with Haff sitting patiently at their feet. The perfect birthday. Life didn't get much better than this.

Suddenly men in strange uniforms rushed from the trees and surrounded them. They fired their guns. Brittany flinched. But instead of bullets, she was struck by paintballs. The impact stung and spattered her with orange liquid. She staggered, more from surprise than anything else.

"Hey!" she shouted. "This is private property."

She looked over at Lynette, expecting her to share her outrage. Her aunt was also covered in orange—but she gaped as if in panic. Rita and Chloe fell twitching to the ground, eyes rolled back to whites, mouths frothing.

"Mum!" Ayanna cried. She rushed across the yard toward her mother, but several orange splotches appeared on her chest. Her steps slowed, and she fell before she could reach her.

"Wait." Brittany cried. "Stop!" She stepped forward, arms out as if she could put everything back together.

A crash made her jump. Pitchers of sweet tea fell from the picnic table as a barrage of paintballs struck. Orange liquid plastered the three men. Cards flew. Dick stood in slow motion then crumpled and fell, convulsing on the grass. Bob collapsed onto the table. Howard toppled backward off the bench then came up sputtering, his face dripping orange.

Cody roared. His arms elongated, and his body swelled.

"No!" Brittany shouted. *Don't turn into your beast! Turn into a wolf. Run away!*

Cody was now at least seven feet tall. Yellowed claws curled from his fingers. Fangs filled his snarling mouth. He thundered toward the soldiers, towering over them. They quailed and scattered.

But there were more soldiers. So many more.

"Cody!" Brittany screamed. "Run!"

The soldiers concentrated their firepower on him. William leaped before them, taking the brunt of the blast. Brittany ran toward him, but

Howard caught her by the waist and wouldn't let her go.

Cody roared again. He charged, striking out with his massive arms. One man cartwheeled through the air. Another flew into five more, knocking them all down.

And still, they fired. Noxious orange liquid drenched Cody's fur. He stumbled to his knees.

"Cody!" She struggled. Tears streamed down her face.

A circle of soldiers converged, peppering him with paintballs. He jerked and snarled with each impact.

She cried. "Let me go!"

Howard looked at her. His face echoed her confusion and horror. He lowered his arms.

Brittany didn't move. She couldn't. A terrible emptiness filled her.

Cody lay on the grass within the ring of soldiers.

Saarsgard stepped from the trees.

"What are you doing?" Brittany shouted and stomped toward her. Two guards stepped up and grabbed her arms.

Saarsgard smiled. "I'm fulfilling the promise I made the last time we met. I'm helping your boyfriend."

"Helping?" she shouted shrilly. "This is helping?"

"*Kapten*," Saarsgard called, and a man stepped obediently to her side. "*Sparra in*."

The man nodded, and soldiers burst from the trees wheeling cages. The cages looked like oversized dog carriers.

"No." Brittany stretched out her hand, but she couldn't stop them.

The two guards marched her to where her friends had been herded. All were splotched with orange. The stink of bitter medicine wafted around them.

The werewolves remained on the ground. Dick convulsed. Cody had returned to his human form. He lay as still as death.

Brittany stepped behind Lynette and slipped her new smartphone from her pocket. She videoed the scene.

They took Dick first, then Bob, cramming them headfirst into their cages. Ayanna was next. Foam streamed from her open mouth as they shoved and folded her inside. Then they rolled two cages to Chloe and Rita and snapped them up.

Cody had not moved from where he had fallen, but when the cage rattled next to him, he groaned. One of the soldiers leaped back, gun drawn. Another kicked Cody in the ribs.

Howard stepped forward. "Hey!"

The soldier nearest Howard butt-ended him in the mouth. Blood sprayed. Chelsea cried out and put her arms around him. As if she could protect him. As if any of them could protect the ones they loved.

Tears sprang to Brittany's eyes, but she pursed her lips and hardened her heart. She moved to the other side of her huddled friends, recording everything. The soldier kicked Cody again, and Cody writhed with the blow.

Saarsgard crossed the lawn. She gave William a nasty look but didn't approach him. Instead, she stood over Cody. She smiled with such glee, Brittany felt sick to her stomach. The soldiers took Cody's arms and legs and manhandled him into the little cage. The door latched with a loud click.

Like a gunshot to her heart. Brittany clasped the phone to her chest. Her legs wobbled, and she sat heavily on the ground. They had Cody. What was she going to do?

"Brittany? Are you all right?"

"Brit, can you hear me?"

What was she going to do? He was her

world. Her mate. Her reason for living. And they were taking him from her.

Haff appeared from nowhere and sat beside her. The intruders dragged the clattering cages across the grass and into the trees. An engine roared. There was an overgrown road back there, not much more than a bike trail. How had they known about it? Who could have told them?

She remembered Haff barking...

Barking at Eff. Efrem Higgins. He knew about Saarsgard. He knew about the road. Eff must be the one who ratted them out. And he would pay.

NINE

Brittany lay in bed and stared at the ceiling as it slowly darkened. Downstairs, her friends were leaving. She listened to their sad goodbyes, imagined their solemn hugs. Then they were gone. After a while, Lynette and Myra went to bed. The house grew silent. Cold.

She got up, stripped naked, and slipped on her white ceremonial robe. Like a wraith, she glided down the stairs. She took the ingredients she needed from the cabinets in the kitchen and tiptoed out the back door.

The waxing moon was high. It bathed her in its light. Normally, the potion she intended to make needed to be concocted during the dark of the moon. But not this time. Tonight, she would add the moon's energy to her own. Mother Moon had a part to play in avenging her son.

The next morning, Brittany sat in her car in the school parking lot, eyes on her rearview mirror. Eff backed his truck into a parking spot. She got out and walked to him.

He turned off the engine. "Hi." He smiled as if nothing were wrong. As if he hadn't ruined her life.

And she wanted to throttle him. Wanted to bash his head against the dashboard. She clung to the handkerchief hidden in her hand.

He climbed from the truck.

She backed away. "Eff," she said in a wavering voice she didn't recognize, "did you tell Saarsgard where to find Cody?"

He straightened his shoulders and met her gaze. "Yes."

The word struck like a rock to her gut. She edged farther away.

"It was for the best," he said. "He was a time bomb."

She stared.

He averted his gaze. "She told me you knew all along. What he was."

She stared.

His lip curled. "You should be on your knees

thanking me. I saved you."

And she reached deep into the well of rage and magic to supercharge the already-potent love potion as she flicked the handkerchief and flung the powder directly into his face.

Eff gasped and wheezed, drawing it into his lungs. He stumbled against the truck and rubbed it into his eyes.

Brittany waited for the cloud to settle. In a low voice, she said, "Eff, look at me."

Eff coughed. He brushed at his clothing, causing more of the powder to rise.

"Look at me!"

And he did.

"Brittany," he whispered. "You are so beautiful."

She stared.

"I have to be with you," he said. "Only with you."

"Only me. For the rest of your life."

"Yes." His face was blissful. "I love you."

"But I don't love you. I will never love you. You are the worst person I ever met."

"What? No... I..."

"I despise you, Efrem Higgins. I want you to know that. I want you to spend the rest of your miserable life knowing that." She turned and strode to her car.

"Brittany," he cried. "Don't leave me."

As she drove away, she saw him in her rearview mirror. He was on his knees in the parking lot, clawing at his shirt, red-faced and wailing.

She murmured, "You got off easy, you son of a bitch."

Dr. David Forester liked his new job as Director of Cardiology at Palms West Hospital. But sometimes the paperwork was overwhelming. He sat at his desk behind a stack of files, but his mind wasn't on his work. He was thinking of Cody and his new car, imagining heads turning as he drove to school. His son was a good kid, but he never had a lot of friends. At least, he had a girlfriend.

As if on cue, Brittany burst into his office.

Angie was on her heels. "I'm sorry, Dr. Forester."

"That's all right, Angie," he said. "Close the door for me, would you?"

Looking pensive, Angie closed the door.

David raised his brows. "Morning, Brittany.

What's up?"

"This is all your fault." She leaned toward him across the desk. "If you hadn't contacted Saarsgard in the first place, none of this would have happened."

"Saarsgard? What are you talking about?"

"She took Cody."

"Took?" He leaped to his feet. "You mean kidnapped?"

"I mean she stuffed him in a cage and carried him away."

"No, no." He smiled, trying to calm her. "Why would she do that? She's a professional. A doctor."

Brittany took her phone from her back pocket and circled the desk. She showed him a video. A horrifying video.

"Oh, my God." David gasped. *What were they doing to his son?*

Dr. Saarsgard came on the screen. Brittany's hand shook, so David took the phone from her. He stared at the doctor's face. She looked deranged.

"This can't be happening."

"Oh, it happened." Brittany sank into a chair. "They put him in a cage."

"You wanted to send him there. Tried to talk

him into going." She looked up with bloodshot eyes. "You should've done your research. The Lindgren Institute isn't a spa or a resort. They experiment on werewolves. They torture them. Murder them." A sob escaped her, and she covered her face. "I'll never see Cody again."

He put his hand on her shoulder and held out her phone. "We'll take this evidence to the police."

"The police can't do anything," she snarled. "Saarsgard is authorized by the government. The FBI is probably filling out the paperwork for her right now."

He recoiled. "FBI?"

"Clueless." She snatched back the phone. "Do you at least know where the institute is located?"

"Yes. It's in the Fjallen Mountains on the border between Norway and Sweden."

She stood. "Can you be any more vague?"

He opened his mouth then closed it. He didn't know exactly where it was. He didn't question Marie. He never questioned Marie. She was his wife. Why would he question her?

Brittany gave him an exasperated look and headed for the door.

"What are you going to do?" he asked.

She paused. "I don't know." And she stormed out.

David closed the door and pressed his forehead against it. Why had he gone along so meekly when Marie wanted to place Cody in that institute? He always did whatever she said.

No more.

He took out his cell phone and dialed her number. He was surprised when she answered after only three rings and stunned when she knew it was him. He'd gotten a new line when they'd separated, and he'd never given it to her.

"Hello, David."

"You knew, didn't you?" he said, impressed with his own daring. "You knew they were experimenting on people at the Lindgren Institute."

"Experimenting is a strong word. We both knew they were trying to find a cure."

"Well, our son was just drugged, caged, and carried away."

"What?"

"They put him in a cage, Marie. Like an animal. No regard for human rights. And you wanted to give him to them."

"I assure you—"

"How could you do that to your only son?

What kind of mother are you?" There. He said it. After all these years.

The phone was silent for so long he thought the call might have been dropped.

Quietly, she said, "There must be some mistake."

"No mistake. She had soldiers with her. A lot of them."

"Very well. I'll contact Congressman Everett."

"What good will that do? Saarsgard has contacts in our government."

"I have contacts, too. But I need proof. Something tangible."

"There's a video."

"Send it to me."

He winced and nodded. "I'll get a copy. And when you find your contacts are worthless?"

Her voice became manic. "Then I will fly to Gothenburg and get our son back."

"Fine." David glanced around his office. "I'm going with you."

Brittany sat at the table in Eileen's little kitchen and buried her face in her hands. She was tired.

So tired. What was she going to do?

Eileen sat next to her. "Did you find out where it is?"

"All he knew was that it's in the mountains between Sweden and Norway."

"Okay." She wrung her hands. "William and I were up all night, and here's what we decided to do. At the wedding, we were given gifts of money to put toward a honeymoon. So, what's to stop us from taking our honeymoon in Norway? I have cousins there. I'd love to meet them. They might even know where this institute is. Then we will spend a week or two backpacking in the Scandinavian mountains. It's not that unusual."

"That's fine for you," Brittany said, "but I can't go on your honeymoon."

"We'll think of something. Tell them it's a tradition to bring a friend to assist us. A lady-in-waiting. To take care of troublesome details, you know? They won't know any better."

Brittany leaned back. Norway? How much money could she borrow from Lynette?

The front door opened, and William entered the room. He crossed to the refrigerator and took out a can of Coke.

Eileen said, "Find out anything?"

The Coke fizzed as he opened it. "It takes three days to get an expedited passport." He took a drink. "But you have to prove you have family there. And you have to visit them at least once."

"Then it's doable." Eileen nodded as if to herself then looked at Brittany. "You already have a passport, don't you Brit?"

"Yes, I got one for that cruise we took as a school trip."

Eileen smiled. "Guess I'd better call and introduce myself to my distant relatives. Next stop, Norway."

Tears sprang to Brittany's eyes. *Hang on, Cody. We're on our way.*

TEN

I cracked my eyes open. I couldn't focus. A moan rumbled in my throat.

"It's waking up," someone said.

The voice seemed to echo. Like I was hearing it twice. I turned my head toward the sound.

"It is. It's waking."

"What should we do?"

"Oh, Lord."

I tried to lift my hand. It was strapped down. An IV line prickled in my arm. Was I in a hospital?

"I'll handle this."

Keys jangled.

No. Not a hospital. I was in a jail cell. Tied to a cot. My body ached.

"What are you doing? Don't go in there. It

might be faking. Just waiting until you get close enough. And bam! It'll rip you limb-from-limb."

"What do we do then?"

A pause.

"Call the doctor. Let her take the risk."

Another pause.

"What, are you afraid?"

"I'm just as much afraid of her as I am of that thing."

"Go on. I'll keep it covered."

A click. Was that a gun?

I tried to speak, but my mouth was dry. So dry. My lips cracked. Blood seeped into my mouth.

I had to wake up. I had to get out of there. My pack... Brittany...

The bars rattled. Someone opened the door.

"Don't worry," said a new voice. A woman's voice. "He can't get free."

Fingers touched my face. Pulled open my eyes. A light shone in. White hot lightning.

I wanted to recoil. I tried. I jutted out my chin. My fingers twitched.

"Well, Mr. Forester," the voice said. "It appears the drip is insufficient. We'll have to mainline."

Fire erupted in my arm. My muscles seized.

My throat convulsed, making a ga-ga-ga sound.

"Yes. Hurts, doesn't it?"

The fire spread. Consuming my body. I imagined my skin crisping. Turning black. My mouth opened. Lips peeled back. But I couldn't catch my breath enough to scream.

"That will put an end to his nonsense. Call me if anything else happens. We can't have him drowning in his own blood."

My back arched. Straining against the restraints. My feet drummed upon the cot. I caught a whiff of urine. Oh, God. I peed myself.

Bars rattled. Keys rang. Footsteps receded. Receded.

Brittany... Help me... My wolf is gone...

Then everything went black.

🐺🐺🐺

Brittany took a step back from her aunt's wrath.

"Norway?" Lynette roared. "What kind of cockamamie plan is that?"

"It's my only hope."

"And how do you expect to find him in all of Norway?"

Brittany glanced toward Myra for support. Her friend sat at the kitchen table looking only mildly interested.

"Well," Brittany said in a quavering voice. "I'll start at the Lindgren Institute."

"And you expect them to just release him, do you?"

"I have to do something. Saarsgard will kill him."

"Kill you, too, most likely. The way Cody talked, she's a real piece of work."

"I have to try." She began to cry. "If I don't... I could never live with myself."

"No. You're my responsibility. I'll not have you traipsing off to another country by your lonesome."

"I won't be alone. Eileen and William will be with me. And Eileen's already spoken to her cousin."

Lynette paced. "What would we tell your ma?"

"The same thing we told Eileen's aunt. Eileen and William are going backpacking on their honeymoon, and I'm going along as a sort of lady-in-waiting. She'll buy it. She knows I've always wanted to travel."

Silence fell over the kitchen. Lynette continued to pace. Brittany looked toward Myra. Isis, the three-legged cat jumped into Myra's lap, and Myra stroked the dark fur.

"I don't know." Lynette leaned against the stove and folded her arms. "What about your studies? You were just starting to make real headway."

"I won't be gone long. I promise. And when I get back, I'll study twice as hard. I'll get a degree in herbology and anything else you think I need. I'll be the best witch you've ever seen. My word of honor. Only, I need to do this first."

Lynette blew out a breath.

Brittany took a step toward her. "I know it will be an imposition, but any money you can lend me–"

"Ha!" Lynette shouted.

In a quiet voice, Myra said, "As it turns out, Lynnie and I have had a recent windfall. The Georgia coven bought out our interests in the candle shop. I would be happy to fund this worthy cause."

"Fool's folly, you mean." Lynette speared her with a beady eye.

Myra got up and slid her arms around Lynette's neck. "She loves him, Lynnie. Wouldn't you do the same for me?"

Lynette scowled. She said, "Yes," as if the word were bitter. She looked at Brittany. "All right. You can go. But I still say you'll never find the boy."

🐕🐕🐕

I opened a bleary eye. Where was I? What was happening to me? I tried to move. My arms and legs were heavy. Strapped down. Yet I was moving. A cold breeze touched my cheeks. Wheels crackled on cement.

I was in a wheelchair. My eyes widened but failed to focus. Where were they taking me? Where was Brittany? My God, if anything happened to her... And my pack.

Where was my pack? I reached for the *link* but couldn't sense anybody. Were they all dead?

My head lowered. My chin bounced on my chest. I'd failed them. All of them. I didn't protect them, didn't defend them from... Who? Someone attacked Brittany's birthday party. Why would they do that?

The chair rolled up a ramp. I gasped. Wake up, stupid! Do something!

"He's moving," a man said. Only that wasn't what he said. His words were foreign, but I heard English in my mind.

"I doubt it," a woman answered. "We gave him enough to drop an elephant."

They were speaking a different language. Swedish? Oh God oh God. I knew only one villain who spoke Swedish.

"Where do you want him?"

"Over there. By the restraints."

The man wheeled me to a wall and secured the chair. I was in the cabin of a personal jet. Saarsgard had me. She was the one who attacked the birthday party. She was taking me to the Lindgren Institute. To experiment on me. Dissect me.

What was I going to do?

"Ah, Mr. Forester. You're awake." Saarsgard's face loomed out of the dark.

Only it wasn't dark. Sunlight streamed through the little portholes.

I peeled my tongue from the roof of my mouth. "Where's Brittany?" I croaked. "If you hurt her—"

"She's fine." Saarsgard sat across from me in a plush chair. "Probably scouting out alternative prospects for the prom as we speak. You may as well put her out of your mind. You will never see her again."

"Because you're going to kill me?"

"Kill?" She put her hand on her chest dramatically. "I'm not going to kill you. You're my star acquisition. Your mother never told me you were a super wolf."

With a shuddering thud, the hatch closed. My ears popped. They were pressurizing the cabin. Oh God oh God. I had to get out. But I couldn't move. Couldn't think.

A soldier approached. He wore a uniform I didn't recognize. He held out a tray with a bottle of sparkling water and a glass. Saarsgard took the items. With her eyes on me, she poured the water into the glass.

I licked my lips. They were split and scabbed. But my head was clearing. I had to keep her off-guard until I figured out what to do.

In a crackly voice, I asked, "What kind of uniforms are those?"

She smirked. "Mine."

"Figures. From the country of You."

She sipped the water then held up the glass as if admiring the light streaming through the bubbles. "Yes. The Lindgren Institute is a sovereign state."

"Supported by all the countries of the world." I rolled my eyes.

"Indeed. No one wants filthy lycanthropes in

their midst. And there are always more to be had."

"So then, what is it you do, exactly? Dog catcher?"

"You will learn what I do soon enough."

The engines whined. Taking off. My weakened body deflated further. Oh no. *Brittany*. My eyes stung. I wanted to cry. But I had no moisture for tears.

The tires clicked on the runway. Picking up speed. The wheelchair bobbed and rattled. In a smooth arc, the plane rose. My stomach swooped.

Saarsgard sipped her water.

I said, "Where are my friends?"

She snapped, "You mean your pack?" Then she paused as if to compose herself. "That was quite a trick you played. You and your shaman friend. I truly thought you'd lost your powers."

"I did. They grew back."

She scoffed. "In any case, your pack has gone on ahead of you. They should be settled into the institute by now. There was no problem getting them through customs. No one to speak for them. You, on the other hand, took days of negotiations. Believe it or not, your mother tried to block me. Not in her name, of course, but I know it was her. Who would have thought?"

My mother? She was the last person I'd expect to stand up for me. She had political friends, but she would never tell them she had a werewolf for a son. That would be embarrassing, might even affect her standing on the Board.

The sunlight shifted as the plane banked. Taking me farther from home.

No, it couldn't have been my mother who fought for me. My mother hated werewolves.

David Forester stepped into the coffee shop—and into a barrage of memories. They used to frequent this place when they were young. Before everything went wrong.

He winced. *Steady, David. She has no power over you anymore*.

She sat at a table by the window looking out at Logan International. She acted like she didn't realize he was there. But, of course, she did. He'd never met anyone more aware of their surroundings. It was like she had a sixth sense.

He sat across from her. "Hello, Marie."

"David. You're looking good."

"So, your congressman friend couldn't help us?"

"He took that video to the top. I didn't tell him it was about werewolves, but he knew. They all knew Dr. Saarsgard. She's more powerful than I expected. The most he could do was delay her. It's time for Plan B." She slid an envelope across the table. "We're flying Scandinavian Airlines to Goteburg Landvetter Airport."

"Gothenburg. In Sweden."

"Yes."

"And that's where the institute is."

"Not exactly." She sipped her coffee. "We'll have to rent a car."

The sun was momentarily eclipsed by a passing jet.

"But you know where to go."

"I have a good idea," she said. "I mean, how many roads through the mountains could there possibly be?"

He stared until she met his gaze. "And what will we do when we get there? Pound on the door and demand our son back?"

She set her cup down with a clink. "The Lindgren Institute was established during World War II."

He waved a hand impatiently. "I got all that

from the brochure you were touting."

"Yes. Well, the point is, it's been around for many years and has quite a few employees. Since Dr. Saarsgard took over, she's been recruiting top personnel. Her assistant, Karl, has contacted me on several occasions trying to get me to join her staff."

"How nice for you."

"So, I called him yesterday, told him we were both interested in employment and asked for a tour. That will get us through the door. Then we can locate Cody."

"And Bob," he said. "They took your brother, too, remember?"

She blew out an impatient breath.

He raised his hands. "I don't get it. You dedicate half your life studying endocrinology to find a cure for your brother then abruptly shift focus and become a neurosurgeon. Doesn't he matter to you anymore?"

She leaned forward, teeth bared, face like a skull. "No, he doesn't matter. He's never mattered. He's always been petty and self-centered. But we'll save him, too, if that makes you happy. And then you'd better get out of the way because I'm going to kill Saarsgard."

ELEVEN

Brittany trailed behind William and Eileen as they entered the terminal at Oslo Airport in Gardermoen. She glanced back at the red-nosed Norwegian Air Shuttle. It had been a long flight, made even longer by her impatience, and she was glad to finally be in Norway. She didn't know how she was going to find Cody, but she wouldn't stop looking until she did.

She watched the customs officer rummage through her friends' backpacks. When it was her turn, she plunked her heavy pack on the table. It was industrial-sized and overstuffed but didn't contain anything out of the ordinary. However, she also carried her medical bag filled with vials of herbs.

The officer frowned as he opened the case. *"Docktor?"*

"Not exactly," Brittany said. "I'm studying herbology."

He called another man.

"Ya, ya," the second officer said. "What have we here?"

The first man was taking out bottles and setting them on the table.

Brittany rolled her eyes. She had packed them so carefully. "These are herbs." She pulled a cork out of a bottle and poured the contents into her hand. "For instance, this is lavender. I put a pinch of it in my tea."

"Ya, ya," the officer said. "I am familiar with such things. My grandmother also collects petals and leaves. This is fine. Enjoy your stay."

"Thank you." She repacked her bag then followed William and Eileen out of the building.

The morning was as dark as night. Traffic streamed by.

"All right." Brittany hefted her pack onto her shoulder. "How do we find this cousin of yours?"

"We're supposed to meet him in Forde." Eileen glanced around. "He said to take the Nettbuss Express."

William motioned. "The sign says the Nettbuss is this way."

The signs were in multiple languages.

Everything seemed geared for visitors. Brittany followed William and the signs to the Oslo Bussterminal and boarded the bus for Forde. It was still dark out, nothing to see. She dozed with the swaying of the vehicle.

At eight o'clock, the rising sun illuminated a stunning countryside. The trees wore autumn yellow. The hills rolled one upon the other. Nothing was flat. Here and there, homes showed among the foliage, and Brittany wondered what it would be like to live in such beauty.

The bus stopped at noon for lunch. The cafe sold a variety of sliced cheeses served open-faced on crusty bread. She and her friends stood in line for their food then took the sandwiches outdoors. The sky was blue and cloudless. The sun was white and strangely low for midday. The air was cool and dry, a vast difference from Florida's steamy humidity.

After about an hour, they boarded the bus with the rest of the passengers and continued on their way. The second half of their journey entertained them with waterfalls which twisted like silver ribbons from the rocks. Red deer dotted the hillsides. Eileen swore she saw a reindeer.

They reached Forde at four o'clock in the afternoon, just as the sun was beginning to set. Stiff and aching, Brittany stepped down from the bus. A man caught her attention. He was short, balding, and held a sign: *Cousin Eileen*.

"Cousin Hugo!" Eileen waved and bounded toward him.

His face lit as if he'd waited all his life to meet her. He opened his arms wide and pulled her into a hug, clunking her on the back of the head with his sign. "Cousin Eileen. Welcome to Forde."

She pulled away, cheeks pink, grinning. "This is my husband, Will."

He shook William's hand. "Congratulations on your marriage."

"And this is my best friend, Brittany," Eileen told him.

"You bring a friend on your honeymoon?" His eyes twinkled as he took Brittany's hand. "Are you the stand in?"

"Um." Brittany's tongue stumbled.

Eileen said brightly, "It's a tradition."

Hugo placed his hand on William's shoulder. "I like this tradition." He steered them into the parking lot. "So, you plan to hike the mountains."

"The Sunnfjord area," William said. "Home of

the waterfalls."

He nodded. "It's a good time of year for a walk. It's been fourteen degrees during the day. Of course, it drops off at night. Here we are." He motioned to a Toyota RAV4. It was covered in road dust.

William said, "Nice car."

"It is." Hugo unlocked the doors. "But later this year they will offer a new car called Buddy. It runs on electricity if you can believe it. Oh, I want one of those. Although I'd probably have to carry an extra battery for long trips."

They stowed their bags in the cargo area and climbed into the car. Brittany sat in front with Hugo.

"Is this also your first trip to Norway?" Hugo asked her as he pulled slowly out of the parking space.

Brittany grimaced against an urge to slam her foot on the gas pedal. She didn't have time for small talk. She needed to find Cody.

Eyes closed, she took a deep breath then forced a smile. "Yes, and I'm happy to be here. Forde is a lovely city."

"Ya, we have everything we need." He glanced at her as he pulled into traffic. "You might like to schedule some time here. You are the entertainment director, right?"

"Right. Speaking of which, have you ever heard of a place called the Lindgren Institute?"

"Hmm." He pursed his lips. "There is a medical facility north of here. They call it an institute, but it looks like a military installation. Fences topped with wire. Gates manned by guards."

Brittany said, "You've seen it?"

"No. I just know a man who knows a man. It is snug in the Fells."

"The Fells?" Eileen asked from the backseat.

"Mountains," he told her. "The Fells are not high but very steep. You'd have to be a mountain goat to reach the installation. Were you hoping for a tour?"

"Something like that," Brittany muttered.

They left the city and followed rural roads through the hills. The trees were gold, and the bushes were russet. The sky was red with sunset.

"Look over there." Eileen pointed. "I told you I saw a reindeer."

"A herd migrates through this area," he said. "Very tasty."

Brittany frowned. "You eat them?"

"Oh, ya, ya," he said. "We will get home just

in time for dinner. Quite a few people want to meet you."

"And we want to meet them." Eileen bounced in her seat.

Brittany's temples throbbed.

It was dark when they reached the farmhouse. Lights glowed in the windows. Woodsmoke filled the air.

"Leave your things," Hugo told them. "I will have them moved to the barn for you."

He opened the front door, and about twenty heads popped up from the couches around the crackling fireplace. People stampeded toward them.

"This is my mother, Agnes." Hugo drew an elderly woman forward. "This is her farm."

Eileen hugged her. "Aunt Agnes, I'm so happy to meet you."

Agnes fixed Brittany with a steely eye. "You are the friend they bring on their honeymoon?"

"Entertainment director." Brittany shook her hand.

"This is my son, Dustin," Hugo said.

"Welcome to our home." Dustin had a surprisingly deep voice. He looked to be around nineteen and was quite good-looking.

Hugo made more introductions. They all

spoke English, although they supplemented it with occasional Norwegian words. Brittany felt embarrassed that she only spoke one language.

At last, it was time for dinner. They strolled into the dining room. The table only sat fourteen, so the youngest guests ate in the kitchen. Everyone served themselves from a sideboard. They had meatballs in cream sauce, cod covered in sour cream, stewed cabbage, and three kinds of potatoes—boiled, scalloped, and a cold potato salad. Brittany ate a bit of everything. She was glad there wasn't any reindeer. She wasn't squeamish, but she didn't like the idea of cooking Santa's helpers.

When they finished eating, they passed around a coffee pot. No one seemed inclined to leave the table. But Brittany had been sitting for days. She squirmed in the wooden chair then got up to help clear the table.

The kitchen was large enough to hold another huge table. Kids dawdled over the remains of their meals. There was no dishwasher, and a teenage girl was at the sink with suds up to her elbows.

"Are you really from Florida?" a girl asked Brittany.

"I saw photographs from Florida," a boy said.

"Palm trees and alligators."

Brittany chuckled. "We have plenty of both. Hey, I'm trying to think of things to do around here. Do any of you know about the Lindgren Institute?"

There came a chorus of "No."

But one girl said meekly, "That's the spooky place."

"The spooky place isn't real," a boy snapped.

"Is so." She stuck out her lip. "My brother drives a truck and sometimes he delivers food there, and he told me he heard the spookies howl."

"Your brother is fooling you," the teenage girl said. "Take the cakes out to the table, please."

The little girl left the room balancing a dessert-laden platter.

The teenager looked at Brittany. "I know of this place. My friends go there sometimes to hassle the guards. But you can't get in."

"Where is it?"

"Down National Tourist Road. In the Fells."

Brittany nodded. Norway was covered with mountains. How was she to know which were the Fells?

She went back to the dining room. Nearly everyone still sat at the table. As Brittany took her seat, someone filled her cup with coffee. It was delicious.

"Sadly, my mother wasn't at the wedding," Eileen said. "She died of cancer earlier this year."

"That's a shame," Agnes said. "I met your mother only once. She was still a girl. I was visiting my sister in New York. Such a time we had."

"She told me about that trip." Eileen nodded.

"Did she live in Florida with you?" a woman asked.

"Yes. We were at a naturist resort. No clothes, you know."

William said, "I'll bet you don't have any nudists this far north."

"Then you would be wrong," Hugo said. "Naturists are widely accepted in our country, and we have many nude beaches. Several are near Oslo. Your plane probably flew over them."

William raised his brows. "I thought it would be too cold."

"Cold is a state of mind, not a state of being," a woman said.

"I'll try to remember that at night in your mountains," he told her.

Laughter rounded the table.

At eight o'clock they had another meal, this time with sliced meats and cheeses. Brittany glanced around in surprise.

Hugo said, "We have four meals each day. It gives us something to do."

"It makes you fat." Agnes chortled and poked his belly.

Brittany glanced around. None of them were fat.

Hugo grinned sheepishly. "Anyway, we call this meal *kveldsmat*. It's a tradition."

William layered meats on a slice of bread. "I like this tradition."

Those nearby chuckled.

After *kveldsmat*, the guests began to leave. Every time the door opened, a swirl of cold air made Brittany shiver. She and Eileen finished clearing the table, but Aunt Agnes wouldn't let them wash dishes. So, they said goodnight and followed Hugo to the barn.

Clouds hid the stars. The night was dark and silent. And cold. Brittany silently lamented leaving her coat with her bags. Hugo didn't seem to notice. He held out an oil lamp to light their way, and his arms were bare.

"No heat in the barn," he said, "but it's a nice night, and the blankets are warm."

113

He opened the door, and they scurried inside. The barn was large and shadowy. It smelled like hay. A ladder led to a loft, and a second lamp shone there. A scrawny dog stepped toward them. Brittany knelt to pet him.

Hugo said, "The girls are bedded down for the night, so they'll be no problem."

"Girls?" Eileen asked.

"Cows."

"You have cows?" She clapped and followed him across the barn.

"This is Kelda, Val, and Gudrid." He slapped each cow on the rump as he introduced them. "I don't know why we name them. They never come when they are called."

Eileen squealed. She went into the stall with Kelda and rubbed the cow's wide nose. William smiled with such tenderness it made Brittany's heart twist. She couldn't bear it if anything happened to them.

"They'll be bawling before dawn, so don't expect to sleep in." Hugo walked to the ladder. The backpacks and coats were piled at the base. "Your bed is up there. I left the light on. I fashioned a second bed out of hay." He moved to a pair of bales covered in a thick woolen blanket. "For the entertainment director."

Brittany smiled. "Thank you."

"Then, I'll leave this with you." He handed her the oil lamp. "Don't eat in front of Olaf. He's a mooch." He strode to the door. It rattled with a gust of wind as it closed.

Brittany, Eileen, and William moved closer together.

"Well, here we are," Eileen said.

"I want to thank you again for doing this," Brittany said. "You got me here, and I'll be forever grateful. But now I think we should split up. You continue on your honeymoon, and I'll look for Cody."

Eileen said, "You aren't going to cut out on us, are you? I thought we were a team."

"That's before I found out about the barbed wire and armed guards."

"Well, you aren't leaving me behind." Eileen folded her arms. "Cody is my friend."

"He's my brother." William sat on the dirt floor. Olaf was immediately in his lap.

"That's settled then." Eileen sat next to him. "All we need is a plan for getting past the guards."

William said, "Perhaps I could summon something that would help. I heard they have eagles in Norway."

"Sea eagles. They nest near the ocean." Eileen shrugged at their surprised looks. "What? I can read."

"We're nowhere near the ocean," William said.

Brittany set down the lamp and sat across from them. "Maybe we don't have to resort to brute force. I made a batch of love potion before we left. It's strong. The best I've ever done. We could put it in bean bags and throw it at the guards. It won't matter who they look at first, they'll be out of commission."

"That's a great idea," Eileen said. "And I know the recipe for the sleeping powder the witches used in Georgia. We can put that in bags, too."

William tapped the floor with his finger. "First, we have to discover how to get to the Fells."

"No," Eileen said. "First, we have to be sure that's where Cody is at." She leaned back, snagged her pack, and tugged it to her side. She took out a six-inch hand mirror.

Brittany recoiled as if it were dangerous. "Scrying." She'd never gotten the hang of scrying.

"I've been practicing," Eileen said. "Could you smudge the area for me?"

"Of course." Brittany got up and opened her medical bag. She'd prepared six smudge sticks, little cigars of sage, cedar, and sweetgrass. She removed one and lit the end with a wooden match. It flamed nicely. After several seconds, she extinguished the flames then bathed her hands in the smoke. She took her compass from her pocket. "That's funny. My compass won't work."

William said, "Try tilting it."

She did, and the needle settled as usual. "Why did that work?"

"There's a magnetic dip this far north. Your needle was hitting the glass." He grinned. "I can read, too."

She returned his smile and began cleansing the area with smoke, first to the east, then the south, west, and finally north. Then she stubbed out the smudge stick in a small stone bowl and set it down to cool.

Eileen sat cross-legged before the mirror, eyes closed as if in meditation.

Brittany lowered the flame of the lamp, and the shadows thickened around them. She joined William on the floor. Olaf put his head on her lap, and she stroked his ears absently.

Eileen leaned over the mirror and stared into

it. "I see him," she said in a faraway voice.

"Is he at the institute?" Brittany asked.

"He is barely conscious. In chains. His arms are held wide by a rod. They are dragging him. Dragging. Up. Into a truck."

"What does the truck look like?" William asked.

"Dark. Black. Like a military truck. The kind with a tarp over the back. There is an insignia on the side. I can't quite see it."

"What about Cody?" Brittany said.

"Cody is inside. His arms are suspended. The rod is chained to a strut overhead. A wide belt is being buckled around his chest. Tightly. He can barely breathe. It is chained to the floor. They pull a bag over his head, and—" She leaned back. "That's all I got."

Brittany stifled a sob. "Oh, Cody. Where are you?"

TWELVE

Where was I? Why couldn't I open my eyes? I tried to move, but my arms felt far away. Drugged again. I had to wake up. Had to find a way back to Brittany.

"Delays, delays." Saarsgard's voice drifted to me. "I didn't expect the officials to keep us so long. No matter. We're on the way home now."

A man's voice said, "Package is secure, ma'am."

"Fine. I need to go on ahead. I have urgent business. Inform me when you arrive at the institute. And Gary, take all precautions with this one."

"Yes, Madam Director."

A door slammed. Then a car pulled out. Probably Saarsgard's limo.

I opened my eyes, but all I saw was black. Something was over my face. A bag. A bag was on my head, a foul-tasting gag in my mouth. My arms were spread wide, attached to something that swayed. And I was cold.

Another door slammed. An engine started. I was in a truck. I had to get out.

Wake up, stupid!

I turned my attention inward. I had several drugs in my system. One was similar to Brittany's Wolfsbane Brew. It disrupted my connection to Mother Moon. But Ayanna and I had been working to strengthen that connection. I only needed to concentrate.

Why couldn't I concentrate?

With its gears grinding, the truck rumbled forward. Oh God, oh God.

Stop it! If I let panic take over, I would never get out. I didn't know where I was, but wherever it may be, it had a moon. And I could connect to it.

I tried to meditate, to draw my being into a single point and send it shooting among the stars—but the truck kept bobbing and forcing me to catch my balance. Maybe that's why they kept me strapped in such an uncomfortable position. To keep me off-balance.

Anger sparked then bloomed into a rage. This body was useless. I was drugged and shackled. Blind. I needed to see what was going on. I needed to get out.

And just like that, I hovered outside my body. *What?*

I looked down at myself. I was a ghost. Had I died? I didn't feel dead. A light shone around me. Like the auras that Brittany talked about. I turned to view my mortal body. It hung limply from a rod that was suspended overhead. My back was against the cab. Three soldiers sat in the truck with me, their pop guns held loosely on their laps. The driver sat up front. I saw him as clearly as if the wall were transparent. Another soldier sat shotgun.

A spotted windshield showcased the night. Headlights pierced the darkness. The road was unlit and untraveled. Heavy clouds threatened snow. Above the clouds, the moon beckoned.

My essence shot toward the sky, leaving a glittering trail. Moonlight bathed me. Strengthened me. It lifted me higher. I looked for Ayanna's tether. It was weak, but at least it was there. I couldn't sense the others at all.

What happened to my pack?

With a rush, I snapped back into my body. I nearly groaned. Pain washed over me. My hands felt fat, prickling with pins and needles.

Drool spilled around the gag and down my chin. I couldn't close my mouth.

They'd gagged me so I couldn't speak, blinded me so I couldn't make eye contact. They were afraid I would make them my thralls.

I once met a wolf who was so accomplished in taking thralls, he didn't even have to be in the same room with them. I remembered the pressure of his mind as he tried to take over my thoughts. I had no idea how to do it—but I'd better figure it out fast. If they got me to the institute, I was toast.

I concentrated on my senses then focused on the soldiers. My heightened hearing picked up the sound of their breathing, the swish of blood in their veins. I smelled shampoo and boot polish and the acrid stench of whatever they had in their guns. One man had recently smoked a cigarette. Another had spilled coffee on his pants. With my enhanced sight, I could see their silhouettes through the bag. Not see exactly, but I sensed their heat signatures. Similar to what I'd done with Ayanna in the forest. Did all alpha wolves have such abilities? I didn't think so. Saarsgard called me a super wolf. Let me see what a super wolf could do.

I concentrated on the man nearest me and

thought *Stand up and unbuckle these cuffs*. I repeated the command several times. The most he did was look my way. So much for using the Force. Maybe I needed to start smaller.

I turned my attention to the soldier sitting across from him, projecting an urge to cough. The man cleared his throat. I tried again. He lifted a hand and coughed into his fist—and when he did, I sensed an avenue. Like a door opening in his mind.

I narrowed my concentration. Slowly, he lifted the pistol from his lap and shot the man across from him.

Splat!

Shock and indignation flared in the other man's mind, but I dampened it. He raised his gun and shot his counterpart five times in the chest. The neon liquid showed black against his radiance.

The first man returned fire. They shot about twenty paintballs at each other. Which was excellent. The more ammo they used, the better for me.

The third soldier jumped to his feet. "What the—"

The two entranced guards turned their weapons upon him and hit him with such a barrage, he staggered and toppled right out the back of the truck.

That seemed like a good idea, so I had the other two men leap out after him.

The truck continued bouncing along, the driver unaware.

That left me alone with no one to release me. I really should think these things through. I shifted my weight. Chains dragged at my waist and rattled on the floor. Shackles held my legs apart. I was barefoot—and it was freaking cold.

I tried to turn into my wolf-beast, but I couldn't concentrate because of the pain in my arms. How could they be numb and excruciating at the same time? I tried to reach the bag and pull it off my head, but my arms were spread too wide.

I had no choice but to enlist the aid of my two friends in the front seat.

I saw them as if through someone else's eyes. They bounced and swayed with the movement of the truck. Both wore uniforms. Neither wore seatbelts. Beyond the windshield, the black road curved through even blacker hills. No other headlights.

Stop the truck I thought to the driver. But the truck didn't slow at all. I couldn't find the door that would let me into his mind.

So, I tried the passenger. *Stop the truck.*

"You should slow down," he told the driver. Only he said it in a different language.

The driver glanced at him. "We are already behind schedule. The Director will have our heads."

I tried again but couldn't get through.

My shoulders slumped. It wasn't working. I sucked at taking thralls. I should just give up, let Saarsgard do what she wanted with me. There was no way out of this mess.

I lifted my head as if I could see the moon. As if I could feel its light surround me.

And somehow, I sensed Brittany. It was like she was right there, not an ocean away. She was asleep. Dreaming of me. In her dream, we were kissing. I felt her lips on mine. The warmth of her skin. Her breath soft and sweet.

I had to get out of this truck.

With all my might, I projected the image of a wolf in the road.

"Look out!" The passenger grabbed the steering wheel.

The truck swerved. With a squeal of metal, it toppled onto its side and skidded off the road, down an incline, and crashed headfirst into a birch tree.

The impact nearly wrenched my arms from their sockets. I balanced on one foot, the other foot held in the air. The shackles around my ankles were now hooked to the floor and the ceiling. The rod holding my arms was attached to what had become a wall. The belt around my chest was pulled so tightly I could barely take a breath.

Outside, the radiator hissed and steamed. The reek of fuel rose. I tried to connect with either of the two men. Their minds were blank. No help there.

I closed my eyes and gathered my wolf strength into a little ball inside my chest. I pulled the bar, trying to break the chain that held it. But I was balanced on the toes of one foot. I couldn't get any leverage. Instead, I concentrated on bringing my arms together.

It took several minutes of constant pressure— then the rod began to bend. Slowly at first. Then faster. I gasped and growled, biting hard on the gag. The rod curved into a U. Narrow enough that I could get my hands together. With numb fingers, I fumbled with a buckle to release my right hand.

Pain. I cried out as my circulation returned. I shook my arm, opened and closed my fist a few times, then tore the bag from my head. The gag was Velcroed in back, and I ripped it off. My lungs heaved a heavy breath. I stood for a moment, sucking in the cold air. Then I struggled to unfasten my shackled ankle. I undid the belt around my chest. When it released me, I dropped and caught the edge of a bench with my knee. I struck hard enough to bring tears to my eyes. I curled onto my side, panting, then unbuckled the remaining straps.

I was free. Carefully, I made my way to the opening in the back of the truck. The smell of fuel intensified. Must have ruptured a line. I climbed down as quietly as I could, my senses amped like radar. No one around.

I stepped along the side of the truck. Its headlights speared the hazy steam. The driver was wedged behind the steering wheel. Blood streamed from his mouth. His passenger had gone through the windshield and was in the tree. Both were breathing.

I gazed down the dark, two-lane highway. Now what? Now I save my pack. Good plan. Which way should I go? I glanced around. No traffic. No street lights. What I needed was a road sign: Evil Scientist's Laboratory This Way. I sighed. I should have waited until I was closer to the institute.

Why did everything happen to me?

I wore a jumpsuit. I unzipped and shrugged out of it. Cripes! It was freaking cold. I shivered at the side of the road, my hands covering my shrinky-dink, and tried to shift into a wolf.

I couldn't. Oh God, oh God. What had they done to me? I swallowed my panic and lifted my face.

Mother, please help me.

My connection was strong. It flowed out of me like a million glittering specks, tethering me to the moon. I sensed her light although I couldn't see it. Warmth rolled over me.

And just like that, Mother Moon overrode the chemicals in my system. Fur prickled my skin in silver waves. With a liquid sensation, my ears slid up my head. My muzzle grew.

And I was a wolf. I snorted and kicked some grass in the direction of the truck. Take that, Dr. Saarsgard, wherever you are.

ᘔᘔᘔ

Dr. Saarsgard walked slowly down the long corridor toward her living quarters. Her home was on the same residential floor as her staff.

When she first brought life back to her father's laboratory, she thought she should appear to be one with her fellow doctors. A show of solidarity. The fallacy in that soon became apparent. She was the master of the institute. She was no more one with them than God was to a bumble bee.

She kept her apartment, however. It was three times the size of their common dwellings. She did enjoy her little secrets.

She unlocked the door with her handprint and keycode and slipped inside.

"Mama's home," she called. "Did you miss me?"

The fireplace was blazing—it was on a timer. Orange light danced over the room. The windows were dark, the night sky cloudy.

She dropped her purse and shopping bag on the couch and slung her overcoat over a chair. "I missed you, sweet boy."

She crossed to the liquor cabinet and poured a measure of brandy into a large snifter. "Yes, the trip was a success. Today I righted a terrible wrong done to us." She swirled the brandy around the glass. "Of course, I brought you a gift. Don't I always?"

She set her drink on the counter and opened an armoire. A small light came on inside. It lit a framed portrait of a seven-year-old boy. Shelves beneath the painting held assorted toys—a dump truck, a ball, some deflated balloons. Below that, a few articles of clothing hung from a rack.

Saarsgard smiled. "There's my sweet boy."

She picked up the shopping bag from the couch and sat on a chair facing the cabinet. Out of the bag, she drew a polka-dot-covered box with a large red bow.

"Look what I have for you. Shall we open it?" She unwrapped the gift to reveal a snow globe. Holding it up to the photograph, she said, "Isn't it lovely? It has a palm tree and an alligator. From Florida." She shook it to send the snow flying. "I thought it was comical. It doesn't snow there, you see." Pause. "No, the boys and girls who live in Florida never see snow. Some of them live their entire lives without knowing what it is to be truly cold." Pause. "Yes, you do know about being cold, don't you?"

She stood, moved the truck aside, and set the snow globe next to the portrait. Then she gathered the wrappings and stuffed them into the shopping bag.

"I'm sorry, Christoph, but that isn't possible. You must stay here." Pause. "Yes, because of your health. Now, mama is tired from her trip.

Play with your gift like a good boy."

She retrieved her brandy, downed it in three gulps, and refilled her glass. Humming Christoph's favorite song, she sat in the chair to watch him play.

She was dozing when the intercom made her jump.

"Dr. Saarsgard?"

With a sigh, she crossed to her desk and toggled the speaker. "Yes, Karl?"

"Your presence is requested at the barracks."

"At this time of night? Very well. Tell the commander I'll be right down."

Shaking her head, she toggled off. Couldn't they make a decision on their own? Must she oversee their every move?

Then a thought struck her. "Our new guest must have arrived." She stood before the portrait in the armoire. "I'm quite excited about this one. With his help, we might, at last, realize our dream of producing a vaccine against childhood disease. No one need to go through the horrors of leukemia ever again." Pause. "Yes, my darling boy. You will be cured. It's all I ever wanted. Now, let mama tuck you in." She kissed the painting and pressed her cheek against the frame. "Goodnight, Christoph."

She closed the doors of the armoire.

Dr. Saarsgard stood beneath the harsh exterior lighting of the barracks. She wanted to scream. To kick and bite. But she did none of those things. Keeping her face stoic, she nodded occasionally as the commander related the story. One dead. One critically injured. And three covered in paint.

When she had heard all she could bear, she put her hand up for silence. She approached the three men. They were so splattered, they fairly glowed.

She addressed Captain Nilsson. "Gary, you knew how important this particular lycanthrope was to the project. I warned you to take all precautions."

"Madam Director, I can't explain what happened. But that werewolf couldn't have caused it. He was unconscious. He was gagged and blindfolded and—"

"Yet somehow he escaped."

"I take full responsibility."

"Indeed." She gave him a curt nod and walked back to the commander.

"What should we do with them?" he asked in a low voice.

"Strip them of rank and put them on incinerator duty," she said. "All except that one."

With a single, fluid movement, she drew the little silver pistol she always kept on her person and shot the soldier standing in the middle. It was a small gun, but at that range, it would do enough damage. A black circle appeared on the man's forehead. He wore a bemused expression as he toppled backward.

"You will find Cody Forester, Commander." Saarsgard turned to walk away. "And if you know what's good for you, you will find him before the coming full moon."

THIRTEEN

Brittany opened her eyes. It was dark, but it appeared to be morning. The cows were shifting around. Cold air bit her nose, but her body was warm beneath the blanket. Of course, she also wore all her clothes.

She'd had the most amazing dream. Cody had kissed her. It felt so real.

As their love had grown, a bond had grown between them, too. A sort of connection. She always knew when he was near. But he couldn't be near now. Eileen saw him being loaded on a truck.

She sat, and the blanket slid down her shoulders. Olaf padded over. She stroked his head then climbed out of her warm nest. By the faint gleam of the oil lamp, she folded the blankets. Overhead, the floorboards of the loft creaked. Eileen and William must be awake.

Cousin Hugo came in. He left the barn door open, and fresh, cold air swirled inside.

"Morning," he said. "How did you sleep?"

"Very well. Thank you."

He turned the key on the lamp, and the flame brightened obediently. "Mother is making us a nice breakfast, and then I'll drive you to the nearest trail. But first I have to milk the cows."

"Oh! I want to help," Eileen called down from the loft.

Hugo laughed. "Come along, then."

Brittany said, "I need to use a washroom."

He nodded. "Right next to the kitchen."

She picked up her bags and crossed the yard toward the house. Yellow light spilled from the windows to light her way. She hurried inside. A warm fire and the smell of coffee welcomed her into the snug home.

"In here," Agnes called from the kitchen.

Brittany followed the voice. "Good morning. Can you direct me to the washroom?"

"Just there." Agnes motioned.

The bathroom looked like any other. What had she expected? She cleaned up. When she left, William stood outside awaiting his turn.

"Have a seat," Agnes said as Brittany

returned to the kitchen. "Would you like coffee?"

"I'd love some," she gasped with more gusto than she'd intended.

Agnes gave her an oblique smile.

Brittany sat at a scuffed wooden table. Agnes set a porcelain cup and saucer and a coffee pot in front of her. The coffee was in a percolator. Her grandmother had owned one like it. Brittany remembered watching the coffee grow slowly darker through the little glass dome. She poured herself a cup then inhaled the aroma before sipping.

"You make the best coffee," she said.

"It's our water," Agnes told her. "Very clean." She took the lid off a pot on the stove and stirred the contents.

Brittany smelled oatmeal. Her stomach sat up and begged. "There's something in the air here that makes a person hungry."

"Our air is very clean," Agnes said.

"It's also very thin," William said as he entered the kitchen. He smiled at Brittany as he sat beside her.

Agnes set a cup and saucer in front of him and continued puttering around the stove.

The front door banged. There came quiet laughter, then Eileen and Hugo appeared in the kitchen doorway. Eileen's nose was red, her eyes bright.

She rubbed her arms. "It's nice and warm in here."

Hugo said, "You get cleaned up. After we eat, I'll drive you to the cabin."

Eileen's smile broadened. She carried her backpack into the bathroom.

The front door opened again, and Hugo's son, Dustin, breezed in. He wasn't even wearing a coat. Brawny muscles stood out beneath his t-shirt. "Morning," he said then stepped to Hugo.

They spoke in a language Brittany didn't recognize. Maybe it was Sami. Then he washed his hands at the sink and sat with them at the table. Eileen came out and joined them. William poured her a cup of coffee.

"Who wants oatmeal?" Hugo set a stack of stoneware bowls in front of his son.

Agnes plopped the pot in the center of the table. Dustin portioned the oatmeal into the bowls and passed them around. Brittany had hers with a lump of butter and brown sugar. Agnes also served a platter of open-faced sandwiches—white cheese with a dollop of red jam on top.

"Lingonberry jam," Hugo said as he sat.

"Mother makes it. Rather tart."

"It's delicious," Brittany said and took another bite. "Reminds me of cranberries."

For such a simple meal, the scope of tastes was astounding—bitter coffee, sweet oatmeal, nutty cheese, tangy jam. And all the milk they could drink.

After a few minutes, Hugo took a key from his pocket and set it before Eileen. "Remember, I need it back."

"Of course," Eileen said.

Brittany said, "A key?"

Hugo poured himself more coffee. "The tourist department runs a series of cabins throughout the mountains. You rent the key, and you can spend the night wherever you like. The larders are full of supplies. The blankets are warm. Some have attendants. Some don't." He spread his hands. "You are on your best behavior. Expected to keep it clean. Don't take more than you need."

"Sounds great," Eileen said.

"And you rented a key for us?" Brittany asked.

"Actually, it's my personal key. I'm a member."

William asked, "Is there phone service in any

of the cabins?"

"Some have landlines." He nodded. "Don't rely on your cell phones. Coverage is spotty."

"Anything else we should be aware of?" Eileen asked. "Wild animals?"

"Bears?" William asked.

"There are brown bears in the mountains," Hugo said, "but they won't bother you if you don't bother them. The polar bears are at the coast where there is sea ice. But it's a fourteen-hour drive to see them."

"How about wolves?" Brittany asked.

He looked embarrassed. "There are still wolves in Norway but not many anymore. They live in the southeast near the Swedish border. I wouldn't expect to see one in this area."

Brittany nodded.

They finished breakfast. Eileen hugged both Agnes and Dustin goodbye. Then they packed their things into the back of Hugo's SUV and climbed inside. The sun was just rising, and the hills were brushed with gold. They pulled onto a paved, two-lane highway that wound through the scalloped land.

"What road is this?" William asked.

"This is our National Tourist Road," Hugo told him. "Very scenic. Takes you through the foothills and mountains."

Brittany sat straighter. The girl in the kitchen told her the Lindgren Institute was off National Tourist Road. How would Cousin Hugo respond if she asked him to drive them a little farther up the mountain?

As she opened her mouth to speak, they rounded a bend and saw a black, military-style truck on its side crashed into a tree. The windshield was broken and bloody, although there were no bodies around. A tow truck was parked behind it.

Brittany's stomach clenched. She tossed a wide-eyed look at Eileen.

Hugo chortled. "Ran into a bit of trouble there."

Eileen asked, "What kind of truck was that?"

"I believe it's from that medical facility we were talking about last night."

"The Lindgren Institute," Brittany said.

"Ya. I see these trucks on the road from time to time. Once I saw a silver limousine. That really stood out."

Brittany gulped. She felt such a surge of anxious apprehension she thought her breakfast might come back up.

They turned onto a dirt road and followed it

to a cabin. Flowers grew on its sod roof. A bike rack held several bicycles.

Hugo said, "This is one of the few cabins with indoor plumbing. And there is phone service. Call me when your adventure is over, and I'll pick you up here."

They got out of the car and retrieved their packs from the back.

Eileen hugged her cousin. "Thank you, Hugo, for everything."

"My pleasure. Enjoy your walk."

"See you in two weeks."

"Sooner if the weather turns." He slid into the driver's seat. "Don't make me come out and get you."

Eileen giggled. "I promise."

They waved as he pulled away.

Brittany murmured, "Do you think that was the same truck Cody was in?"

"I'm certain of it," Eileen said.

Brittany blew out a breath. "He's free."

"You don't know that," William said. "That was a bad wreck. He might be in the hospital."

"No." She gazed into the distance. "Cody came to me last night. In a dream. He kissed me. It was so real." They'd always had a bond. Not as strong as his *link* with his pack, but a sort of sense. And she sensed him now. He wasn't at the institute.

"Wishful thinking," Eileen said. "Just a dream."

Brittany glared at her. "It wasn't."

"Well." Eileen hoisted her pack. "I think I'll make use of the indoor plumbing one last time."

She led them around the side of the cabin. The ground dropped away, giving a spectacular view of hills and trees. Eileen whipped out her phone and snapped a shot.

Brittany groaned. "You're actually taking photographs?"

"What?" She shrugged and took another. "This is my honeymoon. People expect pictures."

A couple sat in rocking chairs on the front porch, backpacks on the floor before them.

"Morning." Brittany waved as she approached.

"Morning," said the woman.

"Door's open," said the man.

Brittany clomped up the steps and went inside. The cabin smelled like woodsmoke, although the fireplace was cold. There were two couches that looked like they might pull out into beds. An overstuffed chair with an ottoman. The coffee table held a half-finished jigsaw puzzle. A bookcase held more puzzles and board games.

"This is nice," Eileen said from the front door. She crossed to the kitchen area and opened a cabinet. "The pantry is stocked. I wonder if I should take a couple of these granola bars."

"May as well," Brittany said. "No telling when we'll find another of these cabins."

William stepped to a rack of pamphlets near the door. "Trail maps. Rated from easy to difficult. And all the cabins are marked."

"Take two," Eileen said. "One to use and one to save. What? It's a keepsake." She shoved a handful of granola bars into her pack.

William studied the map. "This route looks promising."

Brittany peered over his shoulder then pointed. "Let's take this one."

"The institute is north. That trail leads south."

"I know." She glanced away. "That's where Cody is."

FOURTEEN

Something was stalking me. Several somethings. They were good at it. Staying downwind. I had no idea what or how many were there. My hackles rose. But I didn't dare run. They would chase me.

I left the trees and followed a line of boulders. All the better to see my pursuers coming. But they knew the land. I didn't. I was in trouble.

Overhead, a hawk screeched. But not the kind of hawk we had in Florida. So many strange animals. Strange smells.

What was I going to do? Something had convinced me to go south. A kind of intuition. I thought I'd find the Lindgren Institute. But no—just more forest. Now, I was lost. Lost and in trouble.

And alone. I'd never been so alone. No

parents, no friends, no *links* to my pack. No one would know if I died here. I didn't even know where here was.

Maybe I should shift into my human form and climb a tree. There were plenty of trees around. But no. I didn't have any clothes. I'd freeze up there. Better to remain a wolf so I could fight.

The babble of water drew my attention. A stream coursed over the rocks ahead. I angled toward it, surefooted on the rough bank, and dipped my nose into the cold, rushing water. A fish jumped. The stream teemed with them in spite of the current.

A sound came behind me. I tensed. My fur stood, making me look larger than I already was. I gazed toward the far bank. Should I try to cross? Maybe I would move out of their territory. But the current was so strong. Better not risk it.

I heard the sound again. Closer. And another straight ahead. I was penned in. I lowered my head, my back to the stream, searching. Where were they?

Then, with a low growl, a wolf stepped around a boulder. He was half my size. Thin and wiry. He wasn't an alpha, but he *was* the pack leader—and he was competent.

From the other direction, a she-wolf

approached. The pack leader's mate, my intuition surmised. Her eyes were on me, her head down as if ready to spring.

I snarled, ears flat, feet braced for the attack. I could take these two. But there were six more wolves in the rocks. If they all rushed at once, I wouldn't stand a chance. They would take me down, and there would be no one save my pack.

I couldn't let that happen.

I faced the leader. Narrowing my eyes, I searched for the door into his mind.

And then I mind-whammied him.

With a whine, the wolf recoiled. He hunched his shoulders. His mate paused, looking confused—so I hit her, too. *Go away*, I projected.

But the two wolves didn't leave. The leader cowered and slunk forward. Relinquishing his pack to me. To me! The last thing I wanted.

The others stepped around the rocks, keeping their distance. They danced in distress. Barking and yipping.

I stared at them—and all at once I realized it was Mother Moon who'd led me south. Here, to this pack. My personal army. And with equal certainty, I knew I now had to go north. I was going the wrong way.

"We're going the wrong way," Eileen said as she walked.

Brittany raised her arms. "I can't explain it. I just feel—"

What? What did she feel? There was an alien coldness where Cody's warmth had been. He was in these foothills. She was drawn to him like a compass. Maybe her needle was stuck.

"All right," Eileen said. "Let's say Cody did free himself and is running around somewhere in these woods. Where are we supposed to look for him? He's not stationary like the institute. Which we haven't found either, by the way."

"Let's not argue." William held out the map. "We're merely taking a detour. We'll continue south until we reach this point, then we'll turn toward the mountains." He spread his arms wide. "How can you be disagreeable amidst all this beauty?"

"You're right," Eileen said. "It's gorgeous. I'm sorry I'm being such a grump."

William pulled her into his embrace and kissed her forehead. They both looked at Brittany.

Brittany huffed out a breath. She wasn't

there to sightsee. She had a mission. But the colors of autumn surrounded her. Golden trees. Green pine. Ahead, a waterfall fell in threads from the rocks.

She'd always wanted to travel. Now, here she was in Norway. *In Norway!* She would never have gotten this far if it weren't for Eileen. She bit back her frustration. "Like he said. We'll go this way a little farther then turn north."

So, they continued walking. The breeze smelled like spruce. The day became warm enough to unzip her parka, although the sun remained low in the sky. It could only be seen in flashes through the trees.

At lunchtime, William and Eileen munched the granola bars she'd taken from the cabin. Brittany didn't feel like eating. Terrible hopelessness gnawed her stomach.

Because Eileen was right. Where in this immense forest should they search? She had no idea where Cody had gone. All she had was a vague sense that he was south. It would take a miracle to find him.

"Ugh." Eileen chuckled. "Up boulders. Around boulders. I'm used to everything being flat."

"There were hills in Georgia where I grew

up," Brittany said, "but nothing like this." She didn't add that her leg muscles burned, and it was an effort to keep from stumbling.

"We can stop for the night." William pulled out the map again.

Brittany felt a sudden urge to make him eat that guide map.

Eileen leaned close, peering around his arm.

He shook his head. "There are no cabins in this vicinity. If we stop now, we'll have to camp in the open."

"Fine by me," Eileen said.

"Let's keep going," Brittany said. "We can stop when it gets dark."

No one objected, so they walked on in silence. After a while, they came upon a field of wildflowers spilling down a gentle slope. The flowers were dry and withered. Brittany had a strange impulse to walk among them.

She sidestepped her friends. "Let's take a shortcut."

"We should stick to the trail," William said. "It leads this way."

"You two go ahead. I'll catch up."

"Brittany," Eileen said. "What's going on?"

"Nothing." She avoided her gaze. She couldn't explain it to herself. She just had to go find... "Thistles. I want to pick some thistles. For my supplies. You know."

Eileen and William stared at her. Like she was the crazy one.

She motioned at the trail. "Keep moving. I won't be long."

William said, "I don't think we should split up."

"So, we'll go with you." Eileen smiled.

Brittany led them into the field. The flowers rose to mid-thigh. Their brittle stems rattled in the breeze. She gathered dry flowerheads and seed pods, but her attention ranged ahead. What was here? Why was she drawn to this place?

"Oh, my goodness." Eileen chuckled. "You don't even have to hunt for thistles. They adhere themselves to your pants."

"For you, my lady." William presented her with a bouquet of dried blooms.

"Thank you," Eileen crooned. "I love them."

They kissed.

Brittany edged away. From her vantage on the hillside, she could see for miles. Trees and rocks. A glittering lake. Clouds billowed on the horizon, obscuring the sun. The breeze turned gusty and cold.

Then she saw wolves. Wild wolves. With teeth. Brittany froze. Only her eyes moved. Nowhere to hide. Nowhere to run.

Beside her, Eileen whispered, "What are they doing here?"

"They aren't supposed to be here. We're too far north."

"What are we going to do?"

The wolves lay half concealed in the tall grass. There were nine of them. Scrawny and brown. With one silver...

Suddenly Brittany dropped her doctor's bag and ran. Toward the wolves.

"No!" Eileen gasped. "Brittany! Stop!"

The wolves leaped up and faced her. They bared their teeth. Brittany focused on the largest wolf. The silver wolf. The one with a short tail.

As she approached, the wolf morphed into a boy. *Cody.*

Still running, she launched herself into his arms. "I thought I'd never see you again."

He hugged her close, kissing her forehead, her temples. "I can't believe you're here. I can't believe it."

She clung to him, eyes shut tight. Was she dreaming? Wishful thinking like Eileen said?

Eileen screamed. "Cody!"

She and William stood a short distance away. The wolves surrounded them. Snarling. Ready to pounce. Cody looked at them.

And they backed away.

"William?" He gasped. "You came, too?"

William straightened his shoulders. "You are my brother."

Cody wrapped an arm around Brittany and walked toward him. He shook William's hand then hugged Eileen.

Eileen squealed. "You're like ice."

"Oh!" Brittany opened her backpack. "I brought clothes for you." She pulled out jeans, a sweatshirt, a thin, hooded parka like hers, and hiking shoes.

Cody shivered as he dressed. Through chattering teeth, he said, "These aren't mine."

Brittany said, "We got them from Howard. Thankfully, he knew your size."

"Your house burned down," Eileen blurted. "There's nothing left."

Cody paused then nodded.

Brittany was glad he didn't ask about the car. But he probably knew.

"That's it, then." Eileen looked from one to the other. "We found him. Now we can all go home."

Cody said, "I can't go without my pack. No telling what Saarsgard is doing to them." He looked at William. "I know I don't have any right to ask, but I could really use your help."

They held each other's gazes for a moment.

In a low voice, William said, "Bob and Rita are my parent's best friends. They are part of my childhood. I couldn't live with myself if I left them in that place."

"What about you?" Brittany asked Eileen. "You and Ayanna were becoming friends."

"Yes." She looked apprehensive. "Of course, I'll help."

William asked Cody, "Have you been in contact with Ayanna?"

"The *link* is weak," Cody shook his head. "But she's alive. She must be at the institute. Saarsgard said my pack had gone ahead. She said I was delayed because someone spoke out for me. Was it you?"

"Who would listen to us?" William said. "We don't have that kind of clout."

Brittany looked from person to person. "I wonder who it was?"

FIFTEEN

David Forester held out his hand, and Saarsgard's assistant, Karl, shook it in greeting. Marie sniffed impatiently. She didn't offer her hand.

"I'm happy to meet you," Karl said in English without a trace of an accent. "Dr. Saarsgard is actively recruiting new personnel. However, she expressed concern that two such eminent physicians as yourselves would leave your practices to join us in research."

"Actually," Marie said, "I started out in research. It's my first love."

"Not so exciting as a patient with a brain tumor or a heart attack."

David chuckled. "Less stressful, to be sure."

"Of course." He spread his hands as if switching to tour guide mode. "As you can see, this is our main lobby."

"Impressive." David nodded.

Everything was white and chrome. Coupled with a fifteen-foot-high wall of glass, the room appeared spacious.

"The front desk is staffed during normal working hours." Karl nodded to the pretty blond woman who sat behind the desk.

She smiled and went back to her computer screen. David wondered what the duties of a receptionist would be. He doubted they had many visitors in such a remote area.

Karl motioned above them. A chrome and glass veranda overshadowed the desk. "Up there are our second-floor meeting rooms. The rooms are used primarily for presentations to prospective clients, although we enjoy our staff meetings there, too."

There were two magnificent curved staircases, one on either side of the lobby. David glanced around as he climbed, impressed in spite of himself.

Karl said, "I believe this year we will have our Christmas party in one of these rooms." He paused to allow them a view from the veranda then walked to a door. "I think... yes, this one is empty."

He held the door wide, and they peered in at a normal conference room.

"Very nice," David said. "How many are there?"

"We have six conference rooms. Our security offices are also on this level."

"This is all well and good," Marie snapped, "but I'm not interested in conference rooms. I want to see the inner workings of this facility."

"Of course, ma'am." He led them to a bank of elevators and pressed his palm against a touchpad. "The elevators are for authorized personnel only. They are voice activated." The door opened, and he ushered them inside. A soothing instrumental played as they entered the car. He looked toward the ceiling and said, "*Tredje Etasje.*"

The elevator went up a floor, and the doors opened onto what looked like an upscale hotel. Oil paintings lined the walls. Potted plants framed a window.

"This is staff residential," Karl said. "The rooms consist of a living room, bedroom, and small kitchenette. Enough for a coffee pot."

"Where do we eat?" David asked.

"The staff restaurant is on four."

They went up another floor. It looked

identical to the one below it.

"More residences in that direction," Karl said as he stepped out. "And this is our restaurant."

He stood in the doorway of a large, dimly lit room. The tables were round and large enough to seat six people. They had linen tablecloths and crystal goblets. Servers moved silently through the shadows.

"They're setting up for lunch," Karl said, "so we won't bother them. They have a large menu..." He glanced around. "Somewhere. But they will prepare pretty much whatever you ask for."

Marie asked, "Do the inmates eat here as well?"

"We refer to them as clients. And no, they are allowed on floors five, six, and seven only. They have a canteen upstairs."

David smiled. "I'd like to see that."

They returned to the elevator. This time it opened onto a large, sunny lobby. David stepped out eagerly. The room was pleasant enough. Two hallways led away. A glass wall framed the mountains. But there were no clients around. He swallowed his disappointment. He couldn't expect to find Cody that easily.

David glanced back at Marie and noticed two

armed guards standing on either side of the elevator. Instead of commenting on them, he said, "Nice view."

"Yes. Our clients are not allowed outdoors, so we try to bring the outdoors in." He walked past what appeared to be a check-in table and opened one side of large double doors. "Here's the canteen."

David looked in at long, metal tables and bench seating. "A standard cafeteria. Smells good."

"Again, they are getting ready for lunch." Karl returned to the lobby. "Down that hallway are the group therapy rooms. They are in session, so we can't go down there. The pool is this way." He entered the opposite hallway.

The pool room was immense. An Olympic-size pool. Potted palm trees. Glass walls on two sides making it seem even larger. A white-smocked attendant manned a counter with fresh towels. Two brawny men swam laps. A third sat in a lounge chair, apparently asleep.

No Cody.

"Not many people here," David said.

"This time of day, they're usually in the recreation room. It's one flight up. Would you like to see it?"

"Yes," David said.

At the same time, Marie said, "Certainly not. Again, what I wanted was—"

"I think we should see everything, don't you?" David gave her a pointed look.

She glared but relented.

He chuckled inwardly. *Not used to me talking back to her. She'll find I'm quite different now that we're apart.*

They went up another floor to the recreation room. A buzz of laughter and conversation greeted them. People strolled by. David stepped deeper inside. Marie hung back, looking apprehensive, but he was used to being surrounded by werewolves.

The room seemed divided into three areas. In one, flat-screen televisions showed a soap opera to empty couches. There was a game area with tables and a few people playing cards. And a crowded area with ping-pong tables. It looked quite inviting.

But all the inmates wore the same blue jumpsuit. Their laughter sounded forced. More white-smocked attendants walked around, but they were given a wide berth. And two more armed guards stood like sentries at the elevator.

Karl said, "The residential area is on the

seventh floor. I'll take you up there."

David's shoulders slumped. Where was Cody? He ran his gaze over the many faces but didn't see anyone he recognized. What had he expected? He returned to the elevator.

Inmate residential had no windows. The walls were gray, the hallways narrow.

Karl opened a door seemingly at random and showed them a sparse cell with a cot, a chair, and a toilet.

"Rather austere," Marie said.

"We want our clients to socialize, not stay in their rooms and brood."

"They don't lock their rooms?" David asked.

"We lock them. At night," Karl said. "The control room is on eight." He stepped back into the elevator.

David hesitated. No one was in sight, but he heard muffled voices. A woman crying. "How many rooms are there?"

"One hundred."

He winced. He couldn't check every room for his son. He joined his wife, and the elevator took them to the eighth floor.

They entered a small, well-lit lobby with paintings on the walls. There were three corridors.

"The control room I mentioned is straight ahead," Karl said. "It is manned twenty-four hours a day. The rest of this is offices."

They passed several closed doors, all with a keypad and a handprint scanner. Windows faced out into the corridor showing the offices behind them. Desks and cabinets. People sat with their unblinking eyes glued to computer screens.

Marie said, "Will I have an office here?"

"Of course."

She stopped walking. "But where do I do more… hands-on research?"

Karl smiled. "The labs are in the basement."

David sighed and followed them back into the elevator. Where was Cody? Where was his pack? He thought he'd see someone he knew.

🐺🐺🐺

Ayanna stood before a wall of floor-to-ceiling windows and looked out at brown, craggy mountains. She was in a cage. A glass cage. It smelled faintly antiseptic. Her captors warned her to cooperate. Her parents pleaded with her to cooperate. But she had no intention of doing so. She would learn all she could about her prison, and she would escape.

A burst of laughter came behind her. Insignificant sheep. Playing cards. Playing ping-pong. There were more than enough inmates to overthrow the guards. Yet they did nothing. They didn't deserve to be wolves. When she freed herself of this prison, she would leave them to their fates. All of them.

Even Cody? Her stomach twisted. Cody had been captured when she was. He must be in this building. But she'd heard nothing from him. Nothing about him. Was he dead?

No! She couldn't allow herself to think that. The *link* was still there—but faint. He was alive. Why couldn't she contact him?

Because they were drugging her. Trying to keep her calm. If she could strengthen her tether to Mother Moon, she would throw off the drugs. That would be her first goal. She and Cody had spent hours in the woods strengthening their defenses against Brittany's Wolfsbane Brew. This would be no different.

"Hello." A woman stepped beside her. "I'm Malonnie."

Ayanna glanced at her. She had been pretty once. Now her hair was straying from her braids, and her eyes were shadowed.

"I haven't seen you here before. Just get out of quarantine?" Malonnie asked. "They usually take a few days to process the newcomers. Are you alone?"

Ayanna winced. She may as well be alone. Bob was in his quarters doing his nut, and her parents and Rita were trying to calm him before anyone heard. They sent her away. So, she came here. To the recreation room. Alone.

Malonnie shrugged. "I'm alone. I was with someone. My pack leader. But they took him away. No one comes back from the basement."

Ayanna stared at the mountains.

"They're beautiful, aren't they?" Malonnie said. "I love mountains. I'm originally from California. The Sierra Nevada Mountains. But they picked me up in South Florida."

Ayanna's gaze snapped to hers. "That's where I'm from. South Florida. They took my whole pack."

Malonnie's face melted from friendly to horrorstruck. "You're with the super wolf? Cody?"

"Do you know him?" Ayanna gasped. "Where is he?"

A new voice said, "Ayanna?"

Ayanna turned. A boy stood behind her. He

was her age with black hair falling over one eye.

"Remember me?" he said. "Tommy Lee."

She frowned. "The boy from Georgia?"

He grinned. "That's me."

Ayanna's hand shot out. She grabbed him by the throat and slammed him against the window. "It was you. You're the minger who told them about us."

Tommy Lee said, "Gak."

Malonnie tugged her arm. "No aggression. Don't let them see."

Ayanna's blood surged. Her fingernails grew long and yellow. She was losing control. A death sentence in this place.

She tossed Tommy Lee, and he scurried away like a rat. She curled her claws into fists, breathing hard, and for the first time since she'd arrived, she felt alert. Drug-free.

Malonnie whispered, "You can't do things like that. They'll flag you with a yellow wristband."

She snarled, "When I find out who told them where to find us, I will kill them."

"There have been deaths here. Sometimes the white-coats show up in blue jumpsuits. Like they've been demoted. They don't last long." She met her gaze. "But I wouldn't risk it. The life you had before is gone. This is what you have now. And the only way out is through the basement. No one comes back from there."

David took Marie's arm and lagged behind Karl as they exited the elevator. "What are you doing?" he said in a harsh whisper. "Cody won't be in the basement."

"That's the only place where he *would* be," Marie whispered back. "Besides, we have to keep up pretenses. A prospective researcher would be interested in the labs."

"This way," Karl said.

He led them down a shadowed hallway with several closed doors. One was labeled storage. Another was a stairwell. Ahead, the hallway brightened.

David released Marie, but she took his arm instead. Perhaps she was nervous. He was. He didn't know what he'd do if he found his son in one of the labs.

The corridor widened into a viewing area. A glass partition showed a well-lit room that could only be a morgue. Drawers filled the back wall. A doctor was performing an autopsy at one of the tables. The body he worked on wasn't quite human. It was covered in sleek black fur, and the limbs bent in awkward places.

The next room was an operating room. It was filled with equipment so advanced David didn't recognize all of it. A team of doctors and nurses surrounded a naked man who was strapped to the table. He wasn't anesthetized. He writhed and kicked as much as the straps would allow—but his screams couldn't be heard through the partition.

David asked, "Why isn't that patient asleep?"

Karl paused. "Much of our research deals with the endocrine system. Which hormones the Lycans have that the average person does not. That sort of thing. And, as you know, fear and pain trigger chemicals that are not present otherwise."

He continued walking. David and Marie exchanged a look then followed. They passed three more operating arenas, all in use. The last one was letting out. The team laughed together as they filed through the door.

Marie asked, "Does everyone here speak Swedish?"

"For the most part," Karl said. "We have one team that prefers Sami. And a few Germans here and there. They all speak English as well, of course. But Swedish dominates."

A clean-up crew rushed to the room. When they opened the door, David heard a low moan. The patient stirred against his restraints.

"What do you do with the bodies?" David asked.

"Incinerators. A funny story, that. This place is state-of-the-art, yet the incinerators are left over from World War II. It takes a special crew to run them."

They turned down another hallway. More glass walls showed the laboratories.

Lab1 was a clean room. The researchers who scurried around inside were gowned and masked.

"Our equipment is cutting edge," Karl said as he strolled along. "Special needs can be requisitioned."

They passed *Lab 2*. It brimmed with people and computers.

"How many labs are there?" Marie asked.

"Five. Which means that doctors have to share space. Sensitive data should be kept in your office."

"What's in there?" David motioned to a room without a glass partition.

"I'll show you." Karl opened the door.

It looked, smelled, and sounded like a kennel. Three white-smocked attendants looked up from a desk. Behind them was a wall of four-foot cages. The creatures inside the cages were not human, not animal. They were monsters. They barked and howled.

Karl said, "This is where we keep our test subjects."

David scowled. "When do you stop calling them clients?"

"When they come here." Karl smiled. "This concludes our tour. Do you have any questions?"

David walked slowly along the line of cages. He'd seen Cody transform a number of times—he was certain he would recognize him. But he wasn't there. A mixture of relief and disappointment filled him. Where was his son? How was he going to find him?

"I think we have everything we need," Marie said.

"Excellent." Karl headed for the door. "Dr. Saarsgard is waiting for you in the penthouse."

SIXTEEN

I held Brittany's hand as we walked through the forest. I didn't want to let her go. If I did, I might wake up and be alone again. It was a miracle she was there. A miracle they'd found me. I couldn't believe it.

Couldn't. Believe.

"Are you okay?" Brittany asked.

I nodded, not trusting my voice.

"You look like you lost weight." She nudged me. "Didn't they feed you while you were in custody?"

I swallowed before answering. "No."

"No?" Eileen cried behind us. "Cody, it's been a week."

A week—was that all it had been? A week ago, I'd been happy. I had a new car. Brittany said she'd marry me. Life couldn't get much better. How could things go so wrong so fast?

"They kept me unconscious," I said. "Didn't want me causing trouble. I woke up once with an IV line in my arm. I guess they were giving me fluids."

"That and more drugs," Brittany muttered.

"I ate a little something this morning. And by something, I mean I couldn't identify the animal. Talk about being a stranger in a strange land."

"That's for sure." Brittany gestured. "Look at this place."

The forest had thickened as we walked. Dark green. Almost black in places. It smelled like spruce. Thick moss covered everything. The ground. The rocks. The sides of trees. The wolves kept their noses down as they picked their way through.

"Ugh," Eileen said. "I don't know where to put my feet in all this."

"We need to get back on the trail." William pulled out a map.

I don't know why that surprised me. They seemed so organized. So prepared. While I was floundering.

"We left the trail here," he said. "Traveled straight north. We'll pick it up again here. That should make the trek a little easier."

By the time we reached William's trail, blisters had formed on my heels, and I longed to return to my wolf form. The clouds lowered, and the day grew chilly.

"I thought there would be more animals," Eileen said.

"We're surrounded by animals," I told her. "There was a fox there a moment ago. Some deer passed by over there."

"I didn't see that. Are they hiding from us?"

"They don't like the company we keep," William said.

I heard the rebuke and sent a mental command to the wolves to keep close.

Several minutes later, I paused. "I smell smoke."

William whipped out his map then grinned. "Cabin up ahead."

"Ooh." Eileen took Brittany's arm. "Let's hope it has a bathroom."

They picked up their pace and led the way, chatting quietly.

The cabin was made of weathered wood. Moss climbed up one side. Smoke drifted from the chimney. Just as I was about to ask *now what*, Eileen clomped up the steps, inserted a key into the lock, and opened the door. I couldn't even respond.

"Come on, Cody." Brittany motioned from the doorway.

What was this place? How did they get a key? I shook off the questions and went inside.

A woman sat at the fireplace. She smiled and closed her book. "*God eftermiddag.*"

"Hello," Eileen said. "Is there a bathroom here?"

"And a phone charger?" Brittany held out her phone—and I winced at the sight.

She'd gotten it for her birthday. We were at her party. Happy. And oblivious.

"No electricity, I'm afraid," the woman said. "But the lavatory is just there."

The girls rushed to the bathroom together. Why did girls always do that?

"Sit. Sit," the woman said to William and me.

I sat. "Is this your cabin?"

"I'm stationed here for now. Not all the cabins have attendants, of course. Certainly not this late in the season. But the DNT likes to place people with nursing skills here and there just in case." She stood. "Would you care for some coffee? I was about to put a pot on."

"That would be appreciated," William said. "Thank you."

She went into the kitchen portion of the room and measured coffee beans into a grinder.

In a low voice, William said, "I can't believe we found you."

"I can't believe you came at all." I winced.

He leaned closer. "Are you all right?"

I nodded then shook my head. "Why are you here?"

"What do you mean?"

"Do you remember that wolf we met in Georgia? The one who could take people as thralls?"

"How could I forget?"

"He wasn't even an alpha, but he could influence people's minds. Make them do what he wanted them to do."

"Yes."

"That wolf pack out there. I didn't mean to take over. I did a mind whammy on them, but I only wanted to keep them from attacking. I told them to go away. Instead, they followed me. And deep inside, I have to admit that I wanted them to. So, I wouldn't be alone. And now you three are here. And—"

"And you think you did your mind control

thing on us. From halfway around the world. When you were unconscious."

I paused.

He put his arm around my shoulders. "We are here because we couldn't bear for you to live without us. Or us without you."

I swallowed hard.

He jostled me. "You are my brother."

"Here we are," the woman said. She set an old-fashioned percolator on a hook over the fire. "Where are you from?"

"Florida," William said.

"Oh. Palm trees and alligators."

Just then, a helicopter circled overhead.

"Oh, dear." The woman stepped to the window. "That's the third time I've heard them today. They're searching for someone."

William caught and held my gaze. Were they looking for me? I lowered my head and pulled my arms in tight as if I could make myself smaller. As if they would see me through the roof of the cabin. I couldn't let them capture me again.

As the thwap-thwap echoes died away, Brittany and Eileen came out of the bathroom.

"That was refreshing," Brittany said, her face bright and dewy.

Eileen sat on the couch beside William. "We were thinking maybe we should stay here for the night."

"We could," William said. "But we would be wasting time. It's still afternoon."

Brittany said, "I don't relish camping out in that alien rainforest."

"We are quite proud of our boreal rainforests." The woman sniffed. "I'll get the mugs."

Brittany gave an embarrassed smile. "I was joking. I didn't know there were actual rainforests in Norway."

"We're in Norway?" I frowned. "Svalbard."

"What?"

"I visited Svalbard a few years ago with my parents. To see the polar bears and reindeer. You know. And you don't need a visa to go there." Excitement bubbled inside me. "We stayed in Longyearbyen. They had good Internet. Something to do with NASA. I could contact my dad, see if he can help me get home. He probably doesn't even know what's happened."

"Oh, he knows," Brittany said. "I went to his office the day after. He was very upset. I don't think he realized how evil Saarsgard was."

175

"Well," I said, "if he didn't know then, he does now."

David and Marie followed Karl out of the elevator, through a small lobby, and into a spectacular office. The glass walls showed mountaintops, some snow covered, some craggy and brown, and some partially obscured by dark clouds.

Dr. Saarsgard sat behind an enormous desk. Her white, upswept hair looked frozen in place. "Thank you, Karl."

Karl backed out of the room and closed the door.

"Please." Dr. Saarsgard motioned to the chairs in front of her desk.

Marie chose a seat. "Lovely office."

Dr. Saarsgard showed her teeth. "I was surprised to hear from you. My previous attempts at acquiring your services were refused."

"I hope it wasn't a limited time offer."

"What changed?"

Marie hesitated. David sank onto the chair beside her. He hadn't thought this far ahead.

Marie cleared her throat. "You may remember I was researching werewolves when we met."

"And then you went into private practice. Why?"

"Money." She raised her brows. "Now I have money. All the money I could want. And I find that private practice bores me. So, I want to get back into research."

Dr. Saarsgard turned her frigid gaze to David. "And you, Dr. Forester?"

He said, "Those people in the basement—"

"Lycanthropes."

"Yes. They don't look... healthy."

Dr. Saarsgard stood and walked along the edge of her desk. "This is a research facility. We have several teams. One searches for a cure so those afflicted with lycanthropy can live normal lives. That is our public persona if you will. Another group develops weapons to be used against the Lycans in the event of a war with these creatures. My pet project is learning the secrets of super healing and super strength so we may harness such abilities for ourselves. It is based on the research my father started in the war. But where he was more concerned with the military applications, I will share my findings with the world in the form of a vaccine. Childhood disease will become a thing of the past because our children will be able to heal themselves. I'm sure you'll agree that such goals supersede the health of our test subjects."

"Yes, but–"

"Perhaps you don't have the stomach for research, Dr. Forester. In fact, I don't see what benefit a cardiologist would bring to the institute."

"That's the point I'm trying to make. You should have a medical doctor on staff to keep your clients healthy. A strong body would produce more of the hormones necessary for your research."

Dr. Saarsgard nodded as if running calculations in her mind. After several moments, she said, "A worthy hypothesis."

"Thank you. With my background in cardiology, I can–"

"But you aren't here for the health of our clients. You're here for Cody."

David reeled back. A dozen retorts sprang to mind, each more ridiculous than the last.

"I know you came for your son. Perhaps you thought you would whisk him away." Saarsgard leaned against the edge of her desk. "You don't understand. No one leaves this facility. Not the Lycans. And not the doctors."

Marie frowned. "What do you mean?"

"The work we do is sensitive. Everyone is housed on grounds. No one quits. No one retires."

"Then what do you intend to do with us?"

Saarsgard looked at her. "You will join my staff. As one of the basic researchers at first, but I'm sure if you apply yourself you will elevate your station. Your husband will go into general population. As long as you cooperate, no harm will come to him."

"What?" David cried. "I can't go to gen-pop. I'm not a lycanthrope."

"I suggest you don't tell them that."

David looked at his wife. She had gone as still as granite. No expression crossed her stony face. Was she considering Saarsgard's proposition? Would she throw him to the wolves?

"This is ludicrous," he sputtered. "I can't just disappear. I have a life. A job."

"Yes." Saarsgard flipped her hand. "Karl informed me of your new position. You have already tendered your resignation."

His jaw dropped.

"I'm not being unreasonable," she said to Marie. "You came here to disrupt my operations. In response, I am offering you a prestigious job in a cutting-edge facility. All I ask in return is your family. A family, I might add, who has rejected you."

David stared at his wife with mounting horror. "Marie."

And in a quiet voice, she said, "No."

Saarsgard raised her brows.

"No," Marie said again. "I will not be a part of your high-tech barbarism."

"I knew you were the one who opposed me." Saarsgard sneered. "Trying to save your son. But I'll never let him go. You didn't tell me he was a super wolf."

Marie winced and turned away. "I didn't know."

David looked from one to the other. "Super what?"

"It doesn't matter." Saarsgard gave a triumphant laugh. "You'll never see him again. Guards!"

The door flew open, and several burly men burst into the room.

SEVENTEEN

Brittany huddled nearer the fire, as much for warmth as for light. She and Eileen sat within a magical shield dome similar to the one Lynette placed over the house when Bodark's army threatened them. Nothing solid could get inside, so they were safe from predators. But the draft filtering through made her shiver.

She was grinding herbs to a powder with a mortar and pestle and combining them to make a love potion strong enough to use as a weapon. She smiled as she worked, willing her excitement and relief at finding Cody to travel down her arms and permeate the mixture. Strong emotions affected the outcome, so she expected this to be the most powerful batch yet. She had everything she needed. Her doctor's bag was stuffed with vials and packets of herbs.

And she had small, muslin bags to fill with the powder.

On the other side of their meager campfire, Eileen gave an exasperated moan and set down her scrying mirror. "I'm getting nowhere. The images are too fuzzy."

"Keep trying," Brittany said. "We need to know where Ayanna and the others are if we're going to rescue them."

Eileen nodded then sat up as if alerted, gazing at something behind Brittany.

A black bear stepped from the darkness. It lumbered to a pile of unlit firewood then rose up on its haunches and stared at the girls behind the protective barrier. Blood stained the patch of white fur on its chest. Something grisly was under one arm. Then the bear morphed into William. Naked William. He yelped and dove for his clothes.

Eileen got to her feet. "I'm going out there. Cover your herbs."

"Hold on." Brittany scooped the last of the powdered herbs into a muslin bag and folded the top. "Okay, go ahead."

Eileen broke the circle with her foot. The magic barrier dropped. Immediately, the wind picked up. The temperature plummeted. Dry and sharp. Brittany snapped her medical bag shut and hugged her arms.

Eileen hurried to William. "Hello, Sweetie. How was your hunting trip?"

William grunted as he zipped his coat. He knelt at the pile of firewood and stacked it into a cone shape.

Brittany picked a flaming stick from her little fire and walked over to him. He used it to light the larger fire. In minutes, their cozy clearing danced with light.

The grisly thing the bear had been holding looked to be part of an animal's leg. William skinned it with a knife, tied it to a branch, and propped it over the fire.

Brittany stepped nearer the flames, holding her hands out to the warmth. "Where's Cody?"

"He's feeding with the pack." William sneered. "I'm not sure about traveling with those wolves. They're wild."

Brittany chuckled. "They're probably not sure about traveling with two human girls and a boy who can turn into a bear."

He shook his head. "When he said we were going hunting, I thought he meant squirrels or rabbits. They took down an ox."

She crouched next to him and watched the

meat cook. Juices sizzled and spat at the flames. Eileen emptied a pouch of dehydrated vegetable soup into a pot, added water from her canteen, and balanced it on the edge of the fire. The wind gusted, and the flames roared. Brittany's front side was toasty warm, making her backside feel even colder.

This part of the forest was more like the woods back home–trees and bushes and dirt. Mostly birch trees. The thick, dark moss was gone. Now, patches of bare stone showed on the ground.

Yellow eyes appeared in the darkness. The wolves were back. William rose to his feet, one hand on the knife in his belt. Brittany stood beside him and rested her fingers on his arm. None of them would survive if he attacked one of the wolves.

Before things escalated, Cody stepped out of the trees. He was in his wolf-beast form and carried a four-foot log on his shoulder.

"Cody!" Brittany laughed and grasped her chest. "I thought you were a yeti."

He was a good seven feet tall, covered in shaggy fur, looking more like Big Foot than a wolf. It occurred to her that the Big Foot sightings might have been werewolves. That would explain why they disappeared before anyone could document them. They simply turned human once more.

Cody snorted at her as if in amusement. With a thud, he dropped the log near the fire then stalked off into the trees.

Eileen sat on the log. "At least, we won't have to sit on the cold ground."

William remained standing, but his stance seemed more relaxed.

Brittany went back for her backpack and doctor's bag. The little fire had gone out. She scattered the sticks with her boot and kicked dirt over the spot.

Minutes later, Cody returned. He dropped a second log near the first, making a V around the fire. He snagged his clothes in one clawed hand and disappeared again into the forest. When she saw him next, he was a boy in mismatched garage-sale clothing.

Brittany sighed and shook her head. She poured water over one of her muslin bags then stepped close and wiped the blood from his face.

Eileen said, "Ew, Cody. Gross."

Cody blushed, so Brittany kissed his cheek. Wolves prowled the perimeter of their camp.

William pointed at them. "Will they be here all night?"

"I'll be here, too," Cody snapped.

"So, they're under your control?"

Cody blew out a breath and sank onto a log. "I'm becoming everything I hate."

"They seem to like you." Brittany sat beside him.

"Maybe they have to. Maybe I'm forcing them to like me against their will. Taking them from their homes. Putting them in danger."

"That isn't you," she said.

"It *is* me. I made two men jump out of a moving truck. Then I caused the truck to crash."

"We know," Eileen said. "That was some wreck."

"You saw it? Oh, no." He covered his face with his hands.

Brittany put her arm around him. "You need to remind yourself why you're doing this. Try to contact Ayanna."

Cody nodded and closed his eyes.

🐾🐾🐾

Ayanna lay on her cot. It wasn't comfortable. The whole room wasn't comfortable. A jail cell without the bars. The walls and ceiling were battleship gray. No windows. Just a rigid cot and a hardbacked chair. A toilet right out in the open. No wardrobe in which to put her possessions. Of course, she had no possessions. They provided her with a fresh jumpsuit every morning. No smalls to wear under it. Then acted like she should be grateful. But she wasn't grateful. She hated them.

A hot ball of rage swelled in her stomach. She clenched her fists.

Stop it!

If she lost control now, they would kill her. She needed to find the way out, plan her escape. Then she could go all terminator on them. For now, she would meditate. The way Cody taught her. She needed to strengthen her *link* to Mother Moon. Eyes closed, she willed the tension from her body, picturing the tether that connected her to the light.

Mother, please. Wash away these drugs that muddle my mind.

The connection grew. She imagined it like a rope of glittering motes. Hand-over-hand, she climbed from the horrors of reality into a dark and sparkling starfield. Mother's presence poured over her. Healing her body and mind.

Her wolf erupted in a stream of fireworks. Finally, free.

And as if in a dream, Cody came to her.

He was alive. The fear she'd refused to acknowledge dissipated. She bounded toward him, nearly bursting with joy, and their two ethereal wolves danced in the moonlight.

From far away, his voice called *I'm coming for you. Hold on!*

Ayanna's eyes snapped open. She sat up on her cot and stared at her hands. Human again. Had it been a dream? No. He was there. Cody was alive.

She had to tell her parents. She leaped up and crossed the room in two strides.

The door was locked.

Rage rose inside her, urging her to kick down the door. Her vision turned red. *Bloody mingers. Think they can cage me?*

Then above a ringing in her ears, Cody's voice rose sweet and clear—*Hold on!*

She backed away and sat, panting, on the edge of the cot. Cody was coming for her. She could hold on a little longer.

I stared at the campfire, filled with both elation and dread. Ayanna was alive. I had to believe the others were, too. But how could I save them? I'd have to go against Saarsgard's army. Their weapons were customized for werewolves. The situation was impossible.

Brittany's head rested heavily on my shoulder. She gave a jaw-popping yawn.

"Okay, that's it," I said. "Time for bed."

"I can't leave you alone in the cold while I'm snug inside my sleeping bag."

I glanced over at William and Eileen. They were already asleep. Their sleeping bags overlapped as they snuggled together.

I smiled. "I could climb in beside you."

"I got the smallest one I could to conserve space." She shook her head. "I should have bought an extra, but I never expected you to be out here in the wild. I thought you'd be all institutionalized. I only brought clothes because I didn't know what state you'd be in when we found you."

"How *did* you find me?"

"I don't know. Our *link*, I guess. I was drawn to you."

Or maybe I called her to me. I kissed her chilled forehead. "Let's go. You need your beauty sleep."

She climbed fully clothed into her sleeping bag, and I zipped her inside.

"What will you do?" she asked.

"I will watch over you. Now close your eyes." I stroked her hair.

She sighed and nestled deeper into the warmth. Minutes later, she was asleep.

I tossed another branch onto the fire. Sparks flew, glowing gold in the darkness. If I were home, I'd be watching fireflies. I gazed into the sky. The clouds were so low, they felt like a ceiling. But I sensed the moon above them.

And something more. I squinted, trying to make it out. Five wispy lines, like red contrails, pointed to Ayanna and the others. *Hold on*, I sent through the *link*, *I'm coming for you*. But would I be in time?

I stripped and hurriedly dressed in my wolf suit. Dang! It was cold even for a wolf. The pack came out of the surrounding trees and nuzzled me. They wanted me to run with them. I was tempted if only to get my blood moving. But I couldn't leave Brittany. I stepped to the sleeping bag and lay across her feet.

The others milled about, silhouettes black against the leaping flames. I whined to tell them to go without me. Instead, they settled for the night–one against me, two on either side of Brittany, more boxing in Eileen and William. My friends may never know how protected they slept–but I knew.

I awoke to the sound of my name.

"Cody?" Brittany whispered again, sounding a little alarmed.

I stood and walked on all fours up the sleeping bag. Apparently, two-hundred pounds of wolf on your chest is breathtaking.

She gasped. "Get... oof!"

I didn't. I sprawled on top of her and licked her face. She giggled and squirmed but couldn't knock me off because of the wolves lying on either side of her.

Then Eileen shrieked, "Cody! Your wolves!"

I transformed. In seconds, I was a boy. A naked boy with my backside in the wind.

"It's all right," I told Eileen. "They're just keeping you warm."

"Oh. They startled me."

"You're safe with them. You're part of the pack."

I backed off Brittany until I could get to my

feet then grabbed my clothes. My pants felt like ice. I dressed then slapped my arms as I glanced around. It was morning, although the sun hadn't risen.

Eileen sat up in her sleeping bag. She placed one hand on the shoulder of the she-wolf who had guarded her. They just looked at one another as if bonding. Thankfully she didn't pet her like a dog. That wouldn't have gone over too well.

Brittany got up and began rolling her sleeping bag. It compressed well. It was made of that new microfiber material. Thin but weatherproof.

"Need help?" I asked through chattering teeth.

She smiled. "I've been practicing with this thing since I got it. Watch this." She rolled it into a neat package and slid it into her backpack. "Ta-da."

William hunched down and stirred the campfire. The flames had gone out, but when he knocked the ash from the remains, the coals glowed red hot. He added kindling, and in minutes, the fire blazed again.

I crouched next to him, savoring the warmth. "You're really good at that."

"No comments about my heritage," he grumbled.

"Man." I chuckled. "You're a bear in the morning. I just meant—" I leaped up, my ears tuned to a thwap-thwap sound. *Hide!* I sent to the rest of the pack.

The wolves bounded into the trees just as a helicopter slowed overhead. No doubt drawn to William's fire. My heart raced, and I suppressed the urge to run away with the wolves. With my enhanced vision, I saw a man lean out. He wore night-vision goggles. I didn't know if he would recognize me at a distance in the dark. Just in case, I edged up the hood of my parka. The wind whipped around us, so I figured it wasn't too weird a thing to do.

Brittany stepped beside me, and I put my arm around her. William stood with Eileen. The copter hovered over us for another minute then rattled away.

"What was that about?" Eileen said. "Are they searching for a lost hiker?"

William said, "Search aircraft are red and white. That one was black."

"I think they were looking for me," I murmured.

"Not good," Brittany whispered, still staring in

the direction it had gone.

William scowled. "Let's have breakfast and get out of here."

"Yes." Eileen opened her backpack as if relieved to have something to do. "Who would like some oatmeal?"

"I would," Brittany said.

"If you don't mind," I said, "I'd rather have some of the leftover meat from your dinner last night."

"If your wolves didn't get to it," William muttered.

"They aren't *my* wolves."

"Then answer this," he said. "Why are there more than before?"

I frowned. "Why would there be?"

"He's right." Brittany sat on a log. "There were eight. Now there are twelve."

William jutted his finger at me. "You're calling them to you."

"I am not." My glare fell. "Am I?"

Eileen set a pot of oatmeal on the fire. "If you are, they traveled quite a way to find you. My cousin said all the wolves are south near the border. Apparently, they were hunted to near extinction."

"Then we'll have to keep our wolves out of

sight." Brittany smiled and patted the seat beside her.

I sank down. "I don't want to be this way."

"What way?" She nudged me. "Handsome? Debonair?"

"And scary."

Eileen said, "I think it's your scary side that will get us through this."

"But my powers–"

"Are getting stronger. I know." She shrugged. "So, master them."

Brittany took my hand. "Ayanna, Bob, Rita. They're depending on you. Like these wolves. Like me."

The ball of dread that filled my stomach lodged in my throat.

🐺🐺🐺

Ayanna sat on the edge of the cot and stared at the door. She got up and checked the lock again. Then sat down again. Her back ached. It felt like hours had passed.

She strengthened her tether to the moon until she felt like she sat in a spotlight of moonbeams and called to Cody with all her might. But he didn't return. Had it been a dream?

No. She had heard him. Sensed his presence. She still could, although he seemed far away.

The door clicked, making her jump. She rose and tried the handle. It opened. She slipped out of the room into the silent hallway. The lights were on. Between each ceiling panel was a black dome. Cameras.

Ayanna tiptoed to her father's quarters. The door opened. Dark inside. No one home. She went to her mother's room. When she opened the door, the light from the hallway showed her parents sitting on the narrow cot, arms around each other, heads together. Sound asleep.

She hurried inside and switched on the lamp. Their heads popped up.

"What's happening?" her father mumbled.

Ayanna whispered, "Do you feel him?"

"Who? What?" Her mother rubbed her eyes. She looked haggard without her make-up and turban.

"Cody." Ayanna sat next to them. "He's free. He's coming for us."

"A dream," her father said, speaking to her fears.

Had it been a dream?

"No," Ayanna said.

He shook his head. "I don't sense him. The *link...*"

The rage that seemed so close to the surface threatened to boil over. "You've broken the *link*. You've lost faith in him."

"Of course not," he sputtered. "I would never... But after everything that's happened... It would be extraordinary if he..."

Ayanna stood, and her voice rose with the movement. "He *is* there. I feel him."

"No, sweet flower. I know you want to believe—"

"I feel him, too," her mother said in a small voice.

They both looked at her.

"The *link* is faint, but it's there. I can sense his presence." She stood and took Ayanna's shoulders. "If you can reach him, you must tell him not to come for us. If he is free, he must run away."

Her mouth fell open. She wanted to argue— but she couldn't. Of course, he shouldn't come. He'd be foolish to risk it. All her hope, her determination, died like a doused flame.

But a spark remained. "I could tell him to run. I could tell him to leave us to our fates. But you know he won't."

She turned toward the door. There was movement in the hallway. Muffled conversation. People going to breakfast. But that wasn't what alerted her.

Someone knocked. Ayanna glanced at her family then answered the door.

Rita stood outside. Her eyes were puffy and red, her cheeks sunken. "I need help with Bob."

Ayanna's parents rushed to Rita. They stepped into the hallway, moving against traffic. Ayanna followed. She glanced with dread at the dark cameras, certain her family would be noticed. When they reached Bob's quarters, Rita opened the door and hurried them through.

The tiny cell seemed even smaller with four extra people inside. Bob sat in the straight-backed chair, his face slack, unblinking.

Rita hugged her arms. "I'm trying to get him to go down to breakfast. He didn't eat at all yesterday."

Ayanna knelt and whispered, "Cody's coming for us."

His red-rimmed eyes turned toward her. "Cody is dead."

"No. I sensed him. He escaped."

He looked away. "There is no escape."

She stood and backed off. Bob sat before

her. She was looking right at him. But he wasn't there. It was like his wolf had died.

"Bob," Rita said in a commanding voice, "it's time for breakfast. Stand up now and come with us." She reached for his hand, but he snatched it away from her.

"You must come," Ayanna's mother said. "If you stay here, they might think you are a troublemaker."

Her father said, "She's right, old man."

Bob gave a slow shake of his head. "I won't make trouble."

He withdrew so completely, Ayanna thought they could lunge at him with knives and he wouldn't respond.

Rita hiccupped a sob. Ayanna's mother put an arm around her, and they left the room. The gray corridor was long and narrow with many doors. One door was labeled with a small sign printed in another language. The sign said *trapphus*. Perhaps it meant *closet* or *stairwell*. She longed to open it and see what was inside.

She followed Rita and her parents to the lift. It had three buttons—residential, recreation, and canteen—branded in a variety of languages. Elevator music played. Strings and piano. They went down two floors to the canteen.

199

The doors opened to the large check-in room. Tables along one wall were manned by attendants in white lab coats. People queued up before them. Ayanna and her family got in line. Her senses twanged. She was surrounded by werewolves, but they didn't feel right. They weren't really werewolves anymore.

She got to the front of the line, and her stomach knotted. The table was filled with little paper cups, each holding a fat orange pill. They were going to drug her again. How was she going to reach Cody?

The attendant checked her wristband and handed her a paper cup. Ayanna hesitated.

Her father asked the attendant, "What's this, then?"

"Just something to keep you calm," the attendant said.

"It's a different color than yesterday."

She smiled in a most ingratiating way. "We like to switch them up. It's more effective. Where is—" She checked her list. "Bob Nowak?"

Ayanna's mother stepped forward. "He's in his room. Not feeling very well, I'm afraid."

Rita said, "I wonder if I can take him a cup of coffee. Might settle his stomach."

The attendant sat back. "Food isn't allowed

out of the canteen. And lycanthropes don't get sick."

"Perhaps he's having an allergic reaction to all these drugs." Her father gestured at the table.

He spoke in a kindly voice, but his stance was belligerent, and Ayanna was proud of him for standing up to her even if just a little bit. The attendant glared at him, and Ayanna used the opportunity to slip the pill out of the cup and hide it in her hand.

"Very well. I'll send someone to check on Mr. Nowak." The attendant handed out the cups. "I need to see you swallow these."

Obediently, Rita and her parents placed the fat pill on their tongues and showed the attendant.

Ayanna held out the empty cup. "I already swallowed mine."

"I didn't see you." She gave a saccharine smile.

"She palmed it," said the white-coat sitting beside her.

And miraculously, someone took the pill from the hand Ayanna hid behind her back.

Ayanna showed them her empty hands.

"All right. Move along." The attendant gestured. "Next."

Ayanna glanced over her shoulder. The woman with messy braids stood close behind her. Malonnie. They didn't make eye contact.

Ayanna passed through the double doors into a brightly lit room. Her nose twitched with the aroma of strong coffee. The canteen could easily seat one-hundred people. Long rows of aluminum tables stretched away.

Her father breathed in deeply. "I wouldn't say no to some black pud this morning."

They filled their paper cups with coffee and carried them to a table near the windows. The sun wasn't up yet, and the view beyond was as dark as night.

An attendant with a clipboard circled the perimeter of the room like a vulture. He stopped behind them and said something in what sounded like German.

Ayanna's father turned. "Pardon me?"

"Bus your own tables, please."

"Yes. Of course, of course."

The attendant walked on. Ayanna watched him with narrowed eyes. A reek of aftershave and cigarettes trailed him. His shoes creaked when he stepped. She could hear it plainly even over the footsteps and conversations of the incoming inmates.

Her senses were returning.

Her mother stood. "You three hold the table. I'll get brekkie."

As she walked away, Tommy Lee sat next to them. Ayanna glared.

"Tommy Lee, my lad," her father said. "I'm sorry to see you here."

"What happened?" Rita leaned forward. "When we left you, everyone was fine."

He swiped at his mop of dark hair. "A couple of weeks after you went home, soldiers swooped down and swept everyone up. Ma died trying to give me time to escape. But I don't know. When I saw her fall... I couldn't leave her that way, so I went back for her, and they got me."

"My deepest condolences."

He nodded. "Is Cody with you?"

Ayanna growled. "No."

Her father glanced at her as if surprised she wasn't giving him a warm welcome. "We were separated. No idea where he is."

"That's too bad," Tommy Lee said. "They must've taken him to the basement. No one comes back from there." He looked up as Ayanna's mother set a tray of bread and sausage on the table. He stood. "I'll let you eat."

He joined a group of boys two tables over.

Ayanna glared at his back.

"Small world," her father murmured. "I didn't expect to see anyone I knew. Right, flower?"

She sneered. "If I find out he was the one who told them we were in South Florida, I will strangle him."

Across the room, she noticed Malonnie watching her.

EIGHTEEN

I reached for Brittany's hand and helped her up the steep incline. The sun was rising as we crested the hill. Shafts of light turned the mountains gold and filled the valleys with shadow.

To one side, a herd of musk oxen milled about skittishly. They looked like shaggy buffalo. To their credit, they didn't run. I doubt I could have held back the wolves if they had.

Brittany smiled as she looked around. "Beautiful."

"Not as beautiful as you," I said lamely.

She crinkled her nose in the way that I loved.

I took both her hands in mine and stepped close for a kiss—but was interrupted by Eileen.

"Can we take a break?" She panted as she joined us.

"This isn't a good place," I said. "There's no cover."

Brittany gazed toward the golden sun. "On the other hand, we can see for miles in all directions. If another helicopter approaches, we'll know."

"On the *other*-other hand, if we keep stopping, we'll never get there."

Eileen sat on a boulder and pulled off a boot. "Oh, my feet."

"And these are just the foothills." William snickered and sat beside her.

Brittany put her hands on her hips. "I keep saying we should get on that touristy road. The girl I talked to said it led to the institute."

"A secret installation won't be on the main road," I snapped, then amended my tone. "But side roads might lead off of it."

William took out the map. "The National Tourist Road curves around quite a bit."

"Exactly," she said. "The surveyors would have found the easiest way through these hills."

I looked at the sky. I couldn't see the red lines that connected me to Ayanna, but I could sense them. "You might be right," I said, trying to keep the impatience from my voice, "but the only way I know to get there is the direct way. If we veer from the path in my head, we might get lost."

"Your way will take us down into the valley then up again," Eileen said. "I'm not a mountain goat."

William said, "The hiking trails will likewise be scouted out for the best route. This one parallels the road in question. I suggest we follow it."

"All right," Brittany said. "Which way?"

"If we stay on this ridge, we'll run right into it." He motioned to the east and stood.

"Let's go then," I said.

"But... But..." Eileen moaned.

William looked at me. "Brother, can you carry our packs?"

My brows went up. "Sure."

He picked up Eileen on his back. She whooped and laughed.

I slung the packs over my shoulder and walked beside him. "You're making me look bad," I murmured.

William gave me one of his rare smiles.

🐺🐺🐺

Ayanna stood at the wide windows in the rec room looking out at the steep mountains. Cody was out there somewhere trying to get to her. Nothing would keep him away. Yet Mum was right—it was a fool's errand. His life was at risk.

She closed her eyes and tried to contact him, but the noisy room intruded. Sodding ping-pong players. If they put as much energy into trying to escape, they could all go home. But home wasn't safe any longer. And these people weren't really wolves.

The echoing laughter diminished, and the room fell silent. Ayanna turned around. The crowd parted for an odd procession. A guard pushed an empty wheelchair leading a line of two more guards and two white-smocked attendants. The inmates backpedaled out of their way so fast, one woman actually fell. Wide-eyed and hushed. Could they smell themselves? The stench of their fear? Ayanna wanted to rail at them. She jutted out her jaw.

From nowhere, her parents materialized at her side. Her father motioned for silence. Rita and her mother clung to one another.

The procession stopped before a bearded man. His face went ashen. He looked as if he might faint.

"Lonzo Pascal," the lead guard boomed. "You are being remanded to the labs."

"No!" Pascal held out his hands, backing away. "I didn't do anything. I've been good."

The people nearest him edged away. The two guards stepped forward, guns raised. But they were pop guns. They didn't even have bullets. If everyone rushed them, they wouldn't stand a chance.

The two white-coats took Pascal's arms and led him, weeping and trembling, to the wheelchair. They strapped down his arms and legs. Tears and saliva sparkled in his beard. He gaped at his friends, the people who had been laughing with him moments before, but they avoided his eyes as if misfortune were contagious.

"There are three guards," Ayanna said, her voice rising, "and at least seventy of us."

Her father shushed her. Several other people inched back as if she were next.

Lonzo Pascal was wheeled away. They took him to the staff lift, the one with a keypad lock and guards on either side. The one that went to the penthouse—and the basement.

As the doors closed, the people in the rec room came alive once more. A murmur filled the silence.

Ayanna glanced around, fists clenched.

"Happy, are you, that it hadn't been you?"

Rita gawked as if she'd never seen her before. Her mother placed a warning hand on her arm. Her father gasped—but not at her. He took off across the room. Rita and her mother traded befuddled looks and followed, so Ayanna did, too. Her father stopped before two people. Ayanna's stomach dropped.

It was Cody's father. He wore a blue jumpsuit.

"David?" Her father gaped. "What are you doing here? And why are you dressed like an inmate?"

David looked both embarrassed and relieved. He lowered his voice. "We came to break you out, but Saarsgard—"

"You came for us?"

"And Cody. Where is he?"

"He got away," Ayanna said.

Her father glowered as if she'd spoken out of turn. "We aren't certain where Cody is."

David's face fell. "I hope he's all right."

"Where's my brother?" the woman beside him asked.

"This is my wife, Marie," David said.

"Ah." Rita nodded as if a puzzle piece had just fallen into place. She touched the woman's shoulder. "I'll take you to him."

They headed toward the inmate's lift. The one without a keypad. As they waited for the lift to respond, Ayanna noticed a hidden door behind a potted plant. It held a small sign identical to the door in the residential sector. *Trapphus*. That must say *stairwell*. Perhaps it was her way out.

David said, "I don't know what happened. One minute we were touring the facility and—"

"They gave you a tour?" her father asked.

"We saw the whole place. Living quarters for the staff. Research labs."

Ayanna said, "The basement?"

He glanced at her. "Yes."

Her father lowered his voice. "Obviously, Cody wasn't there."

"We couldn't find him anywhere."

"Why will no one listen to me?" Ayanna said.

"Hush," her father said as the door to the lift opened.

They stepped inside. The insipid music played. No one spoke. They went up a floor, exited on the residential level, and walked in pairs down the long, gray hallway. Ayanna kept her head down, although she was certain the cameras would recognize her anyway.

211

They entered Bob's room. He still sat in the chair where they'd left him before breakfast. His face was unshaven, his eyes bloodshot.

Marie knelt beside him. "Oh, Bob. What have they done to you?"

He frowned. "Why are you here?"

"David and I came to get you," she said. "All of you. But we can't find Cody."

He huffed a breath and shrugged out of her grasp. "Don't speak to me about that boy. I don't want to hear his name. This is all his fault."

"But you love him."

"I hate him," he spat. "I wish I'd never met him."

"Bob," Rita said, "calm down."

His voice rose. "Why did you send him to me? I had a life. A good life." He burst into tears, sobbing into his hands.

Marie's face twisted. She stood and backed away.

Bob wept, repeating, "I had a life. I had a life."

Rita held him in her arms, making shushing sounds as if he were a child.

He pushed her away. "Get out," he roared. "Leave me alone."

Ayanna's mother embraced Rita. "How about a nice cuppa?" Patting her back, she steered her toward the door.

They filed into the hallway, leaving Bob alone. Rita wept softly. Marie also appeared shaken, and David had his arm around her. Either he still cared for his estranged wife or he was simply a nice sort of bloke.

The lift took them to the canteen level. The pool was nearby, fouling the air with the odor of chlorine—how had she not noticed before? A few inmates strolled in that direction. The only others in the large lobby were the armed guards standing like sentinels on either side of the staff elevator. The white-coats, with their clipboards and pills, were gone.

"The canteen is always open for a sit-down," Ayanna's mother said. "We can stay as long as you like."

She ushered them to the far corner near the windows. The room was silent but for the hum of the fluorescents in the ceiling and the cooling units in the drink dispensers. Ayanna sat next to Marie, glancing sidelong as if the woman were a snake about to strike. David and her father left to fetch the tea.

Rita sniffled. "I don't know how to help him."

Marie said, "I know what you mean. When he gets something in his head."

"It's been a bit of an adjustment for all of us," Ayanna's mother said. "I'm sure he'll come around."

Ayanna watched Marie out of the corner of her eye. Cody rarely spoke about his mother, but she'd heard enough to know she was a vicious, traitorous hag. And yet, she'd come to save him.

David and her father returned carrying three cups of tea each. The tags fluttered as they set the cups on the table.

Her father gave a tentative smile. "Us boys will have a chin wag over there, shall we?"

They took their tea to the other end of the table.

Rita dried her face with the heel of her hand. Marie sipped in thoughtful silence.

After a moment, Ayanna asked, "Are you a werewolf?"

"No." Marie shook her head. "Neither of us are."

Her mother leaned across the table and whispered, "Why are you here then? And wearing blue?"

"Saarsgard." Marie's eyes narrowed and her lip curled. "We pretended to be looking for a job, but she knew why we were here. This is her way of getting rid of us. When the clients find out who we are, they will—"

"But I don't understand," Ayanna blurted. "The werewolf gene follows the mother."

Marie scowled at her, then sipped. "Sometimes it skips a generation."

"Then your mum was a werewolf."

"Not that I'm aware." She took another sip then murmured, "Although I did have an uncle."

Ayanna's mother smiled. "Did you?"

"Uncle Bob. He was Bob's namesake. He—"

Ayanna slapped her hand down on the table. "Then explain to me how Cody can be such a powerful werewolf when his mother has no powers at all?"

"I don't know." Marie leaned away as if alarmed. "The most it ever affected me is that my monthly cycle always lines up with the full moon."

"Mine, too," Rita said.

"Same." Her mother raised her hand.

Ayanna frowned. "You never even had a twinge?"

"I wouldn't allow it," Marie snapped.

Her mother blew over the rim of her cup. "Leave it alone, love."

Ayanna stood. She didn't like Cody's mother.

Didn't appreciate her holier-than-thou attitude. "I need some air." She chucked her cup into a bin by the door and stepped into the lobby.

The two soldiers still guarded the lift. They paid no attention to her. She crossed the room and stood at the windows. The sky was orange. It would be dark soon. Cody was out there somewhere. It didn't matter what the others thought. He would come for her.

"Are you all right?" a woman said beside her.

Ayanna glanced over. "Malonnie, right?"

"Call me Mal. Everyone does."

"Did you take the pill from my hand this morning?"

"I did. And I buried it in that potted plant right there." She indicated the ficus tree that hid the stairwell door. "Poor thing. It's a wonder it's still alive with all the medication we've given it."

"There are others who go off their meds?"

"Whenever we can. I'd estimate a quarter of us are drug-free at any given time. For all the good it does us."

"What do you mean?" Ayanna glanced back at the guards and lowered her voice further. "The full moon will soon be upon us. If enough inmates can shift into their wolf forms—"

"No." She gazed at her solemnly. "Please,

Ayanna. Don't even think it."

"But if we could get away—"

"And go where?" She motioned outside. "There are more soldiers out there. A lot more. Even if we managed to get past them, they would hunt us down. There's a special place in the labs reserved for escapees. Not that anyone has actually escaped."

Ayanna folded her arms.

"Besides," Mal said. "They take extra precautions during the three nights of the full."

"What kind of precautions?"

"After dinner, everyone goes to their rooms. Then they inject us with something to keep us from shifting. Here." She touched a lump on the side of her neck. "They lock us inside to sweat it out."

Ayanna's stomach clenched. If they injected her, she was doomed.

NINETEEN

Brittany sat on a fallen log and watched William build a fire. She knew there was a method of putting sticks and branches together, but his way was an art, and she enjoyed watching him work.

Eileen joined her. "Four o'clock and the sun has set."

"We're lucky to get eight hours of daylight," Brittany said. "At this rate, it will be December before we get there."

"Well, we can't walk in the dark," Eileen said. "Where's Cody? Out with the wolves?"

"Yes." She sighed and searched the shadows for wolf eyes. How their lives had changed. A short time ago, she was opening presents at her birthday party. "I can't believe I'm seventeen."

Eileen laughed. "I can't believe I'm seventeen and married."

Brittany murmured, "I'll be married soon, too."

"He proposed?" She hugged her. "That's wonderful. Have you set a date?"

"Not yet. Part of me wants to marry him as soon as possible. But..." She gave a sheepish grin. "I've always wanted a Christmas wedding. Not this Christmas, of course. I wouldn't have time to plan it properly. Next year. I'd ask Lynette to preside, and I'd wear white, and you would be my maid of honor... Please?"

"Of course."

"You could wear red velvet."

"Ooh, pretty. Any other bridesmaids?"

"Myra, of course. And I thought I'd ask Ayanna."

"Ayanna. That's a tough call."

"I know she loves Cody. And he loves her, too. But not in a physical way. It's—"

"Platonic?"

"Yeah."

"Argh," William growled. "If we don't plan a rescue, there won't be any Ayanna." He struck a match. As if he'd snapped his fingers, flames engulfed his carefully balanced sticks.

Eileen said, "The rescue plan hasn't changed. I'll have bags of sleeping powder, Brit will have the love potion, and we'll toss them at soldiers as we go in."

"You underestimate how many soldiers there might be."

"We don't need to hit them all. Just the ones standing in front of us."

A wolf howled.

All three of them stared out into the darkness.

William sat next to Eileen. "There are fifteen of them now."

Brittany said, "Cody won't let them hurt us."

"There are no sheep up here."

Eileen looked at him. "Are there reindeer? Or those musk oxen?"

The wind gusted.

Brittany hugged her arms. "I'm more worried about freezing to death. You can turn into a bear. Cody can remain a wolf. But Eileen and I don't have fur."

Eileen stood. "We'll feel better after we eat. Who wants soup?"

"The hotter the better," Brittany said.

Eileen smiled. "Boiling hot soup coming up." She pulled the cookpot from her backpack and poured in two packets of soup mix and the rest of the water from her canteen. "I'm out," she said as she tapped the sides.

Before long, the campsite smelled like vegetable broth. It wasn't the best soup, but it was hot. Brittany held the cup to her face and breathed in the steam before each sip.

When she finished eating, she said, "I'll help you wash up."

But William took the cup from her hand. "Better just wipe them dry if we're low on water."

Just then, it began to snow.

"Oh!" Eileen looked up in wonder, one hand outstretched.

"That does it." Brittany stood. "I can't wait for Cody any longer. I'm making a circle."

She took a container of salt out of her doctor's bag and drew a large circle around them, the fallen log, and the campfire. Then she pricked her finger with her knife and touched the blood to the salt.

An invisible dome sprang up around them. The wind cut to a cool draft. Snow stuck to the top.

William said, "I'd like to know how you do that."

Brittany said, "I'd like to know how you call

animals to your defense. We all have a little magic."

They huddled together before the fire.

Brittany woke with a crick in her neck. She still sat on the log, leaning against Eileen. William slept against Eileen's other side. Brittany chuckled. All the fresh air and activity was tuckering them out. They didn't even get into their sleeping bags.

The campfire was cold, yet the dome was warm. Thick snow blocked the windward side. In fact, snow covered the entire dome. They would have suffocated but for a single clear spot letting in the air.

Brittany jostled Eileen. "Um, guys. Wake up."

Eileen groaned, rubbed her eyes, then looked up. "Wow."

Footsteps crunched outside. A hand wiped away a patch of snow, and Cody looked inside. "Good morning."

"Good morning." Brittany smiled. "Were you out all night?"

"When I got back, you were sleeping so peacefully, I couldn't bear to disturb you. Let me clear this away, or it will drop on your head when you lower the barrier."

He used a pine bough to clean off the dome. The snow was heavy and wet. It slid down as if on glass, leaving blurred streaks. Brittany broke the circle, and the remaining slush plopped down.

William filled their canteens from the melting snow. He handed one to Eileen.

She sipped. "Ice water."

Brittany stood and stretched. The sky was blue. The sun had risen. Wolves filled their campsite. "Did you feed your friends?"

Cody nodded. "Deer."

"That's all right for you." Eileen sniffed. "Meanwhile, we're eating granola bars."

Cody grinned and slipped off his parka. The hood was filled with berries. "Ta-da."

Eileen squealed. "You're my hero."

They sat and ate. William supplemented with beef jerky.

Brittany looked up at the jagged brown mountain. "We have a difficult day ahead."

Eileen said, "My cousin told me The Fells aren't particularly high but very steep."

"We'll all be experienced rock climbers before this is done," Brittany said.

"That must be why they chose the site,"

William said. "It's difficult to get to."

Cody shrugged. "There's a dirt road not far from here. Looks like it goes in the right direction. Let's check it out."

They broke camp then followed Cody. As they approached the road, a big semi rumbled by. Branches brushed the top of the truck. It had *Svenson Jordbruksprodukter* printed in orange letters on the side.

"That's a grocery truck," Eileen said.

Brittany said, "Who would need that much food?"

"Someone with a lot of mouths to feed," William said. "A restaurant, perhaps."

Cody grinned. "Or a cafeteria in an institution."

TWENTY

Ayanna sat alone in the noisy canteen. She relished the noise. It kept her from thinking. Her breakfast was a glass of milk and a chunk of cheese, but she wasn't in the mood for either. She stared at Tommy Lee who sat a few tables away.

The woman with the untidy braids slid in next to her. Why did she keep hanging around?

Ayanna sighed and sipped her milk. "All right, Mal?"

"Hello." Mal smiled at her. Then she twiddled her fingers at a blonde attendant and said in a singsong manner, "Good morning, Norma."

Norma appeared disconcerted that she'd been caught staring. "Good morning, Mal. Bus your own table, please." She moved on.

Mal lowered her voice. "Why aren't you with

the rest of your pack?"

"We had a row." Ayanna scowled. "They don't believe in me."

"Oh." Mal blinked as if taken aback. "Well, we aren't allowed to have packs here anyway. Just one big happy family."

Ayanna glared at Tommy Lee's back. "When I find out who turned chirp on us, I will murder them with my bare hands."

Mal leaned closer. "Look, I'm sorry you were picked up. I really am. Cody should have been strong enough to protect you."

Ayanna turned her glare around. "He *is* strong."

"Well, you're here now, and he isn't. So, you need to look after yourself. Murder is not the best way to go about that."

With a huff, Ayanna got to her feet. "I'm going back to my room."

"Okay." Mal smiled. "It's movie night tonight. Maybe we can sit together."

Doubtful. Ayanna looked at the refuse of her breakfast. *Bus your own table.* They could bloody well bus her table for her. Mal could clean it herself for all she cared.

She stomped out of the canteen and into the large, check-in lobby. People still stood in line for their morning pill. Supposed to keep you calm. But her wolf seemed to have overridden it easily enough. She felt she might explode with frustration.

She took the lift up to Residential. People strolled along the hallway in pairs and threesomes. Going to brekkie. Like they were in a bloody hotel. She scowled at them as they passed, then thought better of it. If she didn't check her attitude, the white-coats might double her morning dose.

The suspected stairwell was across the hall and several doors down from hers. There was no keypad. She passed it, then glanced at the camera in the ceiling and turned back. She tried the knob. Locked. To be expected, for sure, but it was no good until she tried.

She went into her quarters and plopped onto her bed. Light seeped around the door frame. It should have been enough to illuminate the entire room, but she couldn't see as well anymore.

Were those sodding drugs doing permanent damage? Was she becoming like the others—not a human, not a wolf? She'd tried to find a way to stash the pill at check-in, but the white-coats had their eyes on her. She had no choice but to swallow it in front of them.

Still, it didn't have the effect they apparently expected. She did not feel calm. And her connection to Mother Moon was as strong as ever. She checked it often, hoping to sense Cody. But the *link* was faint. Was he forgetting about her?

No, he wouldn't do that. She needed to practice her meditation, that's all. She folded her hands over her stomach and slowed her breathing. Tension rushed out of her in a whoosh. In her imagination, she climbed golden tendrils out of her hellhole.

And he was there. *Cody*. A being of light. Dancing in the glittering starfield. Her breath caught in her throat. She froze, listening, hoping he would speak. *Please. Tell me what to do*. He turned his attention to her. A sensation of warmth spread over her incorporeal body.

And the world opened as with a book.

Ayanna gasped. She was standing in the woods behind her house in Florida. Near the swampy pond where they used to meet. It was so real, she could smell the fetid water, hear the buzz of mosquitoes.

Behind her, Cody said, "Hi."

She turned to him. Just a boy in jeans and a

t-shirt. A remarkable boy. Love and pride welled up in her. She wished Mal could see him.

He is strong.

Words clambered up her throat. She wanted to ask if he was somewhere safe. Wanted to tell him how frightened she was.

Instead, she said, "You did all this?"

"I don't know for how long. Are you okay?"

"We are unharmed." But her thoughts continued, *of course, your uncle has gone bonkers.* She hoped he didn't catch that part. At least, he didn't respond to it.

"Where are you?" he asked. "I mean, what floor?"

"No idea. But we appear to be rather high. Like in a tower. Only three floors are open to us. There's a lift—"

"And it only goes three floors?"

"The one we're allowed to use does. The white-coats use lifts that go all the way to the penthouse. I was up there once." She paused, remembering her trip to Saarsgard's office when she'd first arrived. "But you need a handprint, a keycode, and voice recognition to make the lift work."

He blew out a breath and kicked a pebble. Then he looked up. "What do they do with a bunch of werewolves during the full moon? Let you run amok?"

"I'm told we are given a drug to keep us from shifting and locked in our rooms for the night."

"The drug is not an issue for us. They gave it to me, too, but my wolf overrode it. Just keep strengthening your *link* to Mother Moon."

"I will."

"The locked doors will be more of a problem. I'll have to get there before they lock you in."

Her heart leaped. "On the full?"

"That's the plan." He stepped closer and squeezed her arms, and she could actually feel the warmth of his hands on her skin. "Don't lose hope, Ayanna. We're coming for you."

"We?"

He smirked. "Me and over a dozen true-wolves."

The swamp faded. Ayanna was in her room once more. She hugged her arms together as if she were hugging Cody.

🐺🐺🐺

I opened my eyes. I was sitting on a rock near the road. It was sunny, and I had my jacket open despite the remains of snow on the ground.

Beside me, Brittany said, "Where did you go?"

"I was checking in with Ayanna." I didn't tell her I had transported us both back to Florida in my mind. That would be too weird.

She handed me a granola bar. "Have a snack. You need to keep up your strength."

I opened the wrapper. "Is Eileen still crying?"

Her eyes laughed. "Scrying. With an S. I don't know. Let's find out."

We stepped under cover of the forest. The scent of a hundred Christmas trees enveloped me. The babble of water grew. I smelled the wolves before I saw them. They lounged around a little stream. William and Eileen sat together on a large rock that jutted from the bank. Eileen gazed into a mirror.

Brittany called, "Find out anything?"

"Loads of stuff." Eileen grinned.

The sound of a truck interrupted them. Their smiles dropped. I moved to see the road. A semi rattled by, faster now that it was going downhill. "It's the same truck we saw before only going the other way."

Eileen said, "That's because there's only one way in or out. This road leads to the lone gate. It has two guards." She picked up a stick and drew vague lines on the rock she was sitting on. "Once past the gate, the road continues for a distance before it reaches the main building. It's taller than we hoped. Maybe ten stories. There's a smaller one-story building over here. A lot of men around it."

William nodded. "Barracks. Where her army lives."

"That's where her reinforcements will come from," I said. "We'll have to take it out. How do we get into the main building?"

"There's an entrance here." Eileen drew a box. "But over here there's a ramp that goes downward. I saw two jeeps go inside and not come out. I think it's an underground parking garage."

"Underground." William grimaced. "Too confined. Was there a loading dock? For supplies like that truck brought in?"

Brittany murmured, "A little girl told me a story about her brother who made deliveries. He heard the spookies howl."

Eileen set down her stick. "Well, if there is a dock, it must be on the other side. I only saw this part."

I said, "You did great, Eileen. Good work."

She beamed.

Brittany asked, "Did Ayanna tell you what floor they're on?"

I shook my head. "She didn't know. But she told me that to work the elevators you need a handprint from someone in a white coat."

Brittany chuckled. "That shouldn't be too hard. My love potion is stronger than ever. I'm sure we'll find someone to help us out. Right, Eileen?"

I frowned. I hadn't told them yet that I didn't want the girls to come along. Too dangerous.

William looked at me. "Have you given any thought as to how you will get around their ammunition? Whatever they use in those pop guns incapacitated you before."

"They took me by surprise," I said. "I think that if I'm ready for them—"

"Amulet," Eileen whispered.

Brittany pursed her lips.

Eileen said, "It's the right time for it. The moon is waxing."

Brittany nodded thoughtfully. "Let's look by the water."

They walked along the splashing stream, heads down as if searching.

"What are you looking for?" I asked.

"A hag stone," Brittany said. "It's smooth,

worn away by water, and it will have a hole through it."

"Well, there are plenty of stones," I muttered and went through the motions of helping her.

William said, "Let me get this straight. You propose to make a talisman that will—"

"No," Eileen said as she searched. "A talisman is man-made. A silver pendant. Or that bear you carved out of bone. It attracts power. Like strength, wealth, or love. An amulet is a natural object used to repel. We could use a talisman to attract luck, but in this case, I think it would be stronger to use something of Earth."

I said, "You mean it will actually repel the paintballs? Like a force field?"

"That's right." Brittany reached into the water and picked up a stone. It was about two inches across. She held it up and peered at us through a hole in the middle. "A hag stone. Eileen, grab my bag for me. It's over there."

Eileen hurried away. Brittany knelt and rinsed the stone in the rushing water. Her fingers turned bright pink from the cold.

Eileen carried the bag to the bank. "What do you want? Herbs or salt?"

"Salt." Brittany held out the stone. Eileen poured salt over it, and Brittany scrubbed carefully, murmuring something I didn't catch.

Eileen rummaged through the bag, and my heart did a double-take. Brittany's birthday presents were there. The candles from Uncle Bob. Howard's recipe box. The blank books from Eileen and William. So much had changed. All because of Saarsgard.

Eileen pulled out a ball of twine and cut off a length. Brittany held out the hag stone, and Eileen threaded the jute through the hole. Carefully, as if trying not to touch it. Then she tied the amulet around Brittany's neck so the stone hung even with her heart.

Brittany slipped it into her shirt. She squealed and laughed. "It's so cold."

I said, "I thought you were making it for me."

"I need to charge it with my magic. It's a ritual. I just want to warm it up a bit first."

Eileen moved a short distance away. "Here's a good spot," she called.

Brittany grabbed her bag and hurried over. "Perfect."

The ground was relatively flat, although all of Norway seemed to be slanted in one direction or another. The girls policed the area, removing twigs and pebbles. William sat on a nearby boulder, so I joined him.

From her bag, Brittany pulled out the container of salt, four candles, and a compass. She made a circle of salt around herself, sat in the middle, and set the little candles on the compass points.

She struck a long match. "I call to the Elements for help. East, air." She lit the eastern candle. "South, fire." She lit another. "West, water. North, Earth."

She took the amulet from around her neck and held it up. "I place upon this stone my protective power." She cupped the hag stone in both hands and held it to her heart. "Cody will be protected at all times. No harm shall pass this stone's protective shield. Cody will be protected at all times. Heed my words forevermore."

She blew out the candles counter-clockwise starting with the north. "I thank the Elements for their assistance."

She put the amulet around her neck and stepped out of the circle. Eileen swept the area with a pine bough, scattering the salt.

I stepped forward with my hand out. "So, that's it?"

But Brittany didn't hand me the stone. "I'll keep it. I have to do it again."

"For how long?"

"The longer the better. You want it good and charged."

William slid off the rock. "Let's start walking then. We're wasting daylight."

TWENTY-ONE

Ayanna skulked around the recreation room, surreptitiously looking for hidden doors. The inmates seemed especially excitable this afternoon, perhaps in response to the infamous movie night. Two soldiers stood at attention by the staff elevators, staring straight ahead as if they were Queen's Guard at the Buckingham Palace. Outside the glass wall, the mountains were tinged with sunset.

What floor were they on?

As she stood at the windows, Tommy Lee approached. "Afternoon, Miss Ayanna. How are you settling in? Any questions?"

"Yeah, I have a question." She glared. "Did you tell Saarsgard where to find my pack?"

His eyes widened. "Glory, no. I would never– How could you even think–"

"Someone did." She stomped away, aware of his gaze on her back. She was so irritated, she almost missed her father calling her name.

"Where have you been?" he admonished as he caught up with her. "It's time for dinner."

Her stomach quailed. "I'm not hungry." But she knew she had no choice. Even in this place, her father was a stickler about family dinnertime.

With a sigh, she followed him. Inmates queued up outside the lift. David and her mother stood near the potted plant and the hidden door.

Her mother said, "Thank goodness you found her," as if there were a risk of her getting lost.

Ayanna motioned to the sign on the door. "Does anyone know what that says?"

David looked around. "Yes. It says *stairwell*. But apparently, we aren't meant to notice it."

She nodded. As she suspected. Perhaps Cody could use that information as well. "Where's Rita?"

"She's trying to persuade Bob out of his room," her mother said.

"Marie is with her," David said. "Maybe she can help."

They took the lift one floor down to the canteen. The lobby swarmed with people.

Braving the onslaught of noise, they filed into the eatery with the others.

Her father navigated the tray down the food line. "Lots of meat today."

"Looks yummy," her mother responded, not looking at the food at all.

Ayanna winced at the mingled aromas. She couldn't eat. "I'll get some seats. Should I get seven?"

"Four, I think," her mother said. "I doubt our friends will make it downstairs."

As she left the line, Ayanna grabbed a paper cup of milk, thinking of Cody. She claimed four chairs near the windows. Moments later, David and her parents joined her laden with plates of meat, most of it cooked rare.

Ayanna wanted to tell them about her spectral meeting with Cody and what he'd said about coming for them on the full moon. But it would only start another row. They wouldn't believe her. She could scarcely believe it herself. How could he transport her back home like that? It was like she'd really been in Florida.

Conversation buzzed around her. Why did Cody want to know what floor she was on? It must be important. How could she find out?

Her parents stood, startling her.

"Dinner is done, little flower," her mother said. "Come along."

Ayanna sighed. "I think I'll just sit a spell."

Her mother cast an odd look at her father.

"All right," he murmured, leaning closer, "but don't speak to any dodgy people."

She watched them walk away. Many people had left. Most of the tables were empty. She sipped her milk and found it had gone warm.

Mal slid in beside her. Ayanna nearly groaned. The woman probably thought she'd been waiting around for their movie night date, but in truth, she'd forgotten all about her.

"That man you were with," Mal said. "He doesn't smell like a werewolf."

Ayanna wanted to say *neither do you*. She set her cup down and stared out the window.

"What is he?" Mal asked. "A reporter or something? Someone who got too close? I've heard of that happening. You know, when they want someone to disappear. In fact, a few days before you arrived, I saw a man with a broken neck floating in the pool. I recognized him. He was the psychiatrist who ran the group therapy meetings. I was afraid that there would be repercussions. But it was deemed a diving board accident."

A chill washed through Ayanna. Was David in danger? Trying to deflect the conversation away from him, she snorted. "No wonder I haven't been invited to one of those meetings."

"You will be. Everyone is. They're pretty intense. Try to niggle out all your secrets."

"Like what?"

"The whereabouts of more werewolves, mostly."

Ayanna scowled. "I met a pack in Georgia." Tommy Lee's pack.

She nodded. "There are a lot of our kind in the Appalachian Mountains. We're attracted to the mountains. Maybe through necessity or maybe we just like it. For me, it has a calming effect. I like looking at the ones here."

"Wherever here is."

"You poor thing. All this time you haven't known where you were?" Mal patted her arm. "These are the Scandinavian Mountains. I found that out when I met the big lady upstairs."

"You met her, too?"

"Everyone does. She's kind of a hands-on monster."

They laughed together.

An attendant edged nearer, probably trying to find out why they were still hanging around.

Ayanna twiddled her fingers like she saw Mal do before. "Hello, Norma."

Norma looked surprised as if she'd thought she'd been invisible.

"Norma, what floor are we on?" Ayanna blurted.

"The cafeteria is on the fifth floor," she said with a sniff. "Please bus your table."

Ayanna held an inward smile. That meant her room was on the seventh floor. How could she get that information to Cody?

As Norma ambled off, Ayanna murmured, "She said *cafeteria* instead of *canteen*. She must be American."

"I think she's the only American attendant here. Apparently, her town was attacked by a wild pack. She joined the institute because she felt safer with us all incarcerated." Mal stood. "We should get going if we want a seat for the movie."

Ayanna gulped down her tepid milk. She scrunched the cup and tossed it in the bin by the door. The check-in room was silent, the tall windows dark with night. Above the shadowed mountains, streaks of green light lit up the sky.

Ayanna gasped. She stepped nearer to the windows.

"Isn't that pretty?" Mal smiled. "Aurora Borealis. Puts on quite a light show. We'll be seeing it from now until March."

$$🐺🐺🐺$$

Brittany smiled and nestled closer to Cody, looking up at the colors in the sky. "It's so beautiful. Why didn't I see it before?"

"It was cloudy before." Cody kissed the top of her head.

It was easy to believe they were just on vacation. Easy to forget the horror they'd been through.

Eileen sighed. "This is the best honeymoon ever."

William whispered something in her ear. They stood.

"We're going for a walk," Eileen said.

Brittany sat up, looking around at them. "Ah, okay. Be careful."

"They'll be all right," Cody murmured as they strolled away. "They have guardians."

As if on cue, a wolf howled.

Brittany settled into Cody's arms. "We're up to twenty wolves. How can you control so many?"

"I don't know. And it scares me."

"Why scare?"

He hesitated. "Uncle Bob once told me that every alpha wolf he ever met was evil. And that's been my experience, too. Pascal. Bodark. And who was that latest one?"

"Daryl Huntington."

"Right. Now I find out I can do things even they couldn't do. I made men jump out of the back of a moving truck, for Pete's sake. No concern for what happened to them."

"People are going to get hurt in this. They have our friends."

"I understand that. And I'll do anything I can to get them back. But power corrupts. What if my powers keep getting stronger? I don't want to be the bad guy."

"Then don't be." She faced him. "Look. I'm afraid of my powers, too. Even among the freaks, I'm a freak. But you have to embrace it. Learn everything you can. It's the only way to stop being afraid."

He gave her a sad smile and cupped her cheek in his warm hand. "You are the exact opposite of me."

His arms slid around her, and she fell into his scent. His presence enveloped her, making her feel secure and warm.

"You could never be evil," she murmured.

"I hope you're right," he said.

🐕🐕🐕

Ayanna woke to a blinding light and an avalanche of sound. She skittered from the glare, one hand shielding her face, and banged into the wall.

"Wristband," a male voice ordered.

She blinked, rising up on her elbows. "It's the middle of the night."

"Wristband!"

Someone pulled her arm out from under her, making her plop back down again. She couldn't see them. The light was too bright. But she knew when they put a tourniquet on her arm.

Blood. They were taking her blood.

She squirmed away. "I don't like needles."

"Hold still!"

A knee pressed against her chest. They pinned her arm and jammed the needle in. She bit back a gasp of pain. They released her with a shove and switched off the light. Two men stood in her room. One with a gun leveled at her head.

She cradled her bleeding arm. "You took vials of blood from me when I first arrived. Do you think it's changed?"

The needle man sneered. "We're coming up on a full moon. Do you think your blood has changed?"

They backed out of the room, cart jingling. The woman next door shrieked in alarm as they bashed their way in.

Ayanna leaned back against the hard cot and wept.

TWENTY-TWO

The taste of her greasy breakfast was still on her lips as Ayanna walked out of the canteen with her parents. She longed for a bit of Concepcion's cooking, longed to be home. She never appreciated their cook and housekeeper so much as now. Even after the main house was destroyed in the tropical storm, Concepcion had stayed on to keep them all comfortable in the stone cottage. She'd grilled many a patio meal since then. Her breakfasts were never greasy.

It wasn't that the food in this place was terrible. It was her roiling stomach. It was what was being done to them. Her parents' defeatist attitudes. It was that no one would listen to her.

"It's unacceptable," she muttered as they took the lift to Recreation. "They burst into my quarters in the middle of the night and—"

"It was the same for everyone," her mother said in a hushing tone as if she didn't want Ayanna to mention it.

"I think they were surprised to find me in your mother's room," her father said, "but, I say, they have cameras everywhere. They must know where I've been sleeping."

"They have no right to treat us this way," Ayanna said.

"Don't sulk," her mother said.

They took the lift up to Recreation. As they stepped out, Rita met them. Her wild, red hair stood every which way, and her eyes were puffy.

Ayanna's father smiled. "Bob's still on his hunger strike?"

Rita nodded. "I'm so afraid they're going to yellow flag him."

"They won't." He put his hand on her shoulder. "He's harmless."

They walked deeper into the noisy room. The rhythm and roar of a ping-pong game grated against Ayanna's ears. She wished she could go outside. Just a bit of fresh air. Hear the morning birds sing. Did they have birds in the Scandinavian Mountains? How had Cody transported her to Florida? It had seemed so real, so immediate.

Suddenly, the laughter ebbed. The room fell silent. Ayanna glanced around. A wheelchair emerged from the back-pedaling crowd. With mounting horror, she realized it was coming straight at them.

"Richard Richardson," the guard boomed. "You are being remanded to the medical labs."

Her father blinked. "What?"

"There must be some mistake." Her mother stepped to shield him. "He's done nothing wrong."

"Leave us alone!" Rita cried.

The guard sneered. He was a big man with a crooked nose that had been broken one too many times. "This your pack?"

"Not pack." Her father smiled, hands spread. "Family. They're my family."

"Sit in the chair, please," a white-coat said.

Ayanna gasped beneath a terrible weight. She wanted to cry out. Wanted to fight. But her body wouldn't move.

Her father turned his horrified gaze to her mother. Their eyes held.

"Mr. Richardson, please," the attendant said. "Don't make this harder than it has to be."

"But he's been good." Her mother's voice became strident. "All of us have been. We've done everything that you asked."

"You've been fraternizing," the flat-nosed guard bellowed. "Sleeping in another inmate's room."

"But she's my wife. We haven't slept apart in eighteen years."

"Get used to it."

"I won't let you take him." Tears filled her mother's voice. "You can't."

Flat-nose puffed up. Her mother quailed.

Her father said, "I'll go."

"What?" Ayanna said.

"I'll go." He hugged her and kissed her forehead. "Don't make trouble."

"Daddy, no."

He hugged her mother, but she didn't seem able to respond. Just stood limply. Mouth wide in a silent scream.

"It's all right," he murmured. "I'll go." He sat in the wheelchair.

Flat-nose buckled his arms down.

Her father winced. "I assure you, my good man, you needn't–"

The guard punched him in the face.

Her mother screamed. Rita clung to her.

Her father's head drooped. Chin on chest. Blood streaming.

Ayanna glared at the guard. Memorizing. Scars on his face. Scars on his knuckles.

They pulled the chair away. Her mother dropped to her knees. Screaming. Clawing her face. Rita clutching her, looking horrified.

And still, Ayanna couldn't move. The crowd parted as they wheeled her father away. She watched their procession across the room. They turned the chair around so they could back it onto the lift. She met her father's gaze. He gave her a slow nod then disappeared.

🐕🐕🐕

I staggered as a rush of emotion blazed through my mind. The *link*. What was wrong with the *link?* Something happened to Ayanna. Panic rippled through me—some of it hers, some of it mine.

Then, as clearly as if she were standing right there, Ayanna said, "They took my dad."

No. Oh, no. Tears filled my eyes. I stumbled into a tree.

"Cody?" Brittany grabbed me. "Are you all right?"

For a moment, I couldn't speak. Couldn't breathe. Dick was gone. I was supposed to save him. I ran a hand over my sweating face. "We're running out of time. How much farther is this place?"

William unfolded his map. "Evil installations aren't listed here. It's more for hiking trails."

Eileen looked over his shoulder. "I was hoping we'd run into another of their tourist cabins. We're out of granola bars."

Without looking at her, I muttered, "We can't go to a cabin with twenty-five wolves."

I dropped my arms to my sides, willing the tension from my shoulders. The *link* to Ayanna was strong but garbled. I couldn't sense the others at all. *They took my dad.* What did that mean? Had they executed him? Or had they inducted Dick into their mad experiments? How much longer before I lost Uncle Bob—or Ayanna?

Brittany offered me a sip of water, her eyes filled with concern. I wanted to tell her what happened. What I felt. But it was too raw.

I was failing my mission. Failing my friends.

I drank again and wiped my mouth. "Where are we?"

"I believe we're near Bergen," William said.

"Wow," Eileen said. "That's really north."

"If we went in that direction, we'd see polar

bears. Maybe even sea eagles."

"Well, we aren't going in that direction," I said a little testily. "Let's keep moving."

I wiped a sheen of sweat from my face with a shaking hand and filled my lungs with pine-scented air. Still pondering Ayanna's message, I got back on the road. But I hadn't gone ten paces when another message moved up the line.

I froze mid-step. "A truck's coming."

"I don't hear anything," William said.

"Another food truck?" asked Eileen.

"It's a transport."

Brittany looked stricken. "Cody. Hide the wolves."

I wanted to howl at her. Where did she think I got the message? But I told the pack to take cover just the same.

We hurried off the road. As we crouched in the brush, a truck came into view. Large and covered in a black tarp. A troop carrier. Like the truck I'd been in. The one where I was chained to the ceiling. It lurched and whined, gears grinding as it struggled up the steep incline.

With a thrill of alarm, I sensed werewolves inside the truck. Three of them. I saw their spectral images like heat signatures radiating through the dusty tarp. They weren't bound and gagged as I had been. They sat on a bench, chained to the floor and to one another.

As the truck pulled even with our hiding spot, the prisoners became aware of me.

"Help!" a man cried. "Please, help us!"

Two guards sat across from them. One was half-dozing with the rocking of the truck.

The other sat straighter. "Shut it, you."

"Help!" the man cried. "Don't let them take us."

"Help!" the two women with him chimed in.

The sleepy guard stood, brandishing his gun, but he staggered with the movement of the truck and sat down again. The other man hopped out the flap of tarp and walked alongside. The muzzle of his pop gun tracked his gaze into the forest.

I could take him. It would be a simple thing to hop into the back of the truck and free the werewolves.

"Save us! Don't leave us!"

Brittany placed her hand on my arm, and I realized I was preparing to bolt forward.

"Stay on mission," William murmured. "We're here for your pack, not his."

The truck disappeared around a bend of the

winding road. What would happen to them? What had happened to Dick?

"New mission." I scowled at the dissipating cloud of dust. "I'm going to save them all."

Ayanna turned on the lamp and helped Rita usher her mother inside the cramped cell. The blanket was mussed where her father had spent the night comforting her mother. Mum collapsed onto the edge of the bed. She sobbed and rocked, clutching her stomach. Rita sat beside her, cooing and rubbing her back.

Ayanna shook her head. *This couldn't be happening.* She heard herself whisper, "I will fix this."

Only she hadn't fixed it. She hadn't done anything. Stood idly by as they took her father away.

"Mum, listen," Ayanna said. "It's going to be all right."

Her mother let out a keening wail.

Ayanna stepped nearer. "Cody is coming for us. Tomorrow on the full. When we're free, we'll get dad back."

"Stop it!" Rita snapped. "Stop with the false

hope! You know he's not coming. We'll never be free."

Their eyes met like a thunderclap. Ayanna saw fear and despair. And hatred. Rita despised her. As if it were her fault. As if she hadn't lost…

Ayanna rushed out of the room. She leaned back against the wall. Sobs twisted her face and wrenched her throat. *It couldn't be happening.*

But it had.

TWENTY-THREE

I called a halt around four o'clock although it pained me to do it. I'd promised Ayanna a rescue yet still hadn't found the compound. But the sky was red with the setting sun, and it was dark beneath the trees. I didn't want anyone to turn an ankle.

Brittany said, "Do you need to check on the wolves?" Her breath steamed in the crisp air.

I shrugged. "In a little while. Let's build a fire."

She flashed me one of her bewitching smiles, green eyes bright, and I suddenly felt warm all over. We hunted for fallen branches. This part of the forest was less dense, and there wasn't much wood to choose from.

William also rummaged through the brush. He found a straight, four-foot long tree limb. Sitting on a boulder in a patch of sunlight, he stripped the bark off the limb with his knife.

Brittany and Eileen built the campfire. They were getting good at it. They chose a site near an outcropping of rock that worked well as a windbreak.

I said, "I want to thank you, all of you, for sticking with me. I know it's not your fight. Not your pack."

"They're our friends," Eileen said. "Besides, we're not going to come all this way only to leave you on your own."

"We'll get through this together." Brittany embraced me.

I closed my eyes and breathed her scent. Her presence filled my hollows. She'd promised to marry me. I didn't see how that would be possible now.

Brittany, Eileen, and I sat near the fire with our backs to the outcropping. As the sun went down, the stars came out.

Brittany sighed. "I didn't think there could be so many stars."

Eileen said, "I'm going to make soup. Want some?" She lifted her voice. "Will, do you want soup?"

William didn't answer.

"Oh, well." She put the pot over the flames.

"We'll keep some warm for him."

Soon the soup was boiling. We each had a cup. The night closed around us like a black fist.

William brought his stick to the fire. He carved a design into one end, held it into the fire for a moment, then carved some more. Eileen looked at him as if about to remind him about dinner but seemed to think better of it. He was intent on his work.

The moon rose low on the horizon. It felt like a flurry of electric snow. Bright and nearly full. The wolves sang. Brittany nestled against my side. The perfect night.

After a while, she pulled the amulet from around her neck. "This will be the last time I'll charge the stone. I think it's full, and it needs to get accustomed to you."

My brows went up. How could an inanimate object have feelings for me either way? I thought she was joking, so I chuckled.

"I'm serious." She sat on her knees and looked me in the eyes. "When I hand it to you, you need to formally accept it. Say something like I accept this stone and add its energies to my own. And you need to mean it. This could save your life."

I nodded. "All right."

Brittany stood and moved into the shadows. She and Eileen brushed the area clean of sticks and small stones. Amid a circle of salt, Brittany sat on the ground and set the four Elements candles around her.

She held the amulet toward the bright moon. In a commanding voice, she said, "I call upon the power of the moon. Heed my call. Charge this stone with your power so that it may protect your son. May the power of the moon forever charge this stone."

And the stone began to glow. Blue light pulsed between her fingers.

She bowed her head. "Thank you, Mother Moon, for your energy." With her knife, she pricked her finger. "So mote it be." Holding up both her bleeding finger and the amulet, she allowed a single drop of blood to fall upon the stone.

Like an explosion, the blue glow flared into blinding white light.

Eileen gasped and took several steps back. Brittany leaned away, blinking and looking surprised. Slowly, the light faded back into a blue glow.

Eileen stepped around the fire and motioned for me to stand.

Brittany blew out the candles, thanking the Elements as she did so, then carried the amulet to me. She held it in both hands like it was fragile. "I freely give this protective stone to you."

I hesitated. I wasn't sure I wanted to touch it after that display.

Eileen whispered, "Hold out your hands."

So, I held out my hands. "I accept this stone and add its energy to my own."

Brittany laid the glowing amulet in my cupped hands. It felt like ice.

I slipped it over my head. A hum of energy swept my body. I gasped. "Wow."

"Wow is right," Eileen said. "I've never seen it glow like that. You are some strong witch, Brittany Meyer."

Brittany looked embarrassed. "You're a strong witch, too. In fact, I was hoping you'd teach me how to put together some of that sleeping powder."

"By the light of the moon?" Eileen grinned. "That will give it some punch."

The girls sat at the edge of the campfire, pulling things out of Brittany's doctor bag. Across from them, William continued alternately carving and scorching his staff. He chanted beneath his breath as he worked.

I looked at the amulet. The blue glow dissipated, yet power resonated from it like it was alive and aware. I tucked it into my sweatshirt, pressing the icy stone against my skin. I looked from face to face, each focused on their own project. How did I get such good friends?

TWENTY-FOUR

Ayanna sat on her cot in her darkened room. She'd sat there all night. Her cheeks were stiff with dried tears. She never felt so alone.

Where was Cody? Should she contact him? No. He was busy planning her rescue. It wouldn't do to distract him. He would come for her. Tonight, with the full moon.

But what if he didn't? What if he was a dream as her father had said? How could she bear living in this place for the rest of her life?

Her door unlocked. It was morning. She would be expected to go down to brekkie. If she fought back, stepped a toe out of line, they would take her away like they did her father. She thought of his frightened face, the doors of the lift closing.

Cody would come for her. He promised he

would come. She had to believe.

But what if he didn't?

Footsteps passed in the hallway. Low conversation. She should be able to hear every word, but her ears weren't what they once were. She had to stop taking their drugs. They were changing her. Ruining her. Soon she would be less of a wolf. Less of a human.

Cody, please save me.

A dream, her father had said. *I know you want to believe…*

Perhaps *this* was the dream. She would wake in her own bed. She'd tell Cody all about it, and they'd have a good laugh. She only needed to wake.

After a time, she got up to go to breakfast. She didn't want to. Her stomach churned from lack of sleep and the impending full moon. She always felt sick on the full. Her father said it would pass—she hadn't been a werewolf all that long, after all. And Concepcion would make her a cup of tea.

The hallway was crowded. Evidently, everyone was exceptionally hungry. Ayanna queued up then entered the lift. When the doors opened on the canteen level, the lobby was packed with inmates. Long lines led to check-in.

An inkling of panic gripped her. She tried to retreat, to step back into the lift, but the people behind her crowded forward and pushed her out into the room. She bobbed and drifted as if lost at sea. She couldn't do this, couldn't take their pills, couldn't go on with her day. Her father told her not to make trouble. She didn't *want* to make trouble. She wanted to go home.

Jostled and bruised, she made her way to the back of the lobby and pressed against the wall. A scream bubbled up her throat, but she clenched her teeth to hold it in.

Don't make trouble. They'll kill you if you make trouble.

"Ayanna?" Mal appeared beside her. "About your dad, I'm really sorry that they– Are you okay?"

Ayanna gulped. "I can't. Can't take the pills. Not today. Not today."

Mal's face fell. She put her hand on Ayanna's shoulder.

As if summoned, a man appeared. "What's up, Mal?"

Mal said, "Ayanna, this is Tony. He was part of my old pack. He's been here as long as anyone. He'll take you somewhere to hide."

"What?" Tony said.

"She's just a kid," Mal said. "A terrified kid."

A pause. "All right. I'll hide her in the pool room. They always check there last."

Mal tucked a knuckle under Ayanna's chin, looking into her eyes. "Go with Tony. I'll distract the guards."

Ayanna gasped. *Don't make trouble.* "But you'll be sent to the basement."

"Been expecting to ever since we met."

Ayanna frowned. But before she could respond, Mal walked away.

"No more drugs!" Mal shouted as she pushed toward the head of the line.

The crowd picked up the chant. "No more drugs!"

They pumped their fists in the air. Some of the inmates shoved each other. A few people fell. The white-coats looked alarmed. Guards strode forward, but they couldn't get far in the melee.

Ayanna gawked as Mal leaped onto a check-in table and kicked the little paper cups. Pills flew into the crowd.

"No more drugs!" she shouted.

Inmates shouted with her. She waved as if conducting an orchestra.

Tony latched onto Ayanna's arm. He towed

her toward the hallway. The pool attendant and two guards rushed out. Their attention was on the impending riot. Tony and Ayanna ran past unchecked.

The crowd continued yelling. "No more drugs! No more drugs!"

Ayanna covered her ears, panic welling inside her.

🐾🐾🐾

I was hit with such a wave of anxiety and fear, I thought I would explode. I shoved my hands in my hair and growled. "Argh!"

My friends turned to stare at me. Brittany reached for my arm, but I shrugged her away.

"This is taking too long." I kept my voice low, but inside I raged. They were holding me back. If I'd been running with the wolves, I would have found the institute by now. Wolves didn't stop because the sun was going down. They didn't stop because they were tired.

Brittany said, "Did something happen to Ayanna?"

"Yes," I hissed through clenched teeth. But what had happened to Ayanna? I'd told her I'd be there tonight. I'd promised. What was I going to do? "Where is this place, anyway? We're so close I can practically smell it. What is it? Freaking invisible?"

"Cody, calm down." Brittany held out her hands.

At the same time, the wolves whined and danced—and I realized my fangs were showing. My beast was coming out.

I closed my eyes, sagging as the tension left me. "I'm sorry. It's just—"

"It's all right." She embraced me. "We're frustrated, too."

"This map is useless," William said. "We're too far off the hiking trails."

"At least we can follow the road," Brittany said.

"The road is part of the problem," he told her, "the way it snakes around."

"Better than rock climbing."

"I think we all need a hot breakfast," Eileen said. "Let's just take a break and—"

"You don't get it," I shouted. "We're running out of time."

"Stop yelling!" William's eyes flashed. "Truck."

I blinked. He was right. My agitation kept me from hearing it. I sent a warning through my *link* with the wolves. They were so numerous now I couldn't hope to control them individually. I just told them to hide and hoped they complied. Then I hunkered down with my friends in the bushes.

The truck lumbered by. Another transport. There were three people inside—two guards and a werewolf. Then the truck was gone.

Brittany whispered, "That's the second one today."

"I tell you, we're close," I murmured back.

"Let's keep going," William said.

Eileen glanced around. "But, breakfast."

He helped her up. "We'll stop in a little while."

But we didn't stop. We nibbled cheese and cold venison as we followed the winding road through the mountains. Trees became scarce, and the only cover was jagged boulders jutting up on either side. The day warmed to about fifty degrees. Both Brittany and Eileen took off their parkas and stowed them in their packs.

I sensed a warning from the wolves an instant before I heard the truck behind us. "Get off the road!" I cried and herded everyone into the rocks.

The truck lurched by, gears grinding as it disappeared around the bend. But then the sound of the straining engine leveled, idling as if the truck had stopped.

I caught William's eye. Keeping low, we skittered through the rocks until we reached a plateau. There was a field filled with hip-high grass and brown flowers. A distance away was a twenty-foot chain-link fence topped with barbed wire. A sign said *Lindgren Institut*.

I smiled grimly. We found it.

The truck had stopped at a red-and-white-striped gate across the road. There was a guardhouse. Two uniformed guards stepped out. Two others stayed inside—my senses were so amped, I could see their spectral images right through the wall.

The two guards approached the truck. One prowled around as if checking it out. The other spoke to the driver. They were at least fifty feet away, but I heard them as if they stood before me. They used a language I didn't know, yet somehow, I knew they spoke in Sami. I concentrated, and suddenly I was in the driver's head. My internal Babel fish translated his words into English.

"Good afternoon," he said.

"How many are you carrying?" the guard droned in a bored manner.

The driver passed a clipboard through the window. "One. What's going on? Why has the guard been doubled?"

"A truck hit a tree, and an alpha escaped."

"I'm sure it's long gone."

"I think so, too, but I still have to see your cargo."

The driver's exasperation rippled through me. It had been a long drive, and he wanted to get back to the barracks. But he slid down from the truck peaceably. "No problem."

They walked to the rear of the truck and looked inside. I saw the scene through the driver's eyes. A filthy werewolf hung there. She wore a blue jumpsuit unzipped to the waist. Blood streaked her matted hair. Her arms were shackled to a rod over her head, a gag in her mouth, eyes wide and white in the shadows. The two soldiers sitting across from her had their guns on their laps.

Anger roared through me. I clamped my jaw hard. I couldn't help her. Not yet.

From the other side of the truck, the prowling guard said, "Clear."

The first guard signed the form on the clipboard and handed it over. The driver glared as he snatched it back, and I realized my anger was affecting him. I reluctantly disconnected. I'd rather ride with him as he drove into the compound, see what he saw, but he couldn't help me if he was arrested for insolence.

I blinked to clear my vision as I came back to myself. I'd never gone so deeply into another person's mind before. I could see through his eyes, touch through his fingers. Was that what it was like to take a thrall?

The driver got back into the truck. The red-and-white arm lifted, and the truck drove through. I duckwalked through the rocks, trying to get a better view of the compound.

There were no trees beyond the fence. No rocks. Just a wide expanse of grass. The main building was about two-hundred yards away. It was mostly glass. The truck drove straight toward it, past a small parking lot in the front, and disappeared somewhere along the side. Probably the ramp to the parking garage Eileen saw when she was scrying. Three Quonset huts stood on the other side of the road. Several men loitered around them.

Beside me, William said, "The cameras are pointed inward. This won't be a surprise attack even if we go under cover of night."

I looked at the black boxes on the fence. I

hadn't intended a surprise attack. Not with over thirty wolves. Getting past the gate was more of a problem. I looked at the guardhouse. The driver said they'd doubled the guard. I'd influenced two men at once when I forced them to jump out of the truck. I doubted I could do three. I groaned. "There are four of them."

"So?" Brittany said behind me, making me jump. "There are four of us."

"No." I chopped my hand down. "You and Eileen will wait here."

Eileen huffed. "But we can—"

"Absolutely not," William said.

The three of them began to argue. Their voices became distant. The bright, sunlit rocks dimmed. Ayanna's voice called to me through the *link*.

I latched onto her energy and swept her away to our special place in the Everglades. I smelled the black water, heard the buzz of insects. I had no idea how I was able to do it. I just thought of the safest place to be, and it appeared.

Ayanna collapsed in tears against me. "They found me. I tried to hide but—"

I held her at arm's length, looking into her eyes. "Are you all right?"

"They injected me with something to keep me from shifting. I'm drugged. Locked in my room."

I hugged her. "Is everyone in their rooms?"

"They started putting us away this morning, after the... After Mal..." She sobbed. "There was a riot. They took so many of us away. They still are. Breaking into our rooms. I hear people screaming."

I pulled back and gave her a little shake. "Listen to me. The drug is not a problem. They shot me up with it, too. But our connection to the moon is stronger than they know. Paintball fights in the woods, remember? We can override it. Right?"

"R-right."

"All you need to do is strengthen your connection to the Mother."

"But the moon hasn't risen and—"

"You're forgetting Lesson One. The moon is always there. Did you find out what floor you're on?"

"Seventh. But how will you get to me? How will you work the lifts?"

"I don't know yet."

"There's a stairwell, but it's locked."

"That's fine. You got me all the information I

need. I'll take it from here."

"My door is locked, too," she squeaked through her tears.

"You let me worry about that." I kissed her forehead. "I'm on the way. Be ready."

Her image faded.

Rocks materialized where swampy water had been. Brittany, Eileen, and William sat before me, still arguing in hushed voices.

I cleared my throat to no avail, so I said, "We have a problem."

They stopped to stare at me.

Brittany chuckled. "Only one?"

"We can't wait for nightfall. They're in danger now. The guards are picking up people because of some sort of riot. My pack is on the seventh floor. But they're locked tight in their rooms. I can't use the elevators because you need a handprint and a passcode."

"Stairwell?"

"Yes, but it's also locked."

"Fire alarm." Eileen shrugged. "Usually when the fire alarm goes off, all doors unlock automatically."

I grinned. "That's brilliant."

"All right," William said. "How do we set off the fire alarm?"

"There must be a control room," Brittany said. "I can find out."

I stared at her. "How?"

"I'll ask them." She pulled a small muslin pouch out of her doctor's bag and smiled her special smile. The one that drove me crazy.

I sighed. "I'm not going to be able to keep you safe, am I?"

"I can keep myself safe. Trust me."

I don't think I ever loved her more than at that moment. Because she was right. She could take care of herself. And I needed her help. "Fine. You and Eileen find the control room and get the doors open. William, you go with them for back-up. I'll take the wolves to the barracks and make sure you aren't interrupted by reinforcements."

Eileen nodded. "Now all we need to do is get past that gate."

"You're certain this is the only way inside?" I asked.

"Other than ripping out the fence."

"About that," William said. "Let me try something."

We backed away through the rocks until we couldn't be seen from the gate. William stood. He took off his parka and shirt and dropped them on the ground. Eileen picked them up again and brushed them off.

William chanted something soft and melodic. Using his new staff, he scratched a circle around himself in the dirt. The wind picked up. He continued to chant. Grass and gravel swirled around him in a whirlwind. In moments, I could barely see him through the debris.

His voice deepened. "To me."

The wind dropped like a curtain. William stood bare-chested with his staff overhead. The runes he'd carved glowed red hot. Then the staff began to smoke and smolder. He cried out and dropped it. Eileen rushed to him and examined his scorched hand.

"That was pretty impressive," I said. "What were you doing?"

He grimaced. "I was trying to summon bears. Eileen's cousin said there were brown bears in the area. I thought if I got enough of them, they could break down the fence so we wouldn't have to storm the gate."

"It was a good idea," I said.

"A failed idea."

Eileen pulled a first-aid kit from her backpack and dabbed ointment on his hand. "Maybe there just aren't any bears nearby."

"Watch and learn, boys." Brittany took off

her sweatshirt and tied it around her waist. She wore a sleeveless, purple t-shirt underneath. She must've been too warm in the sweatshirt because the t-shirt clung in all the right places. She smirked at Eileen. "Come on, girlfriend."

Brittany and Eileen hopped down to the road and moved toward the gate. They giggled and jostled each other as if they were there on a dare. The guards had gone back into the guardhouse, but as the girls approached, three of them rushed out to greet them.

One said, *"Stanna!"*

I didn't have to get into the man's head to know he said *halt*.

Brittany and Eileen giggled again. The guards grinned. Eileen dropped William's parka to the ground. She made a show of taking off her sweatshirt and tying it around her waist. For someone who spent most of her life not wearing clothes, she certainly knew how to use them to get attention.

Brittany leaned on the striped gate. "Do you speak English?"

A blond guard said, "Ya, of course."

She motioned around her. "What is this place? Is it super-secret out here in the middle of nowhere?"

Blondie's grin fell. He took a step back.

Quickly, Eileen said, "We're lost. Can you help us?" She took the hiking map from William's parka and stepped to the gate.

Blondie grinned again. "Ya, sure."

The guards grouped together to see the map. Eileen stepped back. At the same time, Brittany chucked one of her little muslin bags. It hit Blondie in the chest and exploded in a puff of dust. She threw two more, enveloping the three men in a thick cloud.

When the dust cleared, Brittany said, "Hello, boys."

Two guards stared at her as if she was the most intoxicating woman on the planet. Which, of course, she was. But Blondie fixated on Eileen.

Brittany sashayed forward and booped a guard on the nose. "We need to go to the parking garage. Can you help us?"

The guard she'd booped said, "Mine."

The other guard shoved him.

"No, no. None of that." Brittany held out her hands. "Eileen, try yours."

Eileen smiled at Blondie. "Hi, handsome. You speak English, right?"

He sighed. "Ya."

"You're so smart. My friend and I need to go to the parking garage."

He brightened. "I can take you. In the jeep."

"Oh, would you?" she crooned. "That would be so helpful."

"Ya, ya." He stepped to a control panel and opened the gate.

As the arm went up, the other two guards slammed into each other like rams. They fell and scrabbled in the dirt. I could hear the thud of punches from a distance away.

The fourth guard burst from the guardhouse. He looked angry. He must've been in charge because his uniform had more patches than the others'. And he had a real gun in his holster.

I couldn't have that, so I leaped down to the road and hustled toward him. The man was so enraged at seeing his soldiers wrestling on the ground, he didn't even notice me.

And I rode that anger right into his brain.

He stopped short, slack-jawed and unfocused. So that was how to take a thrall. That wasn't so hard.

I approached him. "After I go, do not let anyone through this gate."

He didn't answer, but there was a subtle straightening of his spine as if he were standing at attention.

Brittany said, "All right, then. We'll go find the control room."

"Can you stow my clothes in your pack?" I asked.

"Can you keep my things, too?" William stepped around the tussling guards.

Brittany unslung her backpack. William and I stripped. He kissed Eileen, handed her his pack, touched his bear-pelt belt, and morphed into a black bear.

I caressed Brittany's cheek, my naked skin chilling in the cool air. All I wore was the amulet Brittany had made me. "Good luck. Stay safe."

"You, too." She leaned to kiss me.

Then I transformed. Even before I'd finished, the wolves bounded from the rocks. They swarmed through the gate, more than thirty of them, leaping over the two prone men.

With a final yip to Brittany, I took off running toward the barracks with my army closing around me.

TWENTY-FIVE

B rittany watched Cody and the wolves streak away through the tall grass. She wished she could go with him. The man Cody had enchanted lowered the gate and stood at attention by the control panel. The two morons she'd put a love spell on still fought each other, although their punches were coming slower now. Maybe they were getting tired.

The cute blond guard grinned at Eileen. He didn't seem to notice that Eileen stood beside a large black bear. Brittany didn't know how he could miss him—William was over six feet tall on his hind legs. She had hoped to catch Will's transformation, but she'd blinked and missed it. One moment he was a boy and the next moment a bear.

"Let's go," she said.

Eileen turned to the cute guard. "We're ready. Can you take us to the parking garage?"

"Ya," he said. "This way."

The jeep was parked behind the guard shack. Eileen sat in front with Cutie. Brittany sat in the back.

As they pulled away, Cutie said, "I think you will like this parking garage. They keep it very clean."

Eileen giggled.

He moved as if looking in the side view mirror. "There is a bear chasing us."

"It's all right," Eileen said. "That's my pet, Fluffy."

He nodded. "Fluffy. Ya."

The jeep neared a row of Quonset huts. Brittany looked for Cody but couldn't see him in the chaos. Men streamed outside, screaming and firing their guns at the attacking wolves.

But the only ammunition they had was the werewolf potion. Something in the concoction drove the wolves insane. The wolves with the most orange splotches were foaming-at-the-mouth enraged.

They went for the soldiers' guts. Blood was everywhere. Fallen soldiers tried to crawl away, dragging their innards behind them.

Brittany gasped. "It's a massacre."

Eileen's face paled. "William said they were wild, but I never thought—"

"Here we are." Cutie grinned as he pulled the jeep down a long ramp.

The bright sunlight cut off. Sounds of the battle faded. They entered a huge, poorly lit garage and joined a group of parked jeeps. Another section held parked transport trucks, and another had fork-lifts. The area was so wide, there was plenty of space between each region.

The truck that had pulled in earlier sat to one side. Soldiers ringed it. They leveled their pop guns at a woman in chains. She was bloodied as if she'd put up a fight.

One of the soldiers noticed their jeep. "What are these civilians doing here?" He walked toward them, gun in hand.

Brittany smirked as she reached for another muslin bag—then froze mid-action. The soldier carried a real gun. With bullets. She'd never be able to toss the bag before he fired.

"Get out of the jeep." He motioned with the pistol.

Brittany and Eileen traded wide-eyed looks. Cutie-boy grinned.

William-the-bear barreled down the ramp and slammed into the soldier.

Cutie pointed. "Fluffy."

Fluffy roared. The man screamed. He hit the ground, and his gun spun from his grasp. The guards at the truck turned toward the commotion. Someone shouted.

The shackled woman shrieked a war cry. She freed one hand and snapped the chain like a whip. It clipped a man in the face and sent another sprawling. She grabbed a third man and used him as a shield.

The ring of soldiers reformed. Half of them stayed with her, but a group broke away and hustled toward William-the-bear. They shot their pop guns at him. The werewolf potion had no effect. Perhaps realizing this, the lead man lowered his rifle and went at him with a knife. William blocked the blow and struck out with his claws. The man fell back with gashes on his face.

Brittany gripped her muslin bag feeling utterly helpless. And stupid. She truly hadn't expected violence. She thought she'd waltz in, toss her magic around, and waltz back out. Now there was a bloody riot outside and the beginning of one in here.

What was she going to do? She never intended to kill.

𝄂𝄂𝄂

I thought that I had been ready to kill. Just rip the soldiers apart. They deserved it. For everything they'd done to me, my pack, and my kind. But I wasn't a killer. Even my inner human didn't want to kill another human being. So, I went into the fracas with the intent to disable only.

I had it under control. At first. But I hadn't counted on what the soldiers' werewolf juice would do to the true-wolves. The more hits they took, the angrier they got. As if they sought retribution for generations of abuse. The rage that roared through the *link* was almost overwhelming. It fed upon itself. And grew. Until I realized I wasn't in control of them at all.

I skirted the skirmish, keeping out of the way. Two wolves followed at a respectful distance. The pack leader and his mate. They had shadowed me since the battle began. As if they'd appointed themselves my bodyguards. I didn't have time to argue about it.

The point of being there was to prevent reinforcements from entering the institute. To that end, I was looking for something the true-wolves wouldn't recognize or understand. Head down, I led my two bodyguards around the corner of a Quonset hut.

Pop. Something ricocheted off my force field. *Pop, pop, pop.* A soldier was on his knees, pointing my way with a short-nosed rifle. He fired at me again. I flinched. Brittany's amulet had protected me well so far, but if even one of those pellets got through, I would be impaired, or worse, immobilized.

Before I could respond, a wolf loomed out of the shadows behind the man and latched onto the back of his neck with his jaws. The man screamed, firing wildly. Paintballs sailed through the air. With a mighty shake, the wolf snapped the man's neck.

I didn't wait to see what happened next. I bounded down a gravel walkway, my bodyguards at my heels, and at last came to a cinderblock building. Its roof was adorned with antennae and a three-foot dish. Just what I'd been searching for.

As I approached the communications building, I scanned for life with my new-found heat sensing ability. The walls were too thick for me to get a clear reading. The door was metal and sturdy—no getting in there. I circled around to the back and found a single window. It was open a crack and, judging by the smell, led to a bathroom. I whined, looking up. It was too narrow for me to get through.

But not too narrow for my she-wolf bodyguard. I looked at her, and she padded over obediently.

My human side blanched. What was I thinking? How could I even consider it? What sort of monster was I?

Yet, I had to get into the building. If I didn't destroy that radio, someone would call for help. I could order the she-wolf inside, but she wouldn't know what to look for. I had to see through her eyes.

Shoving down my misgivings, I searched for the mental doorway into her mind. She was easy to read—almost as simple as the squirrel had been. Loyal. Brave. Eager to comply.

Taking control of her body, I backed her up a few paces and took a running leap at the window. It smashed inward, littering the floor with bright shards. We were indeed in the bathroom. We picked our way over the broken glass and stepped into the main room.

Pfft. A burst of bullets from an automatic

weapon flew overhead. Either the soldier was so startled by our appearance that his aim was off or he expected someone taller.

A low growl issued from our throat. The she-wolf wanted to take out his legs—standard procedure to disable prey. I overrode her. With a bark and a snarl, I sprang at the human and closed our jaws over his forearm.

The pistol in his hand went off again, drawing a line of pockmarks across the room. Papers on a bulletin board twitched. Books on a shelf toppled and fell. Sparks flew as a line of gunfire zipped over the radio we had come to destroy.

But many more bullets ricocheted off the walls and came back at us. In moments, the room filled with whizzing missiles. One grazed our shoulder, etching a fiery furrow. Another hit the soldier in the head.

The gun silenced abruptly. His knees buckled. We rode him to the ground and released his arm only when we were certain he would rise no more.

Overhead, the barrage of bullets stilled. Smoke and bits of paper drifted through the air. The she-wolf licked her wounded shoulder, and the taste of her blood in our mouth was both a comfort and an anathema.

I forced her onto her feet. Several boxes pitted with bullet holes lined the edge of a table. One box had a small black screen with green markings. My inner human scoffed at that. Apparently, the technology wasn't what he'd expected.

We jumped onto the table and knocked everything to the floor. Last to go was a mug of coffee. An acrid smell rose as the liquid struck the hot components. The backside of the radio was a mass of multi-colored cables and wires. Just what I wanted to see.

We bit and clawed at the cables. Some wires pulled free. Others snapped off, leaving twisted tails still attached. When my human was satisfied that we had done enough damage, we picked up a tangled ball of shredded wire, carried it to the bathroom, and dropped it out the broken window.

We took a moment to look outdoors. It was an eerie sensation to see my own body. I simply stood there. As still as death. No sign of awareness in my eyes. The pack leader, however, paced and fretted, urging us to hurry.

It was time to go. We leaped at the window. Too high. We leaped again but could barely get our forelegs on the sill. When we were outside,

we were able to get a running start. But inside...
We looked around. There wasn't enough room.

Something akin to panic rose in our throat.
We couldn't get out. The she-wolf barked and
whined for her mate.

And a little voice inside my head said *she's
served her purpose. Leave her there*.

No! I jerked, feeling her muscles tense. I had
gotten her into this mess. I wouldn't abandon
her.

The door to the bathroom was across from
the window. It would make a fine ramp, but the
she-wolf's meager weight wasn't enough to
break the hinges. The toilet and the sink were on
opposite walls. The sink was too high to make
an effective springboard. We approached the
toilet. Many toilets had lids. This one did not. I
shrugged, drawing a flare of pain from our
wounded shoulder.

We returned to the radio room and nosed
through the debris, looking for items light
enough to carry but large enough to fill the toilet
bowl. We settled on two books and a keyboard.
After we stacked them into the bowl, we backed
out of the room. Head down, we sped through
the bathroom doorway, zigged onto the toilet,
zagged onto the windowsill, and bounded

through the broken window.

We were free.

The pack leader yipped and pressed against his mate, and she responded in kind. I didn't need to be a party to that. My consciousness snapped back into my body with a dizzying sensation. I staggered then shook myself from snout to tail. The she-wolf rubbed against me, acknowledging the weird intimacy of what we'd just experienced. But I was preoccupied with the safety of my own mate.

We didn't have time to stand there. I barked. *We have to go.*

🐺🐺🐺

Brittany slid out the back of the jeep. "We have to go."

"Right." Eileen gave herself a little shake. She turned toward Cutie-boy. "Can you take us to the elevators?"

"Oh, ya." He grinned as if oblivious to the bedlam around them.

Soldiers shouted to one another as they circled the rampaging bear. Several men lay groaning on the floor. William-the-bear roared up on his hind legs. Soldiers shot him with their pop guns, saturating his furry belly with werewolf potion. Of course, it had no effect.

Across the garage, the chained woman continued to fight. Using a paint-spattered man as a shield, she swung her chains like whips and kicked anyone who got close. But her movements had slowed. Brittany winced as the woman finally fell under a barrage of paintballs.

Brittany and Eileen followed Cutie-boy past the shadowed hulks of parked vehicles. The garage was huge. At last, they reached a bank of elevators. There were keypads and places for handprints.

"Here we are." Cutie motioned as if presenting a work of art.

"Can you open it?" Eileen asked.

His smile fell. "Only attendants are authorized to work the lifts."

"Attendants? Who are they?"

"Smart people. They wear white coats."

Brittany glanced around as if an attendant would magically appear.

Eileen whispered, "What are we going to do?"

Just then, the elevator dinged and opened. Brittany threw her muslin bag. She hit a short man square in the face, knocking his glasses askew. He wore a white lab coat.

A puff of dust enveloped him. He coughed and sneezed.

The door closed.

"No, no, no." Brittany stepped forward and slapped the door.

It opened again.

The little man blinked. His glasses were speckled with white. He looked at her, and his face lit like the sun through clouds.

"*Meine Liebe*," he breathed.

Brittany grabbed Eileen's arm, and they piled into the elevator, pushing the man deeper into the car. He sputtered, looking alarmed. Cutie-boy followed Eileen like a happy puppy. The door closed. Elevator music played. Eileen giggled. She sounded slightly hysterical.

Brittany cocked her brow at the attendant. "Do you speak English?"

"I speak many languages." He lowered his voice. "But I prefer the language of love."

"That's sweet. Do you know where the control room is?"

"Of course, my dear. It's on the ninth floor."

"I've always wanted to see it. Will you take me there?"

He sagged and smiled dreamily. "But, of

course." He looked at the ceiling. "*Nionde vaningen.*" The elevator rose obediently. He kissed Brittany's hand. "You, my dear, are the most beautiful girl in the world."

"No!" Cutie shouted. "I have the most beautiful girl."

The two gentlemen squared their shoulders and faced off, breathing hard. Cutie was head-and-shoulders taller than the much older attendant. Brittany and Eileen looked at each other in alarm.

Brittany whispered, "Maybe I tweaked the formula a little too much."

The door opened. Brittany blew out a breath, half in relief, half in exasperation. She took the man's arm and tugged him out of the elevator. They entered a small lobby with paintings on the walls. Three corridors led away—one to either side and one straight ahead.

He escorted her down the hallway straight ahead. "This way, my dear."

Brittany smiled. "You are so smart. I bet you are the smartest person here."

He patted her hand on his arm. "Well, the work I do *is* important."

Behind them, Eileen said, "What is it you do exactly?"

"I assess. When a lycanthrope arrives, I decide whether they should go into general population or directly to the basement." His expression dropped. "In fact, I was on my way to an assessment when I bumped into you. I should be there now."

"But that isn't a problem, right?" Brittany said. "They'll wait for someone as important as you."

"Yes. Yes, of course."

They passed several closed doors, all with keypads and handprint scanners. Windows faced into the corridor. The rooms behind them held desks and cabinets—but only occasional office workers.

"Where is everybody?" she asked.

"It's four o'clock. Dinnertime. They'll all be at the restaurant." With a flourish, he motioned at the last office. "The control room, my dear."

Brittany stepped closer. Through the window, she saw two men in uniform sitting before a bank of monitors. "I'd love to go inside. Can you open the door?"

"But, of course."

He keyed in the keycode. As he pressed his hand on the scanner, Brittany pulled out another muslin bag.

The door clicked open. The two guards

turned to look at her. She threw the bag of herbs like a hand grenade. It hit the control panel and exploded. She pulled the door closed, careful not to let it latch, and looked at her companions. The white-smocked man bounced on his heels like he just saved the world. Eileen looked apprehensive. Cutie stared at Eileen like she was the only person there.

After counting to twenty, Brittany opened the door. The two guards were in a heated embrace, kissing passionately.

"Oops," she said. "I meant to use the sleeping powder."

Eileen brushed past. "Forget them. Help me find the fire alarm."

Brittany entered the room. Their two gentlemen friends pushed in behind her. She gazed at the many monitors. They cycled through different cameras. Some showed empty corridors. The monitors for the parking garage showed unconscious men. No William. But the outdoor cameras held scenes from a horror movie. The wolves attacked as if taking vengeance for every slight afforded them.

She nudged the kissing men out of her way and studied the control panel. It was covered with knobs and idiot lights, all labeled in a language she didn't know.

"I can't read any of this," Brittany said.

Eileen grinned. "Fortunately, the fire alarm is marked in Swedish, German, and English."

She pulled a lever. A claxon sounded, and red lights flashed outside in the corridor.

🐾🐾🐾

Ayanna looked up as the fire alarm went off. Her door unlocked. In an instant, she rushed out of her room, crossed to the stairwell, and yanked open the heavy door. She was down two flights before she heard inmates thundering on the stairs above.

She hurried down two more flights, but as she did, another stairwell door opened. People in white coats burst out. They chatted excitedly in Swedish. Apparently, they were coming from dinner—they smelled of fish and white wine.

Ayanna pushed into their midst. No one seemed to notice. The fire alarm blared. Red light strobed the air. She moved with the crowd down three more floors. They bottlenecked outside another door. Probably the main floor lobby.

She eased past them and ran down another

flight. When she reached the next door, she opened it a crack and peered out. Car park level. Where was the bloody basement? She closed the door and continued on.

Below her, there came a murmur of voices. People moved up the stairs. She looked back the way she came. Nowhere to hide.

🐕🐕🐕

As I slid through the shadows between the Quonset huts, I heard the fire alarm. My mate had done it. She was safe. I paused a second to thank the Mother for watching over her.

It was a second too long. Two men came around the side of a hut, rifles ready. They fired. I flinched. But their little paintballs were no match for Brittany's amulet. The balls hit my force-field and ricocheted with a clang into the side of the metal building.

I leaped at the largest man and latched onto his arm with my teeth. I'd hoped to dislodge the rifle but only succeeded in shredding his hand. He hissed with pain and butt-ended me.

The other man ran, which was a mistake. It drew the attention of the pack leader and his mate. My unofficial guards. They surrounded

300

the man, moving in a well-practiced dance. She distracted the prey while he went for the hamstring. When the man fell, she ripped out his throat. He tore at his gut. It was over in seconds.

The man beside me gave an unintelligible battle-cry and lifted the rifle in his undamaged hand. He got off two shots before I wrenched the gun away. Unfortunately for him, the only thing his ammunition did was whip the true-wolves into a frenzy. Their eyes turned red. Bloody froth dripped from their jaws. In a flash of fur and fangs, they were on him. His screams joined the cacophony rising around us.

It was time to go. But as I turned toward the main building, something like a bee whizzed past me. A microsecond later, I heard a gunshot. A man stood on the hood of a jeep firing a pistol similar to the one the soldier in the radio room had used. The pack scattered from this new threat. One wolf yelped and fell.

A growl escaped me. I veered and ran full speed toward the jeep. The man's eyes widened. He fired in short, controlled bursts. I was twice as big as the true-wolves. A fine target. A bullet grazed my already-notched ear. Evidently, the amulet couldn't protect me against something with such velocity.

The bullets stopped. He was out of ammunition. He ejected the spent cartridge from his gun and fumbled at his belt. I sped up. My plan was to hit him before he could shoot at me again. But he was quicker than I expected. He reloaded and fired.

At the same instant, a wolf leaped between us. It was the she-wolf who had bonded with Eileen. The bullets impacted her side with wet thwacks. She was dead before she hit the ground.

With a snarl, I leaped, striking the man with my full weight. He flew backward as if shot by a cannon. I was so angry, I wanted to rip out his guts myself. But five wolves met him as he fell. They tore him to pieces.

The fire alarm still blared as I ran for the main building. It had a revolving door. Good for energy efficiency. Bad for me. No way I was getting in there. Inside the lobby, people lined the windows, gaping at the bloodbath as if in awe. I threw myself at the glass, and they skittered back.

My guards hit the window with a synchronized running leap. A crack streaked upward in a silvery line. I stared—and hot fury coursed through me.

No! I did not come all this way to be kept out by a pane of glass.

Rage swelled inside me, and my bulk swelled as well. My beast was coming out. I rose to my hind legs, more massive than any man.

The people inside screamed and scattered. I bellowed, sounding louder than King Kong. I raised my fists to the huge, plate-glass window and struck. Once. Twice. Three times. The glass shattered into small cubes, cascading inward.

Before the last shard fell, my guards were inside. They attacked. The people stampeded up a grand staircase. Some were trampled. Others were knocked over the railing to the crowd below.

Most of them wore white lab coats. They worked here. Torturing and killing werewolves. They were as guilty as the soldiers outside.

I roared and stepped through the window, running my gaze over them as if deciding which one I would eat first. They screamed and backed against the far wall. And my guards picked them off one by one.

I had to get to the seventh floor. Where was the staircase Ayanna told me about? My gaze fell on a door labeled *Trapphus*. The people nearest it scrambled to get inside. I swatted them away, took hold of the door, and ripped it off.

The stairwell was jam-packed with people. Awe and alarm crossed their faces as they saw me. They smelled odd. Not quite human. Not quite wolf. Were these the werewolves I'd vowed to save?

They stared at me as if petrified. I didn't blame them. I would have introduced myself, but my fangs got in the way.

"Go," I said in a gravelly voice. It only seemed to make them more frightened.

As I stood there stupidly trying to figure out what to do, someone shot me in the back. With a bullet.

I turned to see a pretty blonde woman in a powder blue suit standing in a shooter's stance and looking down the barrel of a smoking gun. Then my vision dimmed, and I was falling.

🐺🐺🐺

David Forester heard a distant gunshot. He held fast to his wife's hand as he tried to push forward down the stairwell with the other werewolves. People jostled him from behind. The stairwell was packed. Going nowhere.

An attendant shouted, "What's the hold-up here? Let me through." He elbowed his way through the crowd.

An inmate took offense at being forced aside. He punched the attendant in the stomach and threw him over the railing onto the crowd standing below. A free-for-all ensued and quickly escalated into bedlam. Blue-suited werewolves attacked the white-smocked attendants with alarming ferocity.

What would happen when they realized he and Marie weren't werewolves? David looked for a guard. The only one he saw was a floor above.

He leaned close to Marie's ear. "Let's get out of here." He pulled her down a few steps. Amid the shoving and shouting, David escaped through an unmarked door.

They stepped out onto the second floor near the meeting rooms. David sagged against the door and blew out a breath. But before he could get his bearings, a mob of screaming people ran toward them up the curved staircase. What was going on?

"Go back down!" he shouted. "Get out of the building!"

They bowled him over and streamed into a

meeting room. As they slammed the door, he heard a howl. His heart froze. Had one of the werewolves transformed?

Marie helped him to his feet. Her usual stoic face was pale and panic-stricken. "We have to hide," she whispered.

Somehow, her fear made him feel braver.

"No," he said. "We're going right out the front door. We'll find our rental car and get the hell out of this lunatic asylum."

"Without Cody?"

"Cody isn't here. We've looked."

"Right." She nodded. "But what about my brother?"

What? All of a sudden, she cared about her brother? David wanted to shake her. Instead, he hugged her thin shoulders. "We can't help Bob now. We don't even know where he is."

Bob Nowak peered out his bedroom door. The hallway appeared deserted. Red lights flashed. He stepped outside. He felt groggy and weak as if he hadn't eaten for days. Maybe he hadn't.

Where was Rita?

He looked both ways seeing no one. Red

light strobed over the gray walls. He'd dreamed his sister was here. And David. Stupid dream.

Where was Rita?

"Hey." A man in a blue jumpsuit jogged toward him. "You speak English?"

"Yeah."

"You know what's going on?"

"Fire drill?"

The man looked at the flashing lights. "Think they'd turn it off then."

Bob motioned at a medical cart abandoned in the hallway. It had vials and syringes. "What's all this?"

"What, are you new here? That's the crap they give us to keep us from transforming. They hadn't gotten to my room yet."

"Mine, neither."

"Hello?" A man came from the opposite direction. He had a long, blond beard. "Boy, am I glad to see you guys. The elevators won't work."

The other man nodded. "They turn them off during a fire."

"Why don't you use the stairs?" Bob asked.

"What stairs?"

Bob crossed to a door. It had a small sign that said *trapphus*. He didn't know if that meant

307

stairs, but what else could it be? He reached for the knob.

"Don't open that," the bearded man cried. "There's a fire."

"Doesn't feel hot." Bob opened the door. It was a stairwell. Lights flashed and a claxon wailed. He stepped onto the landing. "I don't smell smoke."

However, beneath the wailing alarm, he heard a gunshot. People shouted.

The first man joined him. "Sounds like a friggin' riot."

The bearded man hung back in the doorway.

Bob leaned over the railing, trying to see the floors below. Suddenly, his stomach cramped. His legs went weak. He clung to the rail for balance.

In a raspy voice, the first man said, "The moon is rising." He tore at the collar of his jumpsuit.

"Oh no!" the bearded man cried. He stepped back into the hallway and slammed the door.

Bob tore the jumpsuit from his arms and torso. He dropped to his knees. His joints realigned with painful pops. His muzzle grew. And as his fangs sharpened, so did his senses. He heard angry shouts. Punches being thrown.

He smelled dust and blood and fear.

Beside him, a black wolf struggled to gnaw off his jumpsuit.

Bob snorted. He had to find Rita. And Cody. He had to rejoin his pack. It sounded like downward was the way to go.

🐾🐾🐾

Ayanna was forced up the stairs by the tide of fleeing people. Some wore white lab coats. Others were in green surgical scrubs. Frustration turned to panic. She flattened against the wall, trying to hold her ground.

"You're going the wrong way," someone told her.

From the floors above, she heard shouts. A gunshot. The people around her paused, looking upward.

"Let me through!" A guard came into view. His face was scarred, and his nose was crooked as if it had been broken one too many times.

It was Flat-nose. The man who took her father.

Ayanna gripped the handrail so hard, it crumpled. Her vision turned red. Rage infused her, coursing through her body like liquid fire.

The conflagration incinerated the drug that held back her beast. Ayanna began to grow.

The woman beside her screamed. Flat-nose looked up. His eyes bulged. He raised a rifle. Ayanna hoisted the screaming woman and held her like a shield. Paintballs splatted against the woman's back.

Shrieks rose as if contagious. People scrambled around her up the stairs. Ayanna continued to swell, doubling, tripling her body mass. The seams of her jumpsuit split. Her fangs grew so large she couldn't close her mouth. Her thick claws dug into the woman's neck. Flat-nose dodged the panicked crowd, leaning for a better shot. He fired again.

Ayanna threw the woman on top of him then roared loud enough to intimidate a Tyrannosaurus rex. She lumbered down the steps, swatting people out of her way. Flat-nose struggled to get out from beneath the dazed woman. He fired his pop gun. Three balls struck Ayanna's chest.

Ayanna laughed. She wrenched the gun from his grasp and slammed it against the wall. Paintballs scattered and bounced down the stairs. With one huge hand, she picked him up and threw him. He struck the landing and bounced up, swinging. She caught his fist and squeezed. He screamed. She twisted his arm, intending to propel him down the next flight, but the arm separated from his body.

Puny human.

She used the arm to beat him around the head. Then she backhanded him. He flew into the air and landed in a tangle of limbs halfway down the stairs. Feebly, he crawled away. She grabbed him by the ankle and swung him. He hit the guardrail so hard, it bent.

Still grasping his leg, she dragged him down the remaining stairs then dropped him. The stairwell door was closed. Her clumsy hands couldn't work the doorknob. She howled and slammed her shoulder into the door again and again until it buckled. Then she grasped the sides and ripped it off its hinges.

She stepped into the basement. Windows faced the hallway, showcasing brightly lit rooms—as if the torture of werewolves were a spectator sport. In each room, a person was strapped to a table. One was sliced open, his organs glistening. Another had electrodes all over his body. Another was covered in black fur—

Oh no. Ayanna stared.

Without warning, the beast left her. She

shrank. Small and skinny. Helpless. The body on the table writhed. She couldn't go in there. But how could she not?

With trembling fingers, she opened the door—then gagged on the chemical stench. She tiptoed toward the table.

"Daddy?"

But it wasn't her father. It was Mal.

The woman struggled against her restraints. She looked at Ayanna. Blood filled the whites of her eyes. She whispered, "Kill me."

"No!" Ayanna yelped. "I'm getting you out of here." She pulled a thick needle out of Mal's neck. Greenish liquid drizzled out.

Mal whimpered. "Ayanna. I'm sorry. I'm so sorry. When I saw you in the rec room… When I saw what I had done…"

"Save your strength." Ayanna unbuckled the strap around Mal's arm.

Mal grabbed her. "I was the one who told them about your pack."

Ayanna recoiled. "What?"

"I'm so sorry. They kept at me and at me. And I thought he could protect you."

Rage turned into a fire in Ayanna's veins. The beast swelled within. With one swipe of her massive hand, she tore off Mal's jaw.

I trusted you. I thought you were my friend.

She slashed Mal's face again and again until it was unrecognizable. Then she picked up the table and threw it into the window. Glass shattered and fell. The table teetered on the sill, Mal's body hanging lifelessly over the side, bloody eyes staring from her mangled face.

Ayanna climbed past her into the hallway. She clenched her clawed fingers and bellowed. Even to her own ears, she sounded terrifying.

She stomped past the operating rooms then rounded a corner and peered into a pair of laboratories. No one there. Where was her father? She couldn't bear it if he was dead.

Voices seeped from an unmarked room. "Let us out!"

Ayanna battered the door with her fists. *Boom. Boom.* She wrenched it open.

It was a detention center. There were two large cells with a wide aisle down the middle. About a dozen inmates were in each jail cell. Her father was not among them. She wanted to weep. Wanted to rip the cages apart. Where was he?

The inmates cringed against the walls as she approached. Ayanna grabbed the bars of the nearest cell and twisted off the door. She stared at the occupants. For a moment, no one moved. Then a woman skittered past and ran. And another. Finally, the rest of them streamed past. When they were gone, Ayanna opened the other cell. These werewolves were bolder. They kept a respectful distance but did not cower.

"Thanks." One man nodded to her before sprinting for freedom.

Ayanna went out into the hall. No one in sight. The only sound was the blare of the fire alarm. The flashing red lights made her head hurt.

She tore open the next door and entered a room. It stank like a kennel. There was a large desk with a computer monitor and eight four-foot cages stacked in pairs. Each cage held a person. But they looked only vaguely human. One occupant was hairless and had fangs and claws. Another had overly long limbs and a tail.

Then she saw her father.

Ayanna gasped. Her hold on her beast slipped, and she shrank, down, down, until she was just a girl once more. She dropped to her knees beside the cage.

"Daddy? Daddy, it's me. Your little flower. I've come to save you."

The thing inside paced back and forth. It

smelled like her father. The *link* told her it was her father.

But it looked more like a panther than a wolf. Its eyes were sickly green, reminding Ayanna of the liquid being pumped into Mal's neck.

She was too late.

"Nooo." She pressed her cheek against the bars and sobbed.

She was too late. Her father was gone. And she hadn't said goodbye. Hadn't told him that she loved him. All those times she poked fun at his clothing. Those times she told him he embarrassed her. But she still loved him. He knew that. Didn't he?

She had to get him to safety. Standing, she lifted the latch of the cage. Her father slinked out. He growled as he prowled the room. He didn't even know her.

"Oh, Daddy." She covered her face, weeping. How could she bear it? How could he? This was worse than death.

She released the other creatures. Some moved on four feet, some hopped on two. One wouldn't come out of the cage at all. She coaxed them out of the room then ushered them through the basement, past the broken doors, the broken glass, Mal hanging precariously from the

315

table. She reached the stairwell, stepped over Flat-nose's body, and led them up the steps. She stopped at the car park level.

The prisoners she'd released had continued up the stairs—she could hear their footsteps above her. She should call them and tell them about the garage. But, no—her responsibility was to her father.

She would set him free. Then she would find her mum. And she would never tell her what she saw.

But when she wrenched open the door, her mouth dropped. A war raged outside. Soldiers retreated down a ramp, firing their weapons at several wolves. The dead and dying lay on the floor.

Was this Cody's rescue? Was Cody here?

Ayanna rushed forward, looking for him. A miasma of blood and chemicals hung on the cold air.

The creatures followed—and went berserk. They charged the nearest soldier, hitting him from behind, tearing him limb from limb. Ayanna froze. For the first time, she realized she was in danger. She headed back toward the stairwell.

But before she could reach it, the blue-suited prisoners she'd released streamed through the door followed by a mob of white-coats and guards. The creatures turned at the commotion—and leaped at their new targets. People scattered, and the creatures chased them down. The guards fired, but their pop guns had no effect.

Ayanna froze, caught between two battles. Then she saw a black bear.

What?

It was William. How was he here?

She ran, waving one arm. "William!"

He looked over at her. In an instant, he morphed into a boy.

She slammed into him, hugging him hard. He was really there. But how? A million questions filled her mind.

She asked the only one that mattered. "Where's Cody?"

ᕼᕼᕼ

I awoke on the floor in all my naked glory. I'd been shot before, but that was with buckshot. So, I was surprised at how much damage a little bullet could do as it rattled around inside my ribs. Fortunately, the amulet kept my connection to Mother Moon strong—she was able to heal my wounds before I bled-out.

I groaned as I sat up. My bodyguard wolves whined and rubbed against me. They were covered in blood—but none of it seemed to be theirs.

Every guard with a weapon sprawled in a bloody puddle. Quite a few people in lab coats had been killed, too. The rest huddled against the wall.

I got shakily to my feet and stepped to the stairwell. The werewolves I'd hoped to save were gone. Either they had run outdoors or they had retreated up the stairs. In any case, the path was clear to the seventh floor where Ayanna and my pack waited for me.

I was about to transform into a wolf when I felt a twinge of pain. A purple knot appeared on my chest. I walked to a desk that was tucked beneath the grand stairway. It was the only piece of furniture still standing. I found a letter opener and stabbed the point into the growing lump. The bullet popped out. The wound closed.

I smiled. Thank goodness for instant heal.

Again, I prepared to transform—but a scent caught my attention. Three scents.

Anger flashed through me like lightning. What were *they* doing here? And with *her*.

My rage was so strong and sudden that instead of a wolf I became the beast. I flipped the heavy desk, sending the pencils and paper clips scattering, and threw the chair for distance. With my two bodyguards at my side, I stomped up the stairs.

My parents stood halfway down a long hallway. They clung to each other. Faces ashen. Terrified of me. Of me! The way they'd been terrified when they sent me away from home. I wanted to howl with fury, wanted to bash the walls with my fists.

But something was wrong. They wore the same blue jumpsuits as the inmates. And my mother's hair was a scraggly mess.

Saarsgard and two soldiers walked up behind them. Saarsgard smiled. Her guards fired their pop guns. Paintballs whizzed toward me as if in slow motion. But the amulet wouldn't let them through. They bounced off my force field and hit my parents instead.

Dad flinched and brushed at the orange splotch.

But my mother fell, jerking and foaming at the mouth.

"Oh, my God." Dad knelt over her. "Marie, what's wrong?"

Saarsgard laughed and clapped her hands. "How delicious."

The wolves lowered their heads and advanced, leaving bloody footprints on the white floor. Saarsgard's goons peppered them with paintballs.

The wolves went wild. They snarled and frothed and snapped the balls out of the air. The men yelped and sped down the hallway. The wolves took up the chase.

Saarsgard's eyes went round. "Get back here!" She looked at me, her perfectly drawn mouth in a little red *oh*.

My mother convulsed on the floor. Why were my parents here? Why was my mother reacting to werewolf juice?

I took a step toward her. And wouldn't you know it, I shrank back into a boy. "Mom?"

"Son," Dad cried.

"Cody Forester." Saarsgard gasped. Then her expression turned to ice once more. She pulled out a gun, strode past my parents, and stopped before me. The gun was small, but she couldn't miss at that distance. "You could have been a part of mankind's greatest advancement. But you had to be difficult. Very well. I will rid myself of you once and for all."

Behind Saarsgard, a huge wolf-beast reared up. It was enormous. Dark fur. Yellow eyes. It growled, "Don't touch my son."

I balked. "Mom?"

Dad yelped and skittered back until he hit the wall.

Saarsgard turned. She lifted the gun, but too late. Mom backhanded her, sending her sprawling. Then she picked her up by one foot and swung her, slamming her head into the wall repeatedly until her face was pulp.

I rushed to my dad, trying to get him up, to get him to run—but he stared as if horrorstruck. He wouldn't move.

Mom lifted Saarsgard's corpse overhead and hurled her off the balcony. Then she turned to me and roared.

Her beast was out of control.

Maybe I would've had a chance if I turned into my own beast. But I couldn't fight my mother. I leaned over Dad as if I could protect him. As if I could do anything at all.

Mom lumbered toward us.

Two wolves barreled down the hallway. They leaped onto my mother, snarling and snapping. She staggered, stumbling back—and fell over the balcony railing.

I sprang up and ran to look. Amid the debris of the floor below, Mom got to her feet. Still in beast form, she leaped out the broken window, my bodyguard wolves on her tail.

I yelled at my dad, "A werewolf? All this time, she was a freaking werewolf?"

"No," he said. Pale and stricken. "She couldn't be. We've been together for twenty years, for God's sake."

"You never saw her... her..." I shook my head. My mom was a werewolf. A super wolf. Even stronger than me. "I never heard of a super wolf so strong they could simply choose not to transform."

"When we first met, she was searching for a cure. She must've found it."

"Suppression is not a cure, Dad."

"She kept me under her spell." He gasped. "I was her thrall. No wonder I felt so oppressed."

I didn't know how to respond to that. I hunkered down next to him. "Look, Dad, I have to go. I have to get to the seventh floor and find Ayanna."

"She's not there. No one is. The whole floor was evacuated. Her mother was frantic, searching for her."

"You were with Chloe?"

"We got separated. On the stairwell. It was a madhouse."

I reached out through the *link,* but my tenuous connection to Ayanna was gone, overwhelmed by the urgent and ferocious needs of the true-wolves.

I plopped onto my butt and put my face in my hands. "Where could they be?"

🐾🐾🐾

Ayanna clung to William, staring aghast at the bedlam around her.

The car park was extensive. It reeked of dust and blood. Wolves prowled the shadows. True-wolves. Did Cody say he had wolves?

One area of the lot held jeeps. Another had transport trucks like the one she'd been in. She spotted Norma, the American attendant, and two others climbing into the cab of a truck—and for some absurd reason, Ayanna felt relieved. At least, Norma would get away. But the truck didn't leave. Apparently, there were no keys. A scrawny gray wolf landed on the hood. Norma's mouth stretched wide as if screaming.

A knot of people ran past the truck. Ayanna saw Tommy Lee, the kid from Georgia.

She waved. "Tommy Lee! Over here!"

He turned toward her voice. His face lit. And at that moment of hesitation, one of the basement creatures slammed into him from the side. He cartwheeled into the crowd and disappeared.

"Tommy Lee!" Ayanna took a hesitant step his way. She'd been so awful to him. And he'd been innocent.

William grasped her arm. He motioned with his chin.

More soldiers rushed down the ramp, bloodied and battered. More wolves followed them down. On the opposite side of the room, another group of white-coats burst from the stairwell only to be attacked by the basement creatures. Their screams echoed.

Still holding her arm, William transformed into a bear. The action seemed to slap sense into her. She should transform as well. For protection. For warmth. It was bloody cold. But mostly because it was difficult to maintain her human form during the full moon.

Her jumpsuit was in tatters, but oddly the zipper was intact. It was also stuck. As she struggled to unzip, a new group of people streamed from the stairwell door. Blue-suited werewolves. Without hesitation, they leaped onto the white-coats, pummeling and pounding, fists flailing.

What were they doing? Didn't they see the creatures? The wolves? This was no time for a common brawl. She wanted to shout at them—but her *link* twanged. Frantically, she ran her gaze over the rioting throng and made out a familiar face.

"Mum!" She waved her arms. "Mum!"

In spite of the tumult, her mother seemed to hear her. Their eyes met. The strain in her mother's face melted into relief. She headed toward Ayanna through the clashing factions, shoving combatants from her path. Rita followed in her wake.

Tears stung Ayanna's eyes. "You're safe."

Mum pulled her into a rough hug. "My flower. Where have you been? I looked everywhere."

Rita stared at the bear. "William? You're here? Then..." She turned to Ayanna. "You were telling the truth. About a rescue." She motioned at the chaos. "Cody is—" She grasped Ayanna's shoulders and gave her a little shake. "But we have to go back. Bob. I left Bob in his room. I got caught in the mob. They pushed me down the stairs and—" She gasped.

Ayanna followed her gaze. A few blue-suited stragglers exited the stairs—and among them were two transformed werewolves. One black, one gray. Her heart leaped. Was that Cody? But, no. It was Bob.

"Bob!" Rita called and ran toward the fracas.

"Wait!" Ayanna yelled.

"Stop!" her mother shouted. "It's too dangerous."

They sped after her. Right into the heart of the riot. Ayanna ducked and elbowed her way through. Just as they reached Bob-the-wolf, Daddy-the-creature leaped out at them.

Mum shrieked and pulled Ayanna back. Bob leaped protectively before them. The other werewolf attacked.

Dad lifted a paw almost in contempt. He removed the werewolf's throat with one swipe. Then he faced Bob, snarling.

Ayanna yelled, "Daddy! No!"

Her mother gasped. Terrible recognition crossed her face. "Dick?"

Dad looked at her. His eyes glowed green. His slit nostrils flared. Then he turned and disappeared into the brawl.

The monitor flashed over a riot.

Brittany gasped and leaned forward. She sat next to Eileen at the desk in the control room, staring at the many screens.

"Where was that?" she asked, searching the panel for the umpteenth time for a way to control the monitors.

As quickly as it had appeared, the riot scene shifted. The screens cycled through empty hallways.

Eileen said, "We'll have to wait until it comes around again."

Brittany drummed her fingers. The institute was huge, and they had cameras everywhere.

One of those cameras touched upon the front lobby. Furniture was broken and upended. Bodies lay in dark pools on the floor.

"My God," Eileen whispered.

The scene changed back to empty hallways. After a few minutes, it again showed the brawl.

"There." Brittany pointed. "It's Ayanna."

"And Will," Eileen cried through a tremulous smile.

The camera shifted again.

"They're rioting," Brittany said. "It looked like the parking garage."

Eileen said, "We should go."

"We promised to stay put. We're safe here."

"But they're not. They could get hurt."

Brittany paused. "We should go."

"Yes." Eileen got to her feet.

Immediately, the cute guard and the flabby attendant were at their sides. Brittany gave a tired nod as her companion helped her from her chair. His chivalry was wearing thin. The other two guards were still in each other's arms, locked in love-potion passion.

"What about them?" Eileen asked.

Brittany waved off a twang of guilt. "They'll be okay."

She stepped into the hallway. Red lights flashed. The alarm rang. She cringed at the noise, but her companion didn't seem to notice.

He took her arm. "This way, my dear."

Eileen said, "I don't think the elevators are working."

"I know." Brittany gnawed her lip.

They strolled along the empty offices.

Brittany motioned to a door. "Are these stairs? Where do they go?"

"All the way to the basement," he said, "but you don't want to go there."

Brittany turned up the charm. "I always

wanted to see your stairs. Will you show them to me, just for a minute?"

"I'm afraid it isn't safe," he whined.

"We won't go to the basement. We'll get out at the parking garage. I promise." She smiled. "After all, you were on your way to an assessment, weren't you? I'd love to see how it's done."

"Yes." He brightened. "Yes, of course."

They entered the stairwell. The alarm seemed even more obnoxious in the enclosed space. She hurried down the steps. Her overweight attendant was breathing hard after two flights. After six flights, he was sweating and pale.

To make matters worse, there were bodies everywhere. Some in lab coats. Some in jumpsuits. A few hung over the railings as if fallen from above.

Even their lovestruck companions couldn't ignore them.

"Oh, dear," the attendant muttered as he stepped around the obstacles. "Who left these here?"

Cutie-boy looked grim as he maneuvered Eileen down the stairs.

After seven floors, the attendant plopped

onto his butt. "I'm afraid I have to stop a moment and catch my breath."

"That's fine," Brittany told him. "You rest here. I'll go on ahead."

He grabbed her arm and looked up at her. "You will come back for me, won't you?"

"Sure, I will."

He smiled dreamily. "Then I shall wait here forever."

She froze. *Oh-oh. What have I done?*

Eileen pushed past. "Come on. We have to find Will."

Brittany gazed at her admirer. Leaning close, she kissed his cheek. He looked enraptured.

"Thank you," she said. Then she hurried down the stairs after Eileen and Cutie-boy.

They were stopped on the next floor. The door had been ripped from its hinges, showing a large room with dead people and broken glass. The wind whistled through the broken window. It was the main floor lobby.

Eileen murmured, "I can't believe this."

Warmth washed over Brittany. A familiar sensation. "Cody's nearby. I can sense him." She stepped forward.

Eileen pulled her back. "He won't be here. Look at this place."

She stared at the destruction then shook herself. "You're right. Let's go."

They rushed down another floor and stepped out into chaos. It was like a huge bar fight. Inmates and attendants and soldiers and guards. Fortunately, no guns were being fired. Perhaps the soldiers were outfitted with paintballs instead of bullets.

Brittany reached into her medical bag. "I can put a stop to this."

"Make sure you use the sleeping powder," Eileen said. "We don't need an orgy."

Brittany threw a pouch like a ball. It flew over the heads of the brawling mob, hit the ceiling, and drifted down in a puff of dust. Anyone beneath the powder dropped where they stood.

Eileen grinned. "It works."

"Help me," Brittany said. "You used to play softball, right?"

They threw more pouches. More people fell unconscious.

Eileen said, "We should have made extra."

"We're running out." Brittany pulled the last pouch of sleeping powder from her bag.

Eileen nudged her.

A bizarre creature stepped toward them over the fallen people. It was pale and hairless with needle-like teeth and overly long limbs. It walked on all fours.

Brittany threw the sleeping powder. The pouch hit it in the chest. The creature shook its head and bared its nightmarish teeth.

With a roar, William-the-bear leaped before them and swatted the thing with a frying-pan-sized paw. It yelped and scampered away.

"Will!" Eileen threw her arms about the bear, barely reaching halfway around his middle.

Brittany stared at the retreating creature. "What was that?"

Rita and Chloe rushed to them. Bob and Ayanna, both in wolf form, took up protective positions around them. Brittany chuckled.

How my life has changed. A year ago, I didn't know about werewolves. Now I can recognize my friends even when they are furry.

Rita hugged her, laughing in a hysterical sort of way. "You came for us. It's a miracle."

"Is everyone here?" Brittany looked around. "Where's Dick?"

"Gone," Chloe said. She appeared stricken, beyond tears.

Oh, no. Are we too late? Is Dick dead?

"Fluffy." Cutie-boy reached up to pat the bear on the head.

William backhanded him. The cute guard sailed through the air and landed hard. He moaned but didn't get up.

"Oh," Eileen said. "There goes my boyfriend."

Brittany said, "Do these vehicles run?"

"No keys," Rita said. "Where's Cody?"

"We left him in the barracks. Let's go."

They ran across the huge garage, dodging people and parked trucks. As they did, three of the true-wolves pulled in beside them. Bob snarled, hackles up.

"It's all right," Brittany told him. "These wolves are with us."

William-the-bear led the way up the ramp. It was windy and cold outside. The night sky was lit with northern lights. The barracks were lit by streetlamps. Bodies were everywhere. Nothing moved.

"Cody!" Brittany strode into the clearing, trying to contain the ball of panic rising up her throat. "Cody, where are you?"

Eileen grabbed her arm as if to hold her back.

Wolves skulked toward them, slinking from the shadows. They were covered in blood.

Cody won't let them hurt us. But where is he?

Shouts came behind them. The rioters had followed them from the parking garage and were spilling out onto the grounds.

"Run!" Eileen yelled.

They sprinted toward a Quonset hut and hid on the opposite side.

"This is insane," Brittany said. "Why are they fighting?"

"Perhaps they couldn't contain their hatred of one another any longer," Chloe murmured. Her voice was cold. Wooden.

Brittany glanced at her. Then she looked at the pack. The bloodstained wolves paced in front of them, noses down, eyes luminous.

Suddenly, their ears perked, and they bolted into the shadows. At the same instant, a helicopter roared overhead. It was Russian military—Brittany recognized the red star insignia—lending credence to Saarsgard's contention that the Lindgren Institute was internationally supported.

A spotlight flashed over them as the copter circled. The wind gusted and peppered them with pebbles. The helicopter lowered to the grassy field.

As the runners touched down, troops leaped out. They fired into the crowd. People screamed.

The soldiers continued firing, walking forward in a line.

Brittany pressed against the wall as if to melt into the metal. They were killing everyone. No witnesses. She was going to die.

🐺🐺🐺

An alert rippled through the *link*. I sensed the pack scatter. At the same instant, a spotlight glanced over the lobby windows. Was that a helicopter?

"Oh, no."

Beside me, Dad said, "Someone must have called the authorities."

"But how? I destroyed the radio."

"There are people in the conference room. They could have used their cell phones."

Oh, crap. I hadn't thought of that. I squeezed my eyes shut. Over the thwack-thwack of the helicopter blades, I heard gunfire.

"Go!" I sprang to my feet and pointed down the hallway. "Get to the conference room with the others. Stay there."

"What?" He stood beside me. "No way. I'm going with you."

I shoved my hands in my hair. No time to

argue. "All right. But grab a jacket. It's freezing out there."

I ran down the grand stairway. The casualties on the first floor made me pause. All that was left were corpses. The survivors had gone to the stairwell—they left bloody footprints like dotted red lines. Mom and the wolves were gone. Saarsgard lay in a mangled heap. I stared at her, not knowing how to feel.

"Ready." Dad snapped me out of my fugue. He was buttoning a white lab coat over his jumpsuit. Not exactly winter apparel, but it would have to do.

I opened myself to the pressure of the full moon and shifted smoothly into my wolf form. With my father behind me, I bounded out the broken window.

The helicopter had landed in the tall grass. The rotor still spun. A line of soldiers fired their weapons into a crowd at the side of the building. People were dying. Both werewolf and human.

My hackles rose. Where were my wolves? We had to stop this.

But before I could move, the gunfire shifted. Soldiers shouted.

A huge polar bear bounded out of the darkness behind the helicopter. It bowled a man over then tossed him through the air. Another bear roared up onto its hind legs—as big as a monster.

"My God!" Dad cried. "Where did those bears come from?"

From the frozen coast, I wanted to tell him. They came in answer to William's summons.

Five bears darted in and out of the darkness, attacking the humans with guns.

The blades of the helicopter picked up speed. The copter lifted from the grass. A bear clipped its whirring tail. It wobbled and struck the ground—and the copter exploded in a brilliant fireball.

The crowd of people gasped and pointed. Then inexplicably they began to brawl. Werewolves pummeled humans. Humans punched back.

I snarled. Enough of this insanity. Enough death.

I padded down the road between the barracks and the building. My father stayed at my side. He wore both the jumpsuit of the werewolves and the coat of their jailers.

I barked for attention, but the fools battled on. Frustration overwhelmed my reason. Against my better judgment, I forged a *link*. And influenced them. All of them. Against their will. As if confused, they stopped fighting mid-punch. Several people stared at me in fear.

I must've looked quite a sight—a huge silver wolf with a puny human beside him, dry grass catching fire behind. I sensed the approach of the polar bears—only four of them now, and I howled for their loss.

The unseen true-wolves picked up the howl and carried it around the compound.

Silence fell over the combatants.

William came out from behind a Quonset hut. He was naked but for his bear hide belt. With his head high, he strode to the bears. He looked ridiculous against their bulk—but somehow majestic at the same time. The bears lowered their heads as if bowing to him, then backed away and disappeared into the night.

William stood beside me. He touched his belt and morphed into a black bear. A few of the humans cried out and backed away, although they must've seen more fearsome things in their time at the institute.

Brittany and Eileen came out from behind the hut. Brittany, my mate. I wanted to run to her, but my attention was on holding the *link* to the combatants.

The true-wolves came out as well. My pack. They stood behind me, adding their feral strength to mine.

Then miraculously, Uncle Bob and Ayanna trotted out, too. They were both in their wolf forms. Rita and Chloe followed. They were human. Drugged. I sensed their wolves deep inside them trying to break free.

Chloe pointed at me, looking at the werewolves in the crowd. "He is alpha."

"Not my alpha," a man shouted back.

The *link* broke. Someone shoved someone, and someone punched back. In seconds, half the crowd was at each other's throats.

Stop, I sent, trying to re-establish the *link. Enough fighting. Enough death*.

They kept fighting.

And I got mad. Fury blazed through my veins as hot as the grassfire raging behind me. My muscles burned and swelled.

My beast was coming out. But this was not like my normal beast. This was larger. More powerful.

I. Said. "Enough!" I roared.

The humans screamed.

Dad rushed forward. "This way! Come on!" He herded them along the wall. "Go to the second-floor conference rooms."

And still, I grew. Brittany's amulet burned like ice on my chest.

"He was dead." One of the werewolves pointed with trembling fingers. "A woman shot him. I saw it."

"He is alpha," someone murmured.

I flexed my muscles and looked at my hand. It was impossibly huge. The ground impossibly far away. The amulet around my neck glowed icy blue as if absorbing the moonlight. My connection to Mother Moon was clearer than it had ever been before.

I looked at the werewolves. They were drugged. Half-alive. Not knowing what it was to be a wolf anymore.

And a voice inside me whispered *kill them. Every last one. Miserable curs*.

But I wasn't a killer. And they didn't deserve what had happened to them.

I was there on a mission. I'd vowed to set them free. And I would fulfill that promise.

Raising my head, I howled. *Mother, please hear me. Help me save them all.*

And the glow of the amulet grew tenfold. Light spread out from me in a wave, flowing over the werewolves, washing away the drugs.

A gift from Mother.

Immediately their inner wolves began to climb, clawing their way out as if from an abyss. As their wolf-selves emerged, the faces of their hosts transported. A cheer rose, a cry of many voices. They wept and hugged each other.

One by one, the werewolves transformed. Gagging and spitting as their bodies twisted into shape. At last, they stood before me as the wolves they were meant to be. The lucky ones had the presence of mind to remove their clothing first.

TWENTY-SIX

I wouldn't let anyone eat the bodies on the ground. Not even the half-cooked polar bear. Instead, I led them away from the barracks across the grassy field toward the fence. The fire from the crashed helicopter burned low, putting out a lot of smoke and stink, and I kept a good distance from it.

When we reached the fence, I was stunned by the damage. The bears hadn't bothered to rip through the chain-link. They'd simply flattened it. The fence posts were either bent forward or snapped in two. I had no problem ushering the weres and true-wolves into the wild.

I took them south over the rocky land toward the forest I'd been in before. The aurora borealis still shone in the night sky, although it was fading. The stars were bright and plentiful but wrong somehow. As if they weren't in the right places.

The tree line was well-defined. We met a few stunted trees then suddenly there was a forest. Pine scent hung in the air. With playful yips, the weres scampered and sped through the woodland. Their joy was infectious. I watched them as a parent might watch his children.

And the amazing thing was the true-wolves played among them. Whoever heard of weres and true-wolves together? The wolves remained devoted to me despite their losses—only about twenty true-wolves survived compared to fifty or so weres.

I trotted deeper into the woods, and the pack followed. I expected to lose a few of the weres but, nope, they stayed together. We came across a herd of reindeer, and I allowed them to take one down. There were so many of us, we could have taken the entire herd, but I warned them not to be greedy. We didn't want our presence known.

As the alpha, I had first dibs on the kill—but I didn't feel like eating. I wanted to be with my mate, make certain she was safe. So, I nuzzled Ayanna, putting her in charge, and returned to the institute.

The night was dark as I left the trees. The lights of the compound glared like their own aurora borealis. I crossed the tumbled boulders to the downed fence then picked my way carefully over the chain-link and barbed wire. The tall grass rattled in the breeze. The fire was out. It left a large, black scar on the ground.

The stench of blood and entrails rose from the barracks like a halo. I trotted through the bodies. So many dead. *They were humans*, I reminded myself. *Evil humans at that.* But it didn't make me feel any better.

"Cody!" Brittany rushed out the revolving door of the main building as if she'd been watching for me. She was followed by a tubby man with glasses. She skidded to a halt and knelt to hug me. "I'm so glad you're okay. Come inside where it's warmer."

She tugged me toward one of the Quonset huts. It was indeed warmer. The hut was filled with both artificial light and artificial heat. The overly dry air made me want to sneeze. There were at least twenty beds, neatly made, in two rows. No soldiers.

Brittany dropped her backpack onto a bed and rummaged inside it. She pulled out jeans and a t-shirt—clothes I recognized as belonging to my human. "Get dressed so we can talk."

I looked at the tubby man and gave a low growl. The man didn't respond—just stood with an insipid smile on his face.

"He's all right," Brittany told me. "He's my boyfriend. Aren't you, Sugar?"

The man said, "Yes, my dear."

Boyfriend? I flattened my ears—which must have looked a little menacing because his smile faltered. He took a step back.

Keeping my eyes trained on him, I transformed into a boy. He acted like he saw such displays every day.

I pulled on my pants. "I didn't realize you had a thing for older men."

"Don't make fun of him," Brittany said. "He's been a big help. In fact, I don't know what we would have done without him."

She smiled at the man, and he looked at her adoringly. I had a sudden urge to smash his face. *He was a thrall. My girlfriend was taking thralls.* I finished dressing.

Brittany lowered her voice. "Cody, I saw Saarsgard's body. Did you do that?"

Her words hit like a slap. Did she think I could beat a woman to a bloody pulp? "No," I said after a moment. "It was my mother."

"What? Your mother is here, too? But how could she... Why would she—"

"She's a werewolf. A super wolf. So strong she learned how to keep from shifting at all."

"Oh, my God." Brittany shook her head. "And she made you feel—"

"I'll never forgive her." I sat on the bed to tie my shoes. The shoelace snapped. "Argh!"

Brittany took the shoe from me before I could throw it across the room. She knotted the shoelace back together. "Where is she now?"

I thought of the two true-wolves who had chased her from the building. The pack leader and his mate. Had they killed her? I was angry, but I didn't want her dead. She was my mom.

With a concussion of sound that shook the metal walls, a helicopter roared overhead. I opened the door a crack and peered outside. The copter circled. A spotlight ran over the bodies in the yard.

My breath hitched in my throat. If they landed, I would have no back-up. How would I protect Brittany? But they didn't land. I rested my forehead against the cold door and listened to them thwap away.

"There are survivors in the conference room," I said, suddenly remembering. "They must've called for help."

She said, "It wasn't them."

"How do you know?" I turned. "Did you turn off the phones?"

"Yes, I did, as a matter of fact. You might notice that the fire alarm is off as well. But the landline isn't the problem. The cell phone coverage here is phenomenal. Eileen and I use different providers, and we both have full bars. They must have a booster tower on the roof or something. But... I'm certain that none of the survivors used their cells."

"And you know that how?"

Her cheeks turned pink. "It's really Eileen's fault. She gave me the idea. We needed some way to keep them distracted. Under control, you know. So, I whipped up a new batch of love potion. It was easy to do with the full moon and all. And I tweaked the formula just a bit. And I... started an orgy."

"You what?"

"Your father's been rounding up the stragglers and herding them to the second floor, and we dose them with it before sending them in."

"So, they're..."

"Busy. Yes."

I suppressed an urge to laugh. She looked mortified—and adorable. "Well, if they didn't call, why is there another helicopter nosing around?"

"Maybe they're checking to see why the first one isn't responding."

I nodded.

"The first one was Russian military," she said. "I know because Butt-Crack used to build models of them."

"Russian?"

"Saarsgard always said this was a global operation. If countries are paying her to take werewolves off their hands, they'll want to know why communications stopped."

"In that case, there will be more. We have to get out of here. Where's my dad?"

"This way." She pushed past me out the door and stepped into the yard.

As she did, my dad came out of the underground parking garage with three women in lab coats. They looked bedraggled and frightened but unhurt. We approached them, Tubby-man in tow.

Dad looked up and smiled as if relieved to see me. He told the women, "Brittany will take you to safety."

Brittany stepped forward. "Hi. The others are

in the conference rooms. Come on, I'll take you up." She and Tubs led them toward the revolving doors.

When they were gone, Dad asked, "Did you see your mother out there?"

"No." I left it at that. I didn't want to share my fear that the wolves had killed her.

From the back of the building, there came the sound of an approaching jeep. I tensed, not sure if I should run or fight. But Dad put a hand on my arm.

The jeep zoomed toward us. It was Eileen and the blond guard I'd seen at the gate—only now he was sporting a massive black eye. Eileen hopped out before the jeep was fully stopped.

"Cody!" she hugged me. "We actually pulled it off. I can't believe it."

Dad said, "What did you find?"

"The loading docks are in the rear of the building right where he said they would be. There were also about twenty-five workers standing around for the *fire drill.*"

"Did you hit them with the orgy powder?"

"I was going to, but I decided to ask for their help instead. Turns out there's a lot of stuff back there. The Laundry. Storage. We found

349

uniforms. Field rations. Blankets. We have the workers filling backpacks. Will is supervising."

"That's great," I said. "We'll need clothing first thing."

She smiled. "That's what I figured."

Dad said, "Does your friend know where they keep the keys to the trucks?"

"Yes, but there's a problem." She looked at the guard. "Come here, Cutie. Tell them what you told me."

The guard turned off the jeep and stepped to her side. "All our vehicles have GPS tracking and monitoring modules."

Dad frowned. "GPS?"

"Ya," he said. "Global Positioning System. They've used it since the nineties. With it, they can track the location of our vehicles within a few meters."

"It's how they found that truck you crashed so fast," Eileen told me.

Dad said, "So if we take their trucks, they'll know exactly where we are."

"Can the module be deactivated somehow?" I asked. "Or removed?"

"Ya, but not by me." He looked at Eileen. "I'm sorry. I failed you."

Another freaking thrall.

"That's okay." Eileen patted his shoulder. "Maybe one of the weres is a mechanic."

I grimaced. "We don't have time to find out."

As if on cue, the helicopter made another pass.

"Get inside!" I hurried them toward the doors.

We entered the lobby just as the copter appeared. It hovered over the yard for a few minutes as if taking photographs. At last, it soared away.

Dad said, "We'd better be out of here before sunrise."

"Sunrise?" Eileen squeaked. "Why sunrise?"

"They won't land until then." Brittany stepped down the grand staircase. "If you saw a courtyard filled with bodies, wouldn't you rather wait until it was light? They'll assume the place is crawling with werewolves."

"The moon is about to set," I said. "I'd better call everyone back. Tell Will to expect us."

Eileen smiled at the guard. "Can you drive me back?"

"We shouldn't move the jeep," he told her. "They've seen it."

She pursed her lips. "All right. Do you know how to get to the loading docks from inside the building?"

He shook his head, looking devastated. "I haven't spent much time inside."

Tubby-man beamed. "I do."

"You're so smart," Brittany cooed. "What would we do without you?"

"Let's go," Eileen said.

Brittany, Eileen, and their two *boyfriends* hurried away.

I looked at my dad. "Keep an eye on things. I'm going to try to contact Ayanna."

I sat with my back to the wall and forced the tension from my body. In moments, I was in the safe spot by the swampy pond in Florida.

"Ayanna," I called.

She appeared in a swath of moonlight. "Cody!" She ran to me and hugged me. What was it with girls and hugging? "You save us. You saved us all."

I hid my embarrassment in a chuckle. "I had a lot of help."

She pulled away, face alight. "You should celebrate with us. Everyone is so happy."

"We're not safe yet. There's been a helicopter hanging around."

She sobered. "We heard it."

"I want you to lead everyone back. But don't force them. If they don't want to come—"

"Of course, they'll want to come. They'll be transforming soon. They won't have any clothes."

"That's first on the agenda," I told her. "Then we have to leave. Before reinforcements arrive. I have a thrall at the gate, but he won't be able to delay them for long."

I expected her to chide me about taking a thrall.

Instead, she murmured, "We'll never be quit of this, will we?"

I shook my head. "There's only one place I can think of to go."

$$\mathcal{H}\mathcal{H}\mathcal{H}$$

Brittany followed Sugar through a maze of gray corridors. They ended up on a loading dock. Carts were lined up along the back wall. She looked out at the cold night. "Wow. Good job."

Sugar rocked on his heels, grinning.

She waved an arm. "But where is everybody?"

Eileen said, "I left them in Storage. This way."

They hurried down a different corridor. Voices echoed in the stillness. They came across a group of people piling bulging backpacks onto a cart. Others stacked uniforms. The uniforms were folded as if freshly laundered.

Will greeted Eileen with a peck on her cheek. "I thought it would be easier to pass things out at the dock, so I'm having them move all the supplies there."

Eileen nodded. "Good idea."

"Yeah, good job." Brittany glanced around, impressed by how organized everything seemed. "Did you hear the helicopter?"

"Yes. It imposes a time limit."

"We have to hurry. Cody's on his way."

Just then, a bony woman with a scraggly bun and fire in her eyes bustled toward them. "There you are!"

Eileen stiffened. "This is Bertha Becker. Head laundress."

Brittany smiled. "I'm happy to meet you, Bertha. I bet you know all about getting out spots."

"I'm not here to exchange laundry tips," she railed, "whoever you are."

Brittany raised her brows. She reached into her medical bag.

"Don't bother dosing her with love potion,"

Eileen murmured. "I already tried it. All it did was make her cough."

Brittany whispered, "The old hag. There's probably no love left in her."

"I demand to know what's going on," Bertha shouted. "Why have you commandeered my employees?"

"I explained to you," Eileen said. "Dr. Saarsgard wants to be certain her soldiers are physically fit, so she is sending them on a hiking trip. Overnight."

Bertha scoffed. "And why would she entrust you with this project? You're no more than children."

Eileen hesitated. She looked at Brittany.

Behind them, Sugar said, "Do you know who I am?"

Bertha jumped as if just noticing him. She blanched then lowered her gaze. "Of course, sir."

Brittany whispered to Eileen, "I wonder who he really is."

He said, "These *children*, as you call them, are consultants. They are not in charge of the project. I am. And I will not have your interference put me off my schedule. If you persist, I'll see you in gen-pop. Is that clear?"

"Yes, sir. I'm sorry, sir. My people will help in any way they can."

"Very well. You will have my supplies moved to the dock immediately."

Bertha motioned frantically. The workers continued filling the carts. Brittany gave a smiling wink to Sugar. He looked like he might faint with delight.

As the carts were rolled outside, William stepped closer to Eileen and Brittany. "The backpacks are all the same. They hold MRE rations and staple items such as matches and canteens. I didn't put clothes in them because we have to pass them out by size. We also have a variety of army boots and dress shoes. I hope we have enough, or we'll be taking them off the dead."

"Any weapons?" Eileen asked.

He shook his head. "They must keep them in a different location. I found five hunting knives with compasses in their handles. Best I can do."

"You did great, Will." Brittany nodded. "You got a lot done in a short amount of time."

They walked to the dock. The carts were lined up, their contents stacked in neat rows.

"Excellent," Brittany told the workers. "Thank you all for your help. Now we need everyone to go to the second-floor conference rooms for a special meeting."

"Meeting?" Bertha sputtered. "I wasn't informed of any meeting."

Brittany nodded. "You'll find Dr. Saarsgard waiting for you. She has the floor."

The workers ambled away, speaking in low voices. But Bertha remained. She stared as if about to go off on another tirade.

Eileen said, "I'll be sure to mention your insolence in my report."

Bertha opened her mouth then closed it again. She turned to leave.

Just then, Cody and his father traipsed up. Behind them came the wolves. Dozens of them. Their eyes glinted eerily in the dock light.

Bertha gasped and pointed. "You aren't outfitting soldiers. You're in league with those filthy werewolves."

Brittany narrowed her eyes. "That's right. So, you better leave before they eat you."

Bertha backed away looking both outraged and terrified. She bolted down the corridor.

Cody smiled and called, "Hello, up there. We have some people in need of clothing."

"You've come to the right place." Brittany smiled back.

Beside Cody, Ayanna-the-wolf transformed. She'd gotten so good at it, she seemed to just stand up as a girl. "Eek!" She laughed. "It's frigid out here. Where are my clothes?"

William said, "The uniforms are in European sizes, so I categorized them my way." He motioned to three carts. "Small, medium, and large." He handed a small to Ayanna.

She dressed then climbed onto the dock. "How can I help?"

He pointed her to the boot cart. "You can be in charge of footwear."

With ugly gagging and popping sounds, two more people transformed.

Cody called, "Try to hold your wolf forms as long as possible. It's cold out here." Then he added as if just thinking of it, "If any of you are still wearing your wristbands, be sure to take them off. They may have GPS transponder chips in them." He hopped up to help pass out supplies.

Each person got a uniform, a jacket, boots, a backpack, and a blanket. A kid with a scarred face leaped up to help Ayanna pass out boots which were more complicated than just small, medium, and large.

As she handed out backpacks, Brittany

asked Cody, "How did the amulet work?"

"Like a charm." He grinned. "I'm never taking it off."

She smiled at him. "Consider it my wedding gift to you."

Just then, a helicopter circled overhead.

Pop! The remaining werewolves transformed all at once and rushed the dock.

"Calm down!" Brittany cried. "One at a time." She looked out to see the sky lightening with the dawn.

William muttered, "It sounded like that helicopter landed."

Eileen said, "I hope they don't talk to Bertha."

"We should have locked her in the storeroom," Brittany said.

"We can't leave through the hole in the fence we used before." Cody frowned then snapped his fingers. "We need bolt cutters."

William's face brightened. "I can do that." He rushed back into the building.

Cody held out his hands as if to calm the frantic crowd. "Break into groups of fifteen," he called. Then he said to Ayanna, "Take group one and run straight west. Wait at the fence."

Cody's dad cried, "They can't go into the open. There are cameras everywhere."

"That doesn't matter," Brittany told him. "There's no one in the control room to see them. I mean, there were two guys, but they're... at the orgy."

"I'll have to ask you about that later." Ayanna hopped down. She smiled at Cody. "Don't be long." She and fifteen weres disappeared into the darkness.

Ayanna's scarred friend kept passing out boots.

Eileen approached Cutie-boy. "There are some soldiers at the front door. Can you ask them to wait for us in the barracks?"

He blushed. "I'm not sure I know how to get back to the front."

"No problem," Brittany said. "Sugar can guide you. Right, Sugar?"

The attendant looked flustered. "But where will you be?"

Eileen said, "We're just going to say goodbye to our friends. We'll be along."

Brittany stepped to the attendant and put her hand on his shoulder. He trembled as if in ecstasy.

"You've been such a big help," she said. "Do this one last thing for me."

"I would do anything for you," he moaned.

Glancing over their shoulders, he and Cutie-boy left.

When they were gone, Cody said to Chloe, "Do you sense where Ayanna went?"

"She's on my radar," Chloe said, then muttered, "I'll never let her off my radar again."

Cody nodded. "You and Rita take group two. We'll be there shortly."

Chloe and Rita left with fifteen weres.

Brittany looked out at the grounds. About twenty people remained. Only a few of them still needed to be outfitted. All the true-wolves had stayed behind as if waiting for Cody.

William rushed from the corridor carrying a duffle bag. "I found this. I think it was left behind by maintenance." He opened it to show a variety of tools, among them a pair of bolt cutters.

"Perfect," Cody said. "You and Uncle Bob take the next group. Open the fence and—"

"I'm staying with my wife," William said.

Bob slung the duffle over his shoulder. "It's all right. I've got this." He left with the third group.

Another helicopter could be heard. The final five weres gasped and huddled together. Two women broke ranks and sprinted after Bob.

Brittany looked into a cart. "We have some backpacks left over."

"I don't want to leave anything behind." Cody frowned and picked up a pack.

The kid who had been helping Ayanna give out boots said, "I can carry extra."

Up close, Brittany saw the scars on his face were fresh. But because he was a werewolf, his wounds had already closed. He looked familiar.

She gasped. "Tommy Lee?"

He smiled at her, making his scars pucker. It was him. The kid from Georgia.

"Howdy-doo, Miss Brittany," he said. "Fancy meeting you here."

"Tommy Lee?" Cody sputtered. "How the heck—"

"It's a long story." He held out his hand to Cody. "One I should regale you with another time."

Cody shook with him. "All right, then. Let's get moving."

They divvied up the remaining supplies.

William handed a bag to Cody and said in a low voice, "You should probably be in charge of this. It's the hunting knives."

Cody slid the bag into his overstuffed backpack. As he leaped down from the dock, the true-wolves stood, ears perked. He said, "Got everything? Then head out."

Brittany grinned, almost giddy with relief. They had done it. They had accomplished the impossible. Now she could go home and plan her wedding.

🐺🐺🐺

I ran across the grassy field with Brittany at my side and my dad just behind. We did it! We'd accomplished the impossible. But the worst was yet to come. I hoped I was strong enough.

My group reached the fence. Traffic was backed up. Uncle Bob held open the hole he had cut and urged people through. But it was slow. They squeezed past the chain-link then ran crouched in single file toward the rocks. I wanted to yell at them to pick up the pace.

My frustration turned to alarm. I looked toward the sound of more helicopters. Two copters flew back and forth over the field, looking like black dragonflies in the brightening sky. Their spotlights speared downward, illuminating the dock we just left.

Dad moved to the hole and pulled the fence farther apart. "Hurry!"

They hurried. Couldn't they go any faster?

Tommy Lee stayed on the other side of the

fence and helped hoist people through.

I watched the helicopters systematically searching the grounds. Someone must have told them where to find us. Brittany's boyfriend? Bertha? What would they do if they caught us?

The last man sprinted away. I held the fence for Dad and Uncle Bob, then threw the duffle bag and my backpacks after them. Then I motioned to the true-wolves. They darted forward as if they'd expected me to forget them. Like that was going to happen.

At last, I climbed through. I joined my dad and uncle. We scurried toward the cover of the rocks where Brittany waited for us. She hugged me then led the way after the others. The true-wolves spread out behind.

Dawn turned into day. We ran due west until we couldn't hear the helicopters anymore then south toward the tree line. When they say tree line, they mean it. One minute there was nothing, then - boom - there was a forest. The trees were one-sided as if turning their backs on the mountains. But they provided shelter from the wind and prying eyes.

It felt good to slow down. To breathe fresh air. The morning was brisk, and the sun hid behind heavy clouds. After a while, we stopped at a rushing stream. The water was cold and delicious. I sat on the lichen-carpeted ground. My friends and family gathered around me, and we watched the weres play. Some of them hadn't seen the outdoors in a very long time.

Suddenly, it began to snow. Fluffy flakes fluttered like confetti as if the sky were congratulating us on our escape. The weres laughed and held out their hands. A few stuck out their tongues like children.

I said, "They seem happy."

"Of course, they are," Ayanna said. "To be shut of that place? You can't imagine what it was like."

"That's it, then." Eileen smiled. "We wish them a happy life. They go their way. We go ours."

And there was my opening. My heart thumped. I took Brittany's hand. "I can't go home with you."

Her face fell.

William groaned.

Eileen said, "If this is because of some sense of misplaced responsibility—"

"No," I said. "I mean, yes, I feel responsible for them. But that's not it."

"Then what is it?" William grumbled.

"First off, how would I get into the country? I don't have ID much less a passport."

"We'll get you fake ID," Dad said.

I ignored him. "Secondly, where would I live? The authorities know what I am now. I'd go straight back into detention."

"Again," Dad said, "fake IDs. For all of you. We'll set you up with whole new lives."

"Do you even know how to do that?" I snapped.

He frowned. "I'll find out."

"It would never work," I said. "We'd spend the rest of our lives on the run."

Brittany turned toward the sound of distant helicopters. "You'll be on the run here, too. They're looking for you."

I nodded. "The whole world knows about the existence of werewolves. They won't stop hunting us just because Saarsgard is dead."

"Then I'm staying with you," Brittany said.

"I can't let you do that. You deserve a better life. Besides, you don't have a permanent visa. If they catch you, you'll be deported. Or worse."

Eileen said, "He's right, Brit."

Brittany began to cry. "But I love you. We came all this way to... to..."

"And I'll never be able to repay you. Thanks

will never be enough." I held her face and looked into her eyes. "But you came too late. I already became a monster. I've become everything I hate. Look at what happened back there. All those people dead."

She pushed my hands away. "And how many did you kill?"

"None. But that doesn't change the fact that they died because of me. I'm not the guy you thought I was. I'm not the guy I thought–"

"Yes, you are. You're not the monster here."

"I am."

"Don't do this to me."

"I'm doing it *for* you." I kissed her face, our tears mingling, salty on my lips. "Go home, Brittany. Make a life for yourself. I will always love you."

"I love you," she whispered.

Eileen pulled her away. Brittany stumbled to her feet, sobbing. My heart wrenched. I stood.

William held out his hand. "Goodbye, brother."

I shook with him, unable to speak. He handed me his dog-eared map.

My father pulled me into a rough embrace. He thumped my back. "Take care of yourself, son. I'm proud of the man you've become."

Then Brittany, Eileen, William, and Dad walked away. I stared, part of me wanting to go after them. Oh, God. What was I doing? I was losing her forever.

I clenched my fists.

One last time. I would hurt her this one last time. Then she would be fine.

I would never recover.

Ayanna moved closer and put her hand on my arm. Uncle Bob looked at me as if about to speak, but he remained silent.

I realized the weres had become subdued. They weren't looking my way, but they knew what had happened.

Of course, they knew. I was broadcasting my pain.

Just then, the two true-wolves who had chased my mother appeared. The leader and his mate. They greeted me, rubbing back and forth against my legs. And just like that, I knew they hadn't killed her. She'd turned into a wolf and ran away.

I rested my hand on the leader's head. I tried to give him back the wolf pack, tried to sever the ties that bound the true-wolves to me, but he wouldn't accept them. I was the pack leader. I was alpha.

God, help me.

I approached the weres on the bank of the stream. They gathered attentively as if they expected a speech, all of them looking to me for guidance. But if I spoke to them, if I took up the mantel, I was a goner. I would never get what I wanted.

Had it been too much to ask? All I ever wanted was to be a normal kid. Hang out with friends after school. Plan date nights with Brittany on the weekends. No worries. No responsibilities.

But that kind of life wasn't for me. I was the amazing wolf boy. Astound your family and mystify your friends. And I had a job to do.

I raised my voice. "I'm going to Svalbard. It's a group of islands north of here. It will be a difficult journey. And living in the arctic will be a difficult life. But I think it's the safest place to be. I'm not asking anyone to follow me. You're free now. If you want to leave, I won't stop you." I glanced meaningfully at my uncle, but he avoided my eyes. "If you want to join my pack, you are welcome. My only rule is no killing humans."

Tommy Lee stepped forward. He grinned broadly. "I always knew you was special."

"He is alpha," cried the man who had denounced me earlier. He punched his fist into the air. "He is alpha."

"He is alpha!" Others picked up the cry. They shook their fists.

I wanted to run—but I didn't. This was my pack. And I would protect them with my life.

As one, they dropped to their knees before me. The *link* flared strong and true.

EPILOGUE

March 7, 2013, Svalbard, Kingdom of Norway

It was a spring snowstorm. Significant snowfall, according to our crank-up weather radio. But I planned to stay outside for as long as I could. I was on guard duty. Again. I took more than my share of guard duty. But what else was there for me to do?

I sat on my favorite rock and watched the snow settle on our squat, yellow tents. We had twenty-five of them now. They were called Arctic Oven Igloos, and they were comfortably warm inside. Easy to set up. Easy to transport. Perfect for our nomadic way of life. Dad sent them a few at a time to the PO Box I kept in Longyearbyen. I had to buy a sleigh to get them to camp—the small sled we used for supplies wasn't large enough. Now we had all the comforts of home. Almost.

I turned toward squealing laughter. Little Lavinia burst out of a tent and streaked across the snow. She was Ayanna and Tommy Lee's daughter. Two years old and a bundle of activity. Chloe followed close behind, growling and making monster hands as she chased her. Chloe took being a grandmother seriously.

When Dad heard that Ayanna was expecting, he sent a ton of baby clothes and toys. Dad would have loved to have been a grandfather. But it wasn't meant to be. With a sigh, I touched the amulet I wore under my shirt. Brittany's amulet.

I thought of Brittany often. All the time, actually. I imagined her going to college, studying chemistry and herbology, maybe becoming the powerful witch queen that Aunt Lynette said she was destined to be. I hoped she was happy. She was my mate. I would take no other, although I'd had plenty of offers. I didn't expect to hear from her. Not really. But I always hoped Dad would mention her in his letters.

Chloe caught Lavinia and carried her home. They spun and danced in the falling snow. Chloe seemed to love being a grandparent. Dick would have loved it, too. But in all the years after the *institute incident*, we never saw him.

I'd seen my mother, though. Dozens of times. She was always a wolf. I didn't think she could shift into a human anymore. Maybe she'd deprived her inner wolf for so long, it wouldn't go back.

I'd tried to invite her into the pack. She'd be safe with us. But she remained on the periphery. A lone wolf. An outcast. Kind of ironic after the way she'd treated me.

The snow became heavier. I raised my hood and ran my gaze over the silent camp. The true-wolves ranged outside the perimeter. Shadows in the haze. They weren't domesticated by any means, but they always stayed nearby. They hunted with us on the full moon, sang to us at night—and kept me company during guard duty. I smiled, taking comfort in their presence.

But then I saw another shadow. Flickering in and out of the blowing snow. A person. Moving toward us.

The wolf inside me leaped to attention. I stood and unsheathed my knife.

Should I sound the alarm? Had the authorities found us? Search parties were rarer now, but they were still a danger.

But no. This person was alone.

Why weren't the true-wolves stopping them?

I wanted to shout *who goes there?* But my mouth was peculiarly dry.

The figure approached. Long, black cloak. Hood up.

Yet, the snow wasn't touching them. The flakes stayed a few inches away, forming a halo.

What the...?

The figure stopped. They lowered their hood.

I gave a strangled cry. Was it a mirage? A snow mirage?

"You're a hard man to find," Brittany said.

And I said, stupidly, "You grew your hair."

"You grew a beard."

I shrugged, suddenly embarrassed, seeing myself as she must see me. "It keeps me warm."

She stepped close, touching my brow. "Now I'm here to keep you warm."

I placed my hand over hers, felt the warmth. "You're real. You're really here."

She smiled, her nose crinkling in the way that I loved. Her green eyes sparkled with tears. "I'm really here."

And then she kissed me.

About the Author

Roxanne Smolen became enamored by werewolves after watching the movie *Abbott and Costello Meet Frankenstein* when she was a girl. The pathos of the wolfman character touched her even then. As she grew into her author shoes, the idea of a conflicted werewolf character grew as well until she knew his story had to be told. Her wolf boy series takes place in Loxahatchee, Florida, not far from her home.

You can connect with her on Twitter, Facebook, and Instagram.

Books by Roxanne Smolen

The Amazing Wolf Boy
The Amazing Wolf Boy
Werewolf Asylum
Wolfsbane Brew
Werewolf Apocalypse
The Bear, the Werewolf, and the Blogger
The Amazing Wolf Boy Box Set

Dark Angel
Satan's Mirror

Colonial Scouts
Alien Worlds
Alien Jungle
Alien Seas
Alien Beginnings

The Resort Debauch Trilogy
Resort Debauch
The Resort Debauch Trilogy

The Violet Series
Violet and the Missing Laptop
Violet and the Missing Puppy

The Adventures of the Power Girls
Keepers of Magic
Island of Magic

Dear Reader,

So ends the story of The Amazing Wolf Boy. If you enjoyed the series, please drop me a line to let me know. It would make my day. After all, my main purpose in writing is to entertain you.

You can reach me at:
smolen.roxanne@gmail.com
or through my website, roxannesmolen.com.

Or better yet, leave a short review. In this world of social media, reviews can elevate a good book. So do your friends and readers like you a favor by bringing The Amazing Wolf Boy series to their attention.

Thank you for reading The Amazing Super Wolf.
Roxanne